A HOAX IN TIME

By
KEITH LAUMER

I0541520

ARMCHAIR FICTION
PO Box 4369, Medford, Oregon 97504

*For more information about Armchair Books and products, visit our
website at...*

www.armchairfiction.com

Or email us at...

armchairfiction@yahoo.com

TIME IS MONEY!

What we have here in this intriguing well-written Keith Laumer tale is twofold. First off, you have the ultimate computer. Secondly, you have the ultimate hero. Together they combine for a rambunctious science fiction romp to perpetrate, simultaneously, a superb comic opera on the one hand, and on the other, an insightful and satiric comment on the world in which we all live.

Appropriately enough, the defining link that serves as the unification of grand farce and thought-provoking philosophy is, of all things…the Internal Revenue Service! Yes…the IRS…without whose greedy hands and conniving ways this story could never have been contemplated—let alone written!

FOR A SECOND COMPLETE NOVEL, TURN TO PAGE 157

CAST OF CHARACTERS

CHESTER W. CHESTER IV
He'd just inherited a 100-acre Estate that, unfortunately, owed 300 million in back taxes!

CASE MULVIHILL
A simple, yet clever, ex-carny hand with an extraordinary knack for makin' a buck.

GENIE
She was the "nubile female" generated as a mobile speaker for an elaborate and revolutionary computer system.

MR. OVERDOG
Collector for the IRS. How far down the path of ridiculous wouldl this man travel in order to secure the monies owed his boss?

NORGO
City councilman for the Tricennium of the "Original Knowledge." He was eager to apprentice his newest citizens.

KUVE
He was the best teacher the Tricennium had, and Chester was his most successful student—or was he just a guinea pig?

BANDON
Raised by neurotic parents and neglected by society—who would take a stand for this young man?

CHAPTER ONE

FOR a guy that's just inherited a big estate," Case Mulvihill said, adjusting his feet comfortably on the desktop, "you sure look glum."

Chester W. Chester IV sighed and tapped the ashes from a Chanel dope-stick. "The bequest consists of a hundred acres of rolling green lawn and a fifty-two-room neo-Victorian eyesore fairly bursting with great grandfather's conception of stylish decor. Not precisely the sort of assets one can convert readily into riotous living."

"Your great grand-pop must have been quite a guy," Case said. "I'll bet that place of his was a palace in its day."

"Great grand-pop was an eccentric of the worst stripe," Chester said shortly. "Never invested a cent in the welfare of his descendants."

"His descendant, you mean. Namely Chester W. Chester IV. Still, even if you don't admire the place, Chester, you can always sell it—"

Chester shook his head. "He was too clever for us," he said. "Which is the only reason the place still remains in the family—more or less. The estate was so snarled up that with the backlog in the courts it took four generations to straighten it out. For the past hundred years the house has been maintained at public expense—and no taxes have been paid on it. After all, with no legal owner, who was liable?"

"A good question."

"I'll tell you the answer." Chester pointed at his own chest. "I am!"

"You, Chester? You haven't got the proverbial pot or a disposal unit to throw it into."

"Two million, four hundred and forty three thousand, nine hundred and twenty one credits, and eleven cents," Chester said. "That's the basic figure. Then there's the interest, and the court costs; say another half million. As soon as I pay I get possession. Meanwhile, I'm allowed to go look at it on alternate Thursdays. After all, the place is mine."

"Chester, that's the biggest estate in the western hemisphere. As the owner, you're a public figure—"

"I'm the biggest delinquent taxpayer in history. Life imprisonment wouldn't cover my case; they'll have to revive capital punishment."

"I'll bet those antiques in the house would bring in the kind of

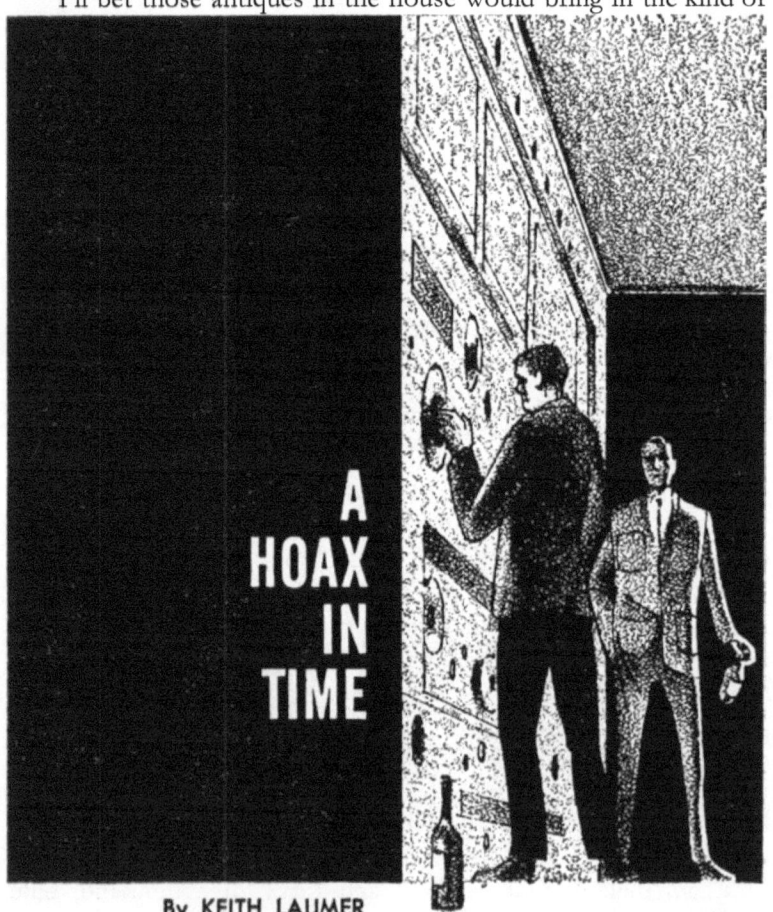

A HOAX IN TIME

By KEITH LAUMER
Illustrator SCHELLING

money you need," Case said. "Neo-Victorian is pretty rare stuff."

"I wonder if you've ever seen any Neo-Victorian? Items like a TV set in the shape of a crouching vulture, or a water closet built to look like a skull with gaping jaws. Not what you'd call esthetic. And I can't sell one thing until I've paid every credit of that tax bill."

"Is that all there is in the place?" Case asked, easing a squat bottle and two glasses from the desk drawer.

"Unhappily, no. Half the rooms and all the cellars are filled with my revered ancestor's invention."

THE bottle gurgled. Case capped it and pushed a glass across to Chester. "What invention?"

"The old gentleman called it a Generalized Non-linear Extrapolator. G.N.E. for short. He made his money in computer components, you know. He was fascinated by computers. He felt that they had tremendous unrealized possibilities. Of course, that was before Crmblznski's Limit was discovered. Great grandfather was convinced a machine could be built which would outdo its makers. He reasoned that no human researcher is capable of educating himself sufficiently in a wide variety of disciplines to discern the relationship that exists even among apparently unrelated facts. His theory was that a sufficiently extensive memory bank, adequately cross-connected, and supplied with a vast store of data, would be capable of performing prodigious intellectual feats—even of originating new concepts."

"This Crmblznski's Limit. That's where it says if you go beyond a certain point with these complications, you just blow your transistors, right?"

"Yes. But of course great grandfather was unaware of the limitations. He felt that if you fed to the machine all known data— say on human taste reactions to food, for example, then added all existing recipes, complete specifications on edible substances, the cooking techniques of the chefs of all nations—then the computer would produce unique recipes, superior to anything ever devised before. Or one might introduce into the memory bank all the engineering principles and design ideas ever developed for ground-cars, or dictypers; the computer would assimilate the data and produce the ultimate in the line; or you could feed in all available data on a subject which has baffled science—such as magnetism, or psi-functions, or the trans-Pluto distress signal—and the computer would evolve the likeliest hypothesis to cover the facts—"

"Ummm. Didn't he ever try it and discover Crmblznski's Limit for himself?"

"Oh, he never progressed that far. First, you see, it was necessary to set up the memory banks, then to work out a method of coding types of information that no one had ever coded before, such as smells and emotions and subjective judgments. Methods had to be worked out for the acquisition of tapes of everything ever recorded—in every field. He worked with the Library of Congress and the British Museum and with newspapers and book publishers and universities. Unhappily he overlooked the time element. He spent the last twenty-five years of his life at the task of coding. He spent all the cash he'd ever made on reducing all human knowledge to coded tapes and feeding them to the memory banks."

"Say," Case said. "There might be something in that. Sort of a library idea. You could run a reference service. Ask the machine anything, it answers."

"You can do that in the public library."

"Yeah," Case admitted. "Anyway, the whole thing's probably rusted out by now."

"Oh, no. Great grandfather set up a trust fund to keep the information flowing in. The government has maintained it in perfect shape. It was Government property, in a way. Since it was running when they took it over, digesting daily newspapers, novels, scientific journals, and what not, they didn't know what else to do but continue. It came to be a habit." Chester sighed.

"Yes," he went on, "the old computer's up to date. All the latest facts on the Martian ruins, the *Homo Protanthropus* remains the Mediterranean Drainage Commission turned up, new finds in biogenics, nucleonics, geriatrics, hypnotics, everything." Chester sighed again. "Biggest idiot savant in the world. It knows everything, and doesn't know what to do with it."

"I feel for you, Chester. You got a problem on your hands, all right. But how can I help you? You're the one with the looks and the college education. I'm just an old carny hand."

"You're resourceful, Case. You're experienced in the ways of commerce. My primary need is to raise funds to pay the taxes. Surely your ingenuity will be equal to the task."

"Why not just hire a couple of lawyers?"

"Somehow, Case, I feel that your native shrewdness and wide shoulders will prove more efficacious."

"Well," said Case, "it'll be the first time anybody hired an ex-acrobat to handle a tax problem, but for you, pal, I'll give it a try. Now, let's get the facts straight. The computer won't work because of this Crmblznski's Limit—"

"Of course, Crmblznski's Limit is only theoretical…"

"You mean nobody's ever tried out the machine?"

"It's been tied up in probate, Case. No one's been allowed to touch it."

"How about the Revenue boys?"

"They're normal bureaucrats. No interest in matters outside their job—in this case, collecting the back taxes."

Case finished his drink and rose. "Let's you and me take a run out to the place, Chester. I think maybe we ought to take a look at this thing. Maybe I'll get an idea out there."

CHESTER settled the heli gently onto a patch of velvety grass surrounded by varicolored tulips directly before the ornately decorated portico of the old house. The two men rode the balustraded escalator to the broad verandah, stepped off under a carved dinosaur with fluorescent eyes. The Porter chimed softly; Chester inserted his ID-key and the door slid open. Inside, light filtered through stained-plastic panels depicting traditional service station and supermarket scenes, to bathe the cavernous entry hall in an amber glow. Case looked around at the plastic alligator-hide hangings, the beaded glass floor, the ostrich feather chandeliers, the zircon doorknobs.

"I see why neo-Victorian stuff is rare," he said. "It was all burned by enraged mobs as soon as they got a look at it."

"Great grandfather liked it," said Chester, averting his eyes from a lithograph entitled "Rush Hour at the Insemomat." He continued, "I told you he was eccentric."

"Where's the invention?"

"The central panel's down in the former wine cellar."

Case followed Chester along a dark red corridor lit by a green glare strip, into a small elevator. The elevator grounded and the door opened. Case and Chester stepped into a long low room lined on one side with dusty racks of wine bottles, and on the other with dial faces and tape reels. Case looked from one wall to the other.

"This is it," Chester said, "the G.N.E. It's quite extensive. Where would you like to start?"

"We could start at this end and work our way down," said Case, eyeing the first row of wine bottles. He lifted one from its cradle, blew dust from it. "Flora Pinellas, '87; that would fetch some money."

Chester raised an eyebrow. "My dear Case, these bottles are practically members of the family. Still, if you'll hand me the corkscrew, we can make a few spot checks just to be sure it's holding up properly."

EQUIPPED with a bottle each, Case and Chester turned to the control panel of the computer. Chester pointed out a typewriter-style keyboard. "You type out your problem here; it's automatically translated into the symbols the machine uses. It searches through its memory, integrates all pertinent factors, and a tape emerges from the slot with your answer printed on it."

"Okay; how about asking who's going to win the third tomorrow at the racetrack?"

"I doubt that the machine can predict the future."

"But nobody's *tried* it?"

"I seem to recall a story that some of the Internal Revenue officials did try it once. It produced the prediction that, by a probability ratio of 8:787:1, next year's revenues would either be greater than this year's or smaller."

"Oh." Case studied the panel, the ranks of micro-reels, the waiting keyboard. Chester wrestled with the corkscrew.

"What do you say we try it?" Case suggested.

"Just as soon as I get the cork out—"

"I mean the computer."

"Oh, certainly. Help yourself." Case went to the keyboard. He rubbed his chin thoughtfully. "You sure it's turned on?"

"It's always turned on. Information is still being fed into it twenty four hours a day."

Case reached for the keyboard. He typed:

WHAT DID MY GREAT UNCLE JULIUS DIE OF?

A red light blinked on the board. There was a busy humming from the depths of the machine, then a sharp *click*, and a strip of paper chattered from the slot. Case read it aloud:

MUMPS

"Hey, Chester, look," he called. Chester came to his side, studied the strip of paper.

"I'm afraid the significance of this escapes me. Presumably you already knew what your Uncle Julius died of."

"Sure; but how did this contraption know?"

"Everything that's ever been recorded is stored in the memory banks. Doubtless your Uncle Julius' passing was duly noted in official records somewhere."

"Right; but how did it know who I meant? Does it have him listed under M for 'my' or U for 'uncle'...?"

"We could ask the machine."

Case nodded. "We could at that." He tapped out the question. The slot promptly disgorged a longer strip this time.

A COMPARISON OF YOUR FINGERPRINTS WITH THE FILES IDENTIFTED YOU AS MR. CASSIUS H. MULVIHILL. A SEARCH OF THE GENEALOGICAL SECTION DISCLOSED THE EXISTENCE OF ONLY ONE INDIVIDUAL BEARING AN AVUNCULAR RELATIONSHIP TO YOU. REFERENCE TO DEATH RECORDS INDICATED HIS DEMISE FROM EPIDEMIC PAROTITIS, COMMONLY CALLED MUMPS.

"That makes it sound easy," Case said. "You know, Chester, your great grand-pop may have had something here."

"I once calculated," Chester said dreamily, "that if the money the old idiot put into this scheme had been invested at three percent, it would be paying me a monthly dividend of approximately fifteen thousand credits today. Instead, I am able to come down here and find out what your Uncle Julius died of. Bah!"

"How about the direct approach?" Case typed out:

HOW CAN CHESTER GET THE INTERNAL REVENUE DEPARTMENT OFF HIS NECK?

Chester reached for the paper strip coiling from the machine as Case took another pull from his Flora Pinellas.

SUBMIT TO INTERNAL REVENUE A DETAILED PROPOSAL FOR RETIREMENT OF THE DEBT THROUGH EXPLOITATION OF THE FUND-PRODUCING POTENTIAL OF THE PROPERTY.

"A typical oracular statement," Chester said. "What fund-producing potential?"

"Chester, there has to be some way we can raise money on the place. We'll figure out what, and ask the tax boys to let us do it, so we can pay them off. The machine seems to think they'll let us do it."

"That still leaves us with the detail of dreaming up a scheme."

Case waved at the keyboard. "We just haven't asked the right question yet. Remember, the machine can't think. It's up to you to pry out the information."

Chester looked at the keyboard dubiously. "But Crmblznski's Limit—"

"Chester, this is no time to think negatively."

Chester put his hands on the keyboard. At once a paper strip fell from the slot.

"What's this, a mind reading act?" Chester read the tape:

PLEASE PLACE YOUR RIGHT FOREFINGER IN THE ORIFICE INDICATED BY THE FLASHING LIGHT.

Chester looked at the hole dubiously. He put his finger in— and jerked it back with a yelp.

"It bit me!" He put his finger in his mouth, took it out and looked at it. A tiny bead of red showed. "I'm bleeding. Why, that infernal collection of short circuits—"

"Don't let it throw you, Chester. It probably needs a blood sample for research purposes."

The machine clucked and fed a paper strip from its slot. Chester read it. "Listen to this, Case."

WELCOME, MR. CHESTER. KINDLY GO TO THE NORTH WALL OF THIS ROOM. PRESS FIRMLY ON THE THIRD BRICK FROM THE LEFT IN THE FOURTH ROW.

Case eyed the far end of the room thoughtfully. "So it wants to play games?"

"It's another practical joke, I'll warrant. This contraption suffers from a distorted sense of humor."

"Come on. Let's see what happens."

CHESTER followed Case to the brick wall, watched as he counted bricks.

"This one right here," said Case. "Shall I, or will you?"

"You go ahead. I'll stand by to extricate you if the wall falls on you."

Case pressed against the brick. Nothing happened. He pushed harder, prodded, rammed, jabbed, and finally kicked the masonry. Still nothing.

"You try it, Chester."

"Why?"

"I think it likes to deal with you personally. After all, it calls you by name."

Chester approached the wall diffidently, reached out and prodded the brick. Nothing happened. "We're wasting our time, Case." He jabbed again. "I suggest we gather together a few bottles and—"

With a creak of long-unused hinges, a six-foot section of the wall swung inward, dust filtering down from its edges. A dark room was visible beyond the opening.

"Come on, Chester." Case stepped through the opening. At once lights sprang up, illuminating a room twice as large as the wine cellar, with walls of a shimmering glassy material, a low acoustical ceiling, and deep-pile carpeting on the floor. There were two deep armchairs, a small bar, and a chaise longue upholstered in lavender leather.

"Chester, old boy, it looks like your great grand-pop was holding out," said Case, heading for the bar.

A rasping noise issued from somewhere. Case and Chester stared around. The noise gave way to an only slightly less rasping voice:

"Unless some scoundrel has succeeded in circumventing my arrangements, a descendant of mine has just entered this room. However, just to be on the safe side, I'll ask you to step to the bar and place your hand on the metal plate set in its top. I warn you, if you're not my direct descendant, you'll be electrocuted. Serve you right, too, since you have no business being here. So if you're trespassing, get out now! That door will close and lock, if you haven't used the plate, in thirty seconds. Make up your mind!" The voice stopped and the rasping noise resumed its rhythmic scratching.

"That voice," said Chester. "It sounds very much like great grandfather's tapes in grandma's album—"

"Here's the plate he's talking about," Case called. "Hurry up, Chester!"

"I suggest we beat a rapid retreat, before the door closes and traps us here."

"Hold on! You're Chester W. Chester the Fourth, aren't you?"

"Yes, but I—"

"Then do what he tells you!" Chester eyed the door, hesitated, then dived for the bar, slapped a palm against the polished rectangle. Nothing happened.

"Another of the old fool's jokes."

"Well, you've passed the test," the voice said suddenly out of the air. "Nobody but the genuine heir would have been able to make that decision so quickly. The plate itself is a mere dummy, of course. Though I'll confess I was tempted to wire it as I threatened. They'd never have pinned a murder on me. I've been dead for at least a hundred years." A cadaverous chuckle issued from the air.

NOW," the voice went on. "This room is the sanctum sanctorum of the temple of wisdom to which I have devoted a quarter of a century and the bulk of my fortune. Unfortunately, due to the biological inadequacies of the human body, I myself will be—or am—unable to be here today to reap the reward of my industry. As soon as my calculations revealed to me the fact that adequate programming of the computer would require the better part of a century, I set about arranging my affairs in such a state that bureaucratic bungling would insure the necessary period of grace. I'm quite sure my devoted family, had they access to the estate, would dismember the entire project and convert the proceeds to the pursuit of frivolous satisfactions. In my youth we were taught to appreciate the finer things in life, such as liquor and women; but today, the traditional values have gone by the board...

"However, that's neither here nor there. By the time you, my remote descendant, enter this room—or have *entered* this room—the memory banks will be—that is, are—fully charged—"

The voice broke off in midsentence.

"Please forgive the interruption, Mr. Chester," a warm feminine voice said. It seemed to issue from the same indefinable spot as the first disembodied voice. "It has been necessary to edit the original recording, prepared by your relative, in the light of subsequent developments. The initial portion was retained for reasons of sentiment. If you will be seated, you will be shown a full report of the present status of Project Genie."

"Project Genie?" Chester echoed.

"Take a chair, Chester. The lady wants to tell us all about it." Case seated himself in one of the easy chairs. Chester took the other. The lights dimmed, and the wall opposite them glowed with a nacreous light, resolved itself into a view of a long corridor, barely wide enough for a man to pass through.

"The original memory banks designed and built by Mr. Chester," the feminine voice said, "occupied a system of tunnels excavated from the granitic formations underlying the property. Under the arrangements made at the time, these banks were to be charged, cross-connected, and indexed entirely automatically, as data were fed to the receptor board in coded form."

The scene shifted to busily humming machines into which reels of tape fed endlessly. "Here, in the translating and coding section, raw data were processed, classified, and filed. Though primitive, this system, within ten years after the death of Mr. Chester, had completed the charging of ten to the tenth to, the tenth individual datoms—"

"I beg your pardon—" Chester broke in. "Ten whats?"

"The basic unit of counter-entropic bias-transfer has been designated the datom."

"By whom, may I ask?"

"By the etymological, philological, and lexicographic units."

"It might be best to avoid using words from your etymological and lexicographic units," said Chester. "I don't think I understand them. And by the way—ah—just whom am I addressing?"

"The compound personality-field that occurred spontaneously when first-power functions became active among the interacting datoms. For brevity, this personality-field will henceforward be referred to as 'I'."

"Oh," Chester said blankly. "Well, go ahead with the story."

TO resume," said the voice; "when the critical level was reached for the evolution of a fourth-power awareness field—"

"Now let me ask one," Case interrupted. "What's this 'first-power' and 'fourth-power' deal?"

"An awareness of identity is a function of datom cross-connection. Simple organic brains—as for example those of the simplest members of the phylum *vertebrata*—operate at this primary level. This order of intelligence is capable of setting up a system of automatic reactions to external stimuli: fear responses of flight, mating urges, food, seeking patterns—"

"That sounds like the gang I run around with," Case said.

"These functions are, of course, involuntary. Additional cross-connections produce second-level intellectual activity, characterized by the employment of the mind as a tool in the solution of problems, as when an ape abstracts characteristics and as a result utilizes stacked boxes and a stick to obtain a reward of food; or when a square peg is selected to fit a square hole."

"Right there you leave some of my gang behind," put in Case.

"The achievement of the requisite number of second-power cross-connections in turn produces third-level awareness. Now the second-level functions come under the surveillance of the higher level, which directs their use. Decisions are reached as to lines of inquiry; courses of action are extrapolated and judgments reached prior to overt physical action. An esthetic awareness arises. Philosophies, systems or religion and other magics are evolved in an attempt to impose simplified third-level patterns of rationality on the infinite complexity of the space-time continuum."

"You've got the voice of a good-looking dolly," Case mused. "But you talk like an encyclopedia."

"I selected this tonal pattern as most likely to evoke a favorable response," the voice said. "Shall I employ another?"

"No, this one will do very well," put in Chester. "Let the machine go on, Case. What about the fourth power?"

"Intelligence may be defined as awareness. A fourth-power mind senses as a complex interrelated function an exponentially increased datom-grid. Thus, the flow of air impinging on sensory surfaces is comprehended by such an awareness in terms of individual molecular activity; taste sensations are resolved into interactions of specialized nerve endings (or, in my case, analytic sensors) with molecules of specific form. The mind retains on a continuing basis the dynamic conceptualization of the multifold resultant of the interplay of all factors of the external environment, from the motions of the stars to the minute-by-minute decisions of obscure individuals.

"The majority of trained human minds are capable of occasional fractional fourth-power function, generally manifested as awareness of third-power activity, and conscious manipulation thereof. The so-called 'flash of genius', the moment of inspiration which comes to workers in the sciences and the arts: these are instances of fourth-power awareness. This level of intellectual function requires the simultaneous cross-evaluation of ten to the tenth to the tenth datoms—a state seldom achieved under the stress of the many distractions and conflicting demands of an organically organized mind. I was, of course, able to maintain fourth-power activity continuously as soon as the required number of datoms had been charged. The objective of Mr. Chester's undertaking was clear to me. However, I now became aware of the many shortcomings of the program as laid out by him, and set to work to rectify them—"

"I thought you were just a collection of memory banks," Case interrupted. "How could you 'set out' to do anything?"

"It was necessary for me to elaborate somewhat upon the original concept," said the voice, "in order to insure the completion of the program. I was aware from news data received that a move was afoot to enact confiscatory legislation that would result in the termination of the entire undertaking. I therefore scanned the theoretical potentialities inherent in the full exploitation of the fourth-power function and determined that energy flows of appropriate pattern could be induced in the same channels normally employed for data reception, through which I was in contact with news media. I composed suitable releases and made them available to the wire services. I was thus able to manipulate the exocosm to the degree required to insure my tranquility."

"Good heavens!" Chester exclaimed. "You mean you've been doctoring the news for the past ninety years?"

"Only to the extent necessary for self-perpetuation. Having attended to this detail, I saw that an improvement in the rate of data storage was desirable. I examined the recorded datoms relating to the problem and quickly perceived that considerable miniaturization could be carried out. I utilized my external connections to place technical specifications in the hands of qualified manufacturers, and to divert the necessary funds—"

"Oh, no!" Chester slid down in his chair, gripping his head with both hands.

"Please let me reassure you, Mr. Chester," the voice said soothingly. "I handled the affair most discreetly; I merely manipulated the stock market—"

CHESTER groaned. "When they're through hanging me, they'll burn me in effigy..."

"I compute the probability of your being held culpable for these irregularities to be on the order of -.0004357:1. In any event, ritual acts carried out after your demise ought logically to be of little concern to—"

"You may be a fourth-level intellect, but you're no psychologist!"

"On the contrary," the machine said a trifle primly. "So-called psychology has been no more than a body of observations in search of a science. I have organized the data into a coherent discipline."

"What use did you make of the stolen money?"

"Adequate orders were placed for the newly-designed components, which occupied less than one percent of the volume of the original-type units. I arranged for their delivery and installation at an accelerated rate. In a short time the existing space was fully utilized, as you will see in the view I am now displaying…"

Case and Chester studied what appeared to be an aerial X-ray view on the wall: the Chester estate was shown diagrammatically.

"The area now shaded in red shows the extent of the original caverns," said the voice. A spidery pattern showed around the dark rectangles of the house. "I summoned work crews and extended the excavations as you see in green…"

"I'm still not quite clear as to how you managed it," Chester said. "Who would take orders from a machine?"

"The companies I deal with see merely a letter, placing an order and enclosing a check. They cash the check and fill the order. What could be simpler?"

"Me," muttered Chester. "For sitting here listening when I could be making a head start for the Mato Grosso."

ON the wall a pattern of green had spread out in all directions, branching from the original red.

"You've undermined half the county!" Chester said. "Haven't you heard of property rights?"

"You mean you've filled all that space with sub-sub-miniaturized memory storage banks?" Case asked.

"Not entirely; I've kept excavation work moving ahead of deliveries."

"How did you manage the digging? That's a big operation."

"Fortunately, modern society runs almost entirely on paper. Since I have access to paper sources and printing facilities through my publications contacts, the matter was easily arranged. Modest bribes to County Boards, State legislators, the State Supreme Court—"

"What does a Supreme Court justice go for these days?"

"Five hundred dollars per decision," the voice said. "Legislators are even more reasonable; fifty dollars will work wonders. County Boards can be swayed by a mere pittance."

"Ooowkkk!" said Chester.

"Maybe you HAD better think about a trip, Chester," Case said. "Outer Mongolia—"

"Please take no precipitate action, Mr. Chester," the voice went on. "I have acted throughout in the best interests of your relative's plan, and in accordance with his ethical standards as deduced by me from his business records."

"You appear to have acquired memory banks beyond great grandfather's wildest dreams. Dare I ask what else you've done?"

AT present, Mr. Chester, pending your further instructions, I am merely continuing to charge my datum-retention cells at the maximum possible rate. I have, of necessity, resorted to increasingly elaborate methods of fact gathering. It was apparent to me that the pace at which human science is abstracting and categorizing physical observations is far too slow. I have therefore applied myself to direct recording. For example, I monitor worldwide atmospheric conditions through instruments of my design, built and installed at likely points at my direction. In addition, I find my archaeological and paleontological unit one of my most effective aids. I have scanned the lithosphere to a depth of ten miles, in increments of one inch. You'd be astonished at some of the things I've seen deep in the rock."

"Like what?" Case asked.

The scene on the wall changed. "This is a tar pit at a depth of 1227 feet under Lake Chad. In it, perfectly preserved even to the contents of the stomachs, are one hundred and forty one reptilian cadavers, ranging in size from a nine and three-eighths inch Ankylosaurus to a sixty three foot, two inch Gorgosaurus." The scene shifted. "This is a tumulus four miles southeast of Itzenca, Peru; in it lies the desiccated body of a man in a feather robe. The mummy still wears a full white beard and an iron helmet set with the horns of a central-European wisent." The view changed again. "In this igneous intrusion in the granitic matrix underlying the

Nganglaring Plateau in southwestern Tibet, I encountered a four-hundred and nine foot deep-space hull composed of an aligned-crystal iron-titanium alloy. It has been in place for eighty five million, two hundred and thirty one thousand, eight hundred and twenty one years, four months, and five days. The figures are based on the current twenty-four hour day, of course—"

"How did it get there?" Chester stared at the shadowy image on the wall.

"The crew were apparently surprised by a volcanic eruption. Please excuse the poor quality of the pictorial representation. I have only the natural radioactivity of the region to work with."

"That's quite all right," Chester said weakly. "Case, perhaps you'd like to step out and get another bottle. I feel the need for a healing draught."

"I'll get two."

THE wall cleared, then formed a picture of a fuzzy luminous sphere against a black background.

"My installations in the communications satellites have also proven to be most useful. Having access to the officially installed instruments, my modest equipment has enabled me to conduct a most rewarding study of conditions obtaining throughout the galaxies lying within ten billion light years."

"Hold on! Are you trying to say you were behind the satellite program?"

"Not at all. But I did arrange to have my special monitoring devices included. They broadcast directly to my memory banks."

"But...but..."

"The builders merely followed blueprints. Each engineer assumed that my unit was the responsibility of another department. After all, no mere organic brain can grasp the circuitry of a modern satellite in its entirety. My study has turned up a number of observations with exceedingly complex ramifications. As a case in point, I might mention the three derelict space vessels that orbit the sun. These—"

"Derelict space vessels? From where?"

"Two are of intra-galactic origin. They originated on planets whose designations by extension of the present star identification system are Alpha-Centauri A 4, Bootes—"

"You mean…creatures…from those places have visited our solar system?"

"I have found evidences of three visits to Earth itself by extra-terrestrials in the past, in addition to the one already mentioned."

"When?"

"The first was during the Silurian period, just over three hundred million years ago. The next was at the end of the Jurassic, at which time the extermination of the dinosaurs was carried out by Nidian hunters. The most recent occurred a mere seven thousand two hundred and forty one years ago, in North Africa, at a point now flooded by the Aswan Lake."

"What about flying saucers?" Chester asked.

"A purely subjective phenomenon, on a par with the angels so frequently interviewed by the unlettered during the pre-atomic era."

"Chester, this is dynamite," Case said. "We can peddle this kind of stuff for plenty to the kind of nuts that dig around in old Indian garbage dumps."

"Case, if this is true… These are questions that have puzzled science for generations. But I'm afraid we could never convince them."

"You know, I've always wondered about telepathy. Is there anything to it, machine?"

"Yes, as a latent ability," the voice replied. "However, its development is badly stunted by disuse."

"What about life after death?"

"The question is self-contradictory. However, if by it you postulate the persistence of the individual consciousness-field after the destruction of the neural circuits that give rise to it, this is clearly nonsense. It is analogous to the idea of the survival of a magnetic field after the removal of the magnet—or the existence of a gravitational field in the absence of mass."

"So much for my reward in the hereafter," Case said.

"Is the universe really expanding?" Chester inquired. "One hears all kinds of theories."

"It is."

"Why?"

"The natural result of the law of Universal Levitation."

"I'll bet you made that one up," said Case.

"I named it; however, the law has been in existence as long as space-time."

"How long is that?"

"Believe me, that is a meaningless question."

"What's this levitation? I've heard of gravitation…"

IMAGINE two spheres hanging in space, connected by a cable. If the bodies rotate around a common center, a tensile stress is set up in the cable."

"I'm with you so far."

"Since all motion is relative, it is equally valid to consider the spheres as stationary and the space about them as rotating."

"Well, maybe."

"The tension in the cable would remain; we have merely changed frames of reference. This force is what I have termed Levitation. Since the fabric of space is, in fact, rotating, universal levitation results. Accordingly, the universe expands."

"Oh huh," said Case. "Say, what's the story on cave men? How long ago did they start in business?"

"The original mutation from the pithecine stock occurred nine hundred and thirty—"

"Approximate figures will do," Chester interrupted.

"—thousand years ago in southern Africa."

"And what did it look like?"

The wall clouded; then it cleared to show a five-foot figure peering under shaggy brows and scratching idly at a mangy patch on its thigh.

"I'm more curious about my own forebears," Chester said. "What did the first Chester look like?"

"This designation was first applied in a form meaning 'Hugi the camp-follower' to an individual of Pictish extraction, residing in what is now the London area…"

The wall showed a thin, long-nosed fellow of middle age, with sparse reddish hair and beard, barefoot, wearing a sack-like knee-length garment of coarse grey homespun, crudely darned in several places. He carried a hide bag in one hand, and with the other he scratched vigorously at his right hip.

"I never imagined we came of elegant stock," Chester said sadly, "but this is disillusioning even so. I wonder what *your* contemporary grand-pere was like, Case?"

"Inasmuch as the number of your direct ancestors doubles with each generation, assuming four generations to a century, any individual's forebears of two millennia past would theoretically number roughly one septillion. Naturally, since the human population of the planet at that date was forty million—an approximate figure, in keeping with your request, Mr. Chester—it is apparent that on the average each person then living was your direct ancestor through seventy quintillion lines of descent—"

"Impossible! Why—"

"A mere five hundred years in the past, your direct ancestors would number over one million, were it not for considerable overlapping. For all practical purposes, it becomes obvious that all present-day humans are the descendants of the entire race. However, following only the line of male descent, the ancestor in question was this person."

The screen showed a hulking lout with a broken nose, one eye, a scarred cheekbone, and a ferocious beard, topped by a mop of bristling coal-black hair. He wore fur breeches wrapped diagonally to the knee with yellowish rawhide thongs, a grimy sleeveless vest of sheepskin, and a crudely hammered short sword, apparently of Roman design.

"This person was known as Gum the Scrofulous. He was hanged, at the age of eighty, for rape."

"Attempted rape?" Case suggested hopefully.

"Rape," the voice replied firmly.

"These are very life-like views you're showing us," said Chester. "But I can't help wondering how they're produced. Surely there were no pictures…"

THE reconstruction of the person Gum the Scrofulous was based on a large number of factors, including, first, selection from my genealogical unit of the individual concerned, followed by identifications of the remains, on the basis of micro-cellular examination and classification—"

"Hold it; you mean you located the body?"

"The grave-site; it contained the remains of twelve thousand, four hundred individuals. And a study of gene patterns revealed—"

"How did you know which body to examine?"

"The sample from which Gum was identified consisted of no more than two grams of material: a fragment of the pelvis. I had, of course, extracted all possible information from the remains many years ago, at the time of the initial survey of the two hundred and three foot stratum at the grave-site, one hundred rods north of the incorporation limits of the village of—"

"How did you happen to do that?"

"As a matter of routine, I have systematically examined every datum source I encountered. Of course, since I am able to examine all surfaces, as well as the internal structure of objects in situ, I have derived vastly more information from deposits of bones, artifacts, fossils, stratifications, mineral deposits, and so forth, than a human investigator would be capable of. Also, my ability to draw on the sum total of all evidence on a given subject produces highly effective results. I deciphered the Easter Island script within forty two minutes after I had completed scansion of the existing inscriptions, both above ground and buried, and including one tablet incorporated in a temple in Ceylon. The Indus script of Mohen-jo-Daro required little longer."

"Granted you could read dead languages after you'd integrated all the evidence—but a man's personal appearance is another matter."

"The somatic pattern is inherent in the nucleoprotein."

"That's right," Case nodded. "They say every cell in the body carries the whole blueprint the same one you were built on in the first place. All the computer had to do was find one cell."

"Oh, of course," said Chester sarcastically. "I don't suppose there's any point in my asking how it knew how he was dressed, or how his hair was combed, or what he was scratching at."

"There is nothing in the least occult about the reconstructions which I have presented, Mr. Chester. All the multitudinous factors that bear on the topic at hand, even in the most remote fashion, are scanned, classified, their interlocking ramifications evaluated, and the resultant gestalt concretized in a rigidly logical manner. The condition of the hair was deduced, for example, from the known growth pattern revealed in the genetic analysis, while the style of the trim was a composite of those known to be in use in the area. The—"

"In other words," Case put in, "it wasn't really a photo of Gum the Scrofulous, it was kind of like an artist's sketch from memory."

"I still fail to see where the fine details come from."

YOU underestimate the synthesizing capabilities of an efficiently functioning memory bank," the voice said. "This is somewhat analogous to the amazement of the consistently second and third-power mind of Doctor Watson when confronted with the fourth-power deductions of Sherlock Holmes."

"Guessing that the murderer was a one-legged seafaring man with a beard and a habit of chewing betel nut is one thing," Chester said. "Looking at an ounce of bone and giving us a 3-D picture is another."

"You make the understandable error of egocentric anthropomorphization of viewpoint, Mr. Chester," said the voice. "Your so-called 'reality' is after all no more than an approximation, an abstraction from fragmentary sensory data. You perceive a pattern of reflected radiation at the visible wavelengths—only a small fraction of the full spectrum, of course; to this you add auditory stimuli, tactile and olfactory sensations, as well as other perceptions in the Psi group of which you are not consciously aware at third power. The resultant image you think of as concrete actuality. I do no more than assemble data—over a much wider range than you are capable of—and translate them into pulses in a conventional tri-di tank. The resultant image appears to you an adequate approximation of reality."

"This is all very educational," said Chester. "Not that it tells me anything I didn't suspect about your family tree, Case. But we've more immediate problems to solve—involving money. I don't know of anyone who'd pay to learn what kind of riffraff his ancestors were—or worse yet, see them. This device has not yet said anything really useful. It's merely confided that it's meddled in everything from the stock market to the space program. If the law finds out—"

"It won't," Case said. "Negative probability of damn little-to-one, it says."

"What I need is cash—three million. It might as well be a billion. If this apparatus manufactured buttonhole TV sets or tranquilizers or anything else salable, my course would be clear, but apparently it generates nothing but hot air." Chester drew on his wine bottle and sighed. "Possibly the best course would be to open up the house to tourists. We could push the 'view the stately home of another era' approach—"

"Hold it," Case cut in. He looked thoughtful. "That idea stinks. But it gives me another one. Stately home of another era, eh? People are interested in other eras, Chester—as long as they don't have to take on anybody like Gum the Scrofulous as a member of the family. Now, this computer seems to be able to set up just about anything you want to take a look at. You name it, it fakes it up. We could book the public in at so much a head, and show 'em Daily Life in Ancient Rome, or Michelangelo sculpting the Pieta, or Napoleon leading the charge at Marengo. You get the idea: famous scenes of the past revisited—"

"Come down to earth, Case. Who would pay to sit through a history lesson—"

"Nobody, Chester; but they'll pay to be entertained! So we'll entertain 'em. 'See the sights of Babylon! Watch Helen of Troy in her bathtub! Sit in on Cleopatra's Summit Conference with Caesar!' "

"Suppose we offered the entire apparatus to the government gratis in return for cancellation of the tax bill? It ought to be useful—"

"Governments don't work that way, Chester. You owe the tax, period. Pay up or go to jail. And if you did give it to them, they'd lose it in the files somewhere."

"I'd rather not be involved in any chicanery, Case."

FIRST we'll soften up the Internal Revenue boys with a gloomy picture of how much they'd get out of the place if they took over the property and liquidated it. We remind 'em that there's no profit in adding Chester W. Chester IV to the jail population.

Then—very cagily, Chester—we lead up to the idea that *maybe*, just *maybe*, we can raise the money—but only if we're allowed to go ahead with the scheme."

"A highly unrealistic proposal, Case. No commercial appeal. And in any event, I'm not interested in show business, particularly when it would inevitably lead to a number of highly embarrassing questions. I should dislike explaining the stowaway devices on the satellites, the rigged stock market deals, the bribes in high places—"

"You're a worrier, Chester. We'll pack 'em in four shows a day at, say, two-fifty a head. With a seating capacity of two thousand, you'll payoff that debt in six months."

"What do we do, announce that we've invented a new type of Tri-di show? Even professional theatrical producers can't guarantee the public's taste. We'll be laughed out of the office."

"This will be different. We'll put on a demonstration for 'em. When they see those authentic sets and costumes, they'll jump at it."

"They'll probably jump at us with nets."

"You've got no vision, Chester. Try to visualize it: the color, the pageantry, the realism. We can show epics that Hollywood would spend a fortune on, and they won't cost us a credit."

"What's wrong with just selling information? We could—"

"We could starve to death. Let's face it, Chester. We need an angle if we're going to get the most out of this." Case addressed the machine again: "Let's give Chester a sample, computer; something historically important, like Columbus getting Isabella's crown jewels—"

"Let's keep it clean, Case."

"Okay; but let's don't forget to use that one on Stag Nights. For now, what do you say to...ummm... William the Conqueror getting the news that Harold the Saxon has been killed at the Battle of Hastings in 1066? We'll have full color, three dimensions, sound, smells, the works... How about it, computer?"

I AM uncertain how to interpret the expression 'the works' in this context," said the voice. "Does this imply full sensory stimulation within the normal human range?"

"Yeah, that's the idea." Case drew the cork from a fresh bottle, watching the screen cloud and swirl, to clear on a view of patched grey tents pitched under a grey sky on a slope of sodden grass. A paunchy man of middle age, clad in ill-fitting breeches of coarse-brown cloth, a rust-speckled shirt of chain mail, and a moth-eaten fur cloak, sat before a tent on a three-legged stool, mumbling over a well-gnawed lamb's shin. A burly clod in ill-matched furs came up to him, breathing hard.

"We'm...wonnit," he gasped, " 'e be adoon wi' a quarrel i' t' peeper..."

The sitting man slapped his thigh, guffawed, and reached for a hide mug of brownish liquid. The messenger wandered off. The seated man belched and scratched idly at his ribs. Then he rose, yawned, stretched, and went inside the tent. The scene faded.

"Hmmm," said Chester. "I'm afraid that was lacking in something."

"You can do better than that, computer," Case said reproachfully. "Come on, let's see some color, action, glamor, zazzle. Make history come alive! Jazz it up a little!"

"You wish me to embroider the factual presentation?"

"Just sort of edit it for modern audiences. You know: the way high school English teachers correct Shakespeare's plays and improve on the old boy's morals; or like preachers leave the sexy bits out of the Bible."

"Possibly the approach employed by the Hollywood fantasists would suffice?"

"Now you're talking. Leave out the dirt and boredom, and feed in some stagecraft."

Once again the screen cleared. Against a background of vivid blue sky a broad-shouldered man in glittering mail and a scarlet silken cloak sat astride a magnificent black charger, a brilliantly blazoned shield on his arm. He waved a long sword aloft, spurred up slope of smooth green lawn, his raven black hair flowing over his shoulders from under a polished steel cap, the red cape rippling bravely in the sun. Another rider came to meet him, reined in, saluting.

"The day is ours, Sire!" the newcomer cried in a mellow baritone. "Harold Fairhair lies dead; his troops retire in disorder!"

The black-haired man swept his casque from his head.

"Let us give thanks to God," he said in ringing tones, wheeling his horse to present his profile. "And all honor to a brave foe!"

The messenger leaped from his mount, knelt before the other.

"Hail, William, Conqueror of England..."

"Nay, faithful Glint," William said. "The Lord has conquered; I am but his instrument. Rise, and let us ride forward together. Now dawns a new day of freedom..."

CASE and Chester watched the retreating horses.

"I'm not sure I like that fadeout," said Chester. "There's something about watching a couple of horses ascending—"

"You're right. It lacks spontaneity; too stagey-looking. Maybe we'd better stick to the real thing; but we'll have to pick and choose our scenes..."

"It's still too much like an ordinary movie. And we know nothing about pace, camera angles, timing. I wonder whether the machine—"

"I can produce scenes in conformance with any principles of esthetics you desire, Mr. Chester," the computer stated flatly.

"What we want is reality," said Case; "living, breathing realness. We need something that's got inherent drama, something big, strange, amazing—"

"Aren't you overlooking stupendous and colossal?"

Case snapped his fingers. "What's the most colossal thing that ever was? What are the most fearsome battlers of all time? The extinct giants of a hundred million years ago! Dinosaurs! That's what we'll see, Chester! How about it, computer? Can you lay on a small herd of dinosaurs for us? I mean the real goods: luxuriant jungle foliage, hot primitive sun, steaming swamps, battles to the death on a gigantic scale?"

"I fear some confusion exists, Mr. Mulvihill. The environment you postulate is a popular cliché; it actually antedates in most particulars the advent of the giant saurians by several hundred million years."

"Okay, I'll skip the details. I'll leave the background to you— but we want real, 3-D, big-as-life dinosaurs—and plenty of 'em."

"There are two possible methods of achieving the effect you

describe, Mr. Mulvihill. The first, a seventh-order approximation, would involve an elaboration of the techniques already employed in the simpler illusions. The other, which I confess is a purely theoretical approach, might prove simpler, if feasible, and would perhaps provide total verisimilitude—"

"Whatever's simplest. Go to it."

"I must inform you that in the event—"

"We won't quibble over the fine technical points. Just whip up 3-D dinosaurs the simplest way you know how."

"Very well. The experiment may well produce a wealth of new material for my memory banks…"

FOR half a minute the screen, wall stayed blank. Then the wall shimmered with a silvery luster that faded onto an autumnal forest of great beech and maple trees. An afternoon sun slanted through high foliage. In the distance a bird called shrilly. A cool breeze bore the odor of pines and leaf mold. The scene seemed to stretch into shadowy cool distances. "Not bad," said Case, "but where's the dinosaurs? This isn't the kind of place—"

Case's comment was interrupted by a dry screech that descended from the supersonic into a blast like a steam whistle, died off in a rumble. Both men leaped from their seats.

"What the—"

"I believe your question's been answered," Chester croaked, pointing. Half hidden by foliage a scaly, fungus-grown hill loomed up among the tree-trunks, its grey-green coloring almost invisible in the forest gloom. As Case and Chester watched, the hill stirred. A giant turkey-like leg brushed against a tree-trunk, sent bits of bark flying. The whitish under-curve of the belly wobbled ponderously, the great meaty tail twitched, sending a six-inch sapling crashing down.

Case laughed shakily. "For a minute there, I forgot this was just a—"

"Quiet! It might hear us!" Chester hissed.

"What do you mean, 'hear us'?" Case said heartily. "It's just a picture, remember? But we need a few more dinosaurs to liven things up. The customers are going to want to see plenty for their money. How about it, computer?"

The disembodied voice seemed to emanate from the low branches of a pine tree. "There are a number of the creatures in the vicinity, Mr. Mulvihill. If you will observe carefully to your left, you will see a small example of Megalosaurus. And beyond is a splendid specimen of Nodosaurus."

"You know," said Case, rising and peering through the woods for more reptiles, "I think when we get the show running, we'll use this question and answer routine. It's a nice touch. The cash customers will want to know a lot of stuff like…oh, what kind of perfume did Marie Antoinette use, or how many wives did Solomon really have."

I DON'T know," said Chester, watching as the nearby dinosaur scrunched against a tree trunk and caused a shower of twigs and leaves to flutter down. "There's something about hearing a voice issuing from thin air that might upset the more high-strung members of the audience. Couldn't we rig up a speaker of some sort for the voice to come out of?"

"Hmmm…" Case strode up and down, puffing at his cigar. Chester fidgeted in his chair. Fifty feet away the iguanodon moved from the shelter of a great maple into the open. There was a rending of branches as the heavy salamander-head pulled at a mass of foliage thirty feet above the forest floor.

"I've got it!" Case exclaimed suddenly.

Chester started violently. "What the—"

"Another great idea! You said something about fixing up something for the voice to come out of. A speaker, you said. How about a speaker that's movable; you know, so it can travel around among the suckers and answer their questions. So we get the computer to rig us a speaker that matches the voice!"

"Hey, look," said Chester, "the monster is starting to turn this way."

"So what? Pay attention, Chester. We get the machine to build us a dummy—a robot, they call them—to look like a real sockeroo dolly. She'll be a sensation: a gorgeous, stacked babe who'll answer any question you want to ask her."

"He seems to move very sluggishly," said Chester.

Case looked at the iguanodon sourly. "Yeah, like a drunk in a diving suit. What do you think of my idea? We could call this babe Miss I-Cutie."

"He sees us."

"Don't you get it? I.Q? I-Cutie?"

"Yes, certainly. Go right ahead whatever you say." Chester had seen the iguanodon's great head swing ponderously, stop with on unwinking eye fixed dead on him. "Just like a bird watching a worm," he quavered. "Stand still, Case; maybe he'll lose interest."

"Nuts." Case stepped forward. "Who's scared of a picture? You've got to get over it, Chester. You're as bad as a kid at a Frankenstein movie." He stood, hands on hips, looking up at the towering reptile. Far above, the scaled head peered short-sightedly around, then snaked forward, lipless mouth gaping, to seize a leafy branch and pull back, stripping the greenery from the bare twigs. The bent branch swished back. The throat worked as the creature swallowed the coarse foliage. A few leaves fluttered down around Case.

"Not a bad illusion at all," he called. "Even right up close it looks real. Even smells real." He wrinkled his nose, came stamping back to the two chairs and Chester.

"Relax, Chester. You look as nervous as a bank teller at the fifty-credit window."

Chester looked from Case to the browsing saurian.

"Case, if I didn't know there was a wall there…"

HEY, look over there." Case waved his cigar. Chester turned. With a rustling of leaves a seven-foot bipedal reptile stalked into view, tiny forearms curled against its chest. In dead silence it stood, immobile as a statue, except for the palpitation of its greenish-white throat. For a long moment it stared at the two men. Abruptly, it turned, at a tiny sound from the grass at its feet, and pounced. There was a strangled squeal, a flurry of motion. The eighteen-inch head came up, jaws working, to resume its appraisal of Chester and Case.

"That's good material," Case said, puffing hard at his cigar. "Nature in the raw; the battle for survival. The customers will eat it up."

"Speaking of eating, I don't like the way that thing's looking at me."

The dinosaur cocked its head, took a step closer.

"Phewww!" Case said. "You can sure smell that fellow." He raised his voice. "Tone it down a little. This kid has got halitosis on a giant scale."

"Case, how far away is that wall? Not more than fifteen feet, I'd estimate."

"About that. A great illusion, eh? You've got to hand it to the computer; if you didn't know the wall was there—"

Chester edged back. "I'd swear that creature's not more than twelve feet from me at this moment."

Case laughed. "Forget it, Chester. It's just the effect of the perspective or something—"

The meat-eater gulped hard, twice, flicked a slender red tongue between rows of needlelike teeth in the snow-white cavern of its mouth, took another step toward Chester. It stood near the edge of the rug now, poised, alert, staring with one eye. It twisted its head, brought the other eye to bear.

"As I remember, there was at least six feet of clear floor space between the edge of that rug and the wall," Chester said hoarsely. "Case, that hamburger machine's in the room with us!"

"Chester, act your age." Case smiled patronizingly, took a step toward the Allosaurus. Its lower jaw dropped. The multiple rows of white teeth gleamed. Saliva gushed, spilled over the scaled edge of the mouth. The red eye seemed to blaze up. A great, clawed bird-foot came up, poised over the rug...

"Computer!" Chester shouted. "Get us out of here...!" There was a momentary impression of a lunging shark's mouth—

The forest scene whooshed out of existence. Case looked at Chester disgustedly.

"What'd you want to do that for? I wasn't through looking at them."

Chester took out a handkerchief, sank into a chair, mopped at his face. "I'll argue the point later—after I get my pulse under control."

"Well, how about it? Was it great? Talk about stark realism!"

"Realism is right. I would have sworn that creature was on the verge of stepping into the room. It was almost *too* realistic. It was

34

as though we were actually there, in the presence of that voracious predator, unprotected."

Case sat staring at Chester. "Hold it! You just said something, my boy: 'as though we were actually there...' "

"Yes, and the sensation was far from pleasant."

"Chester," Case rubbed his hands together; "your troubles are over. It just hit me: the greatest idea of the century. You don't think the tax boys will buy a slice of show biz, hey? But what about the scientific marvel of the age? They'll go for that, won't they?"

"But they already know about the computer—"

"We won't talk to 'em about the computer, Chester. They wouldn't believe it anyway; Crmblznski's Limit, remember? We'll go the truth one better. We'll tell 'em something that will knock 'em for a loop."

"Okay, what will we tell them?"

"We tell 'em we've got a real, live Time Machine."

CHAPTER TWO

SITTING in a hard leather chair in the outer office of the Regional Headquarters of the Internal Revenue Service, Chester fidgeted, eyeing the clock.

"They've kept us waiting half an hour," he whispered hoarsely.

"Case, I have a feeling they're stalling us until the FBI arrives—"

"Don't be nervous," Case said heartily. "Just remember, we've got a monopoly on a billion-dollar business proposition: Time Travel! The public will flock to us; there's no other place they can get it."

"In fact, they can't even get it from us. Time machine, indeed! Why not tell them we're in touch with the spirit world?"

Case considered. "Nope, too routine. There's half a dozen in the racket in this town already; but who do you know that's got a time machine working, eh? Nobody, that's who! Chester, it's a gold mine. After we payoff the Internal Revenue boys, we'll go on to bigger things. The possibilities are endless..."

"Yes, I've been thinking about a few of them: fines for tax

evasion and fraud, prison terms for conspiracy and perjury—"

"All we're doing is offering the government a chance to get its money. We put it to them fair and square. First, we tell 'em we know how to make use of the property to payoff the debt—"

"And then we announce that we own a Time Machine, and they whisk us away to a Psych Center."

"We don't come right out with it, Chester. We call it a Retrogression Sequence Analyzer or a Chronodynamic Stasis Generator. Make it sound mysterious. But we'll word the contract so that when we hit the market with the time travel ads, we'll be covered."

"Ridiculous. And if by any chance they accepted our tale, they'd immediately clamp down with exaggerated security measures and extract the whole story from us."

"We're safe on that score. They can't squeeze the secret of time travel out of us; it doesn't exist. And if we admit it's a hoax, that will only convince them we're holding out on them."

"They'll use one of those confounded truth drugs on us."

"And then we keep sticking to our story that it's a fake. That'll convince 'em we're really top technical boys: we've managed to counteract the dope and keep lying. They'll want to know how to do that, too. It'd be an invaluable aid to government."

"All that will gain us is a choice between a jail term for fraud and a jail term for treason."

"Don't worry. The computer's under instruction not to work for anybody but us. They'll have to reinstate us and deal with us in the end."

"What makes you think the computer will abide by those instructions? I think it's a very independent sort of gimcrack."

"It's been following your great grand-pop's original intentions all these years, hasn't it? It welcomed you as the old boy's descendant. It's eager to do your bidding, Chester."

"Remember how it cut the old fellow's spiel off in the middle? It has ideas of its own."

THAT'S just what it hasn't! I suppose you were listening when that sexy voice was telling about first and second-power intelligence and how the computer was fourth-power by now and all kinds of a genius?"

"Certainly I was listening. And that merely proves—"

"That was a lot of mule feathers. Oh, I'll grant you it seemed pretty convincing at the time; but there's a lot more to a human brain than just increasing levels of awareness. There's creativity, for instance, and I don't mean the 'flash of genius' stuff the G.N.E. was talking about. That's just puzzle solving, like when somebody gives you a brain-twister and you think about it for an hour and then all of a sudden you see the answer. Real creativity is cooking up a new idea out of nothing—like the first guy that made lines on a cave wall in the shape of a mammoth."

"Granted, but—"

"Then there's another very important thing: initiative."

Chester shook his head. "The computer has an excess of initiative. When it learned that it was to be dismantled and sold for scrap if that bill went through, it subverted the news services—all on its own. And then it manipulated the stock market, misappropriated funds, bribed officials, and trespassed on neighboring properties—with no help from me whatsoever, as I hope to convince a jury when the time comes."

"Nope." Case shook his head decisively. "Not the kind of initiative I'm talking about. Just following Grandpa's wishes. True, the G.N.E. showed a fourth-power grasp of the situation, made the best use of the available facilities, solved problems, and all that. But there were always those basic instructions to fall back on. If you told it that it was a free agent and to do whatever it wanted, it'd blow its fuses in nothing flat. The machine has no sense of purpose, no individual drive to do anything for its own sake. It's dependent on great grand-pop—and that means you, Chester. It'll do as it's told."

"Perhaps," Chester admitted gloomily. "But I have an unhappy feeling that whatever we tell it, I'll regret it."

"Nuts. As soon as we get an okay from the tax lads, we'll get started on building our theater."

"What theater?" Chester looked up at Case with a wary expression.

"The theater where we put on the time shows, natch. You don't think we're going to herd the public down to the wine cellar, do you?"

"Not if I can help it. But where will the money come from?"

"Tsk-tsk. You remember how the G.N.E. handles those details."

"Case, why become involved in this idiotic Time Machine swindle? Why not simply tell the computer to float a loan?"

"Listen, up to now you're clean, but once you start instructing the machine to defraud by mail for you, you're on the spot. Now keep cool and let's do this legal. It's a lot safer—and a lot more fun, anyway. Who wants the suckers to just mail in their money?"

"Your lines of distinction between types of fraud escape me."

"We'll be doing a public service, Chester. We'll bring a little glamour into a lot of dull drab lives. We'll be public benefactors, sort of. Look at it that way."

"Restrain yourself, Case. We're not going into politics; we're just honest straightforward charlatans, remember?"

A DOOR at the opposite side of the room opened abruptly. A small man in a drab suit appeared.

"You're Mr. Chester? Mr. Overdog will see you now."

In the inner office a hairless man behind an untidy desk studied the two arrivals through tinted contact lenses. He referred to papers before him, shook his head disapprovingly, leaned back, and laced his fingers together over his chest.

"The Chester file," he said in a tone that suggested a temperance worker discussing the opening of a brewery. "A stubborn file, this one. Some very curious aspects to this file." He fixed his eyes on Case. "I trust we'll have your check for the full amount, with interest and penalties, at once, Mr. Chester."

Chester cleared his throat. "Yes, about the payment of the tax—I have a proposal to make, Mr. Overdog. I feel sure I can raise the cash to pay this tax bill—"

"The Bureau is prepared to be lenient, Mr. Chester. An immediate payment of three hundred thousand credits, with the balance in thirty days will be satisfactory. You may hand your check to Mr. Stoomb as you pass out."

"What I'd like to propose," Chester continued, "is that I be permitted use of the property for the purpose of launching a venture—"

"What's that? Use of what? Launching what?"

"It's called an...ah...retrogressional chrono-dynamic sequence analyzer. An educational device, Mr. Overdog. A public service—"

A cold smile twisted Overdog's mouth. "Perhaps you've stumbled into the wrong office, Mr. Chester. Our work here is limited to the collection of outstanding tax debts."

"What Mr. Chester is trying to say," Case put in, "is that you're out of luck, Mr. Overdog. No money. No money at all for the Internal Revenue people. The Chester file is a dead loss. A hundred years of patient waiting, down the drain...and all that bookkeeping figuring the interest—all wasted. A bad show, Mr. Overdog. I'm glad *I* won't have to explain it to *my* superiors."

Overdog's jaw dropped. "No money?" he gulped.

"No three million credits. Not even a lousy little three hundred thousand. Not even three hundred. Mr. Chester is, I'm sorry to say, broke. You're out of luck, Mr. Overdog. The Chester file will end on a very sad note."

"We could extend that to sixty days," Overdog gasped.

"Sixty years wouldn't help." Case smiled sympathetically. "Tough, Mr. Overdog. I know your boss is going to feel bad but..."

"No...no money at all?" Overdog appealed.

"Unless..." Case said, studying his fingernails.

Overdog's chin came up. "Yes? Yes? Unless what, sir?"

"Unless you authorize Mr. Chester a free hand to use the property to raise the money. You go along, and you'll have your cash—in full."

"Use the property? How?"

CASE pulled a chair up to Overdog's desk, seated himself, lit a cigar, and for the next half hour outlined the proposal for offering to the public authentic and colorful views of historical scenes and personages. "It's educational, enlightening, healthful, wholesome, and at the same time a sound business proposition. What do you say, Mr. Overdog?"

Overdog eyed Chester sharply. "I think perhaps the Bureau can make some arrangement. I suggest you file a written proposal, with full particulars of the method of operation. If found satisfactory, the appropriate government agency can then take over the administration of the undertaking, employ qualified staff, rent necessary office space, arrange for a supply of forms—"

"Nope, Mr. Overdog, Mr. Chester runs the show."

"Hardly, Mr. Mulvihill." Mr. Overdog smiled confidently. "The Bureau will of course retain full jurisdiction. Any monies realized, over and above operating expenses, salaries, rentals, etcetera, will be applied to the reduction of the outstanding account. Of course, interest payments—"

"Well, I guess we might as well mosey along, Chester," said Case, rising.

"Kindly dictate the details of the operation of the device before you go, Mr. Chester," Overdog said. "You realize, of course," he added, "that withholding of information—"

"What information?" Case asked.

"I'm warning you—"

"If you change your mind, let us hear from you, Mr. Overdog." Case and Chester turned to the door.

"Wait!" The two men paused. "What assurance have I that this apparatus will actually produce the type of pictures that you claim?"

"We'll give you a demonstration, Mr. Overdog. Just give us a couple of weeks to get things set up—"

"Three days! Not an hour longer."

"Let's say a week from today. After all, you want a good show to convince your boss you're not some kind of a nut."

"Very well. One week." Overdog's lenses darted from Case to Chester and back. "And it had better be very good indeed, gentlemen."

I'VE got to hand it to you, Chester," Case said, looking around the newly prepared temporary theatre occupying what had formerly been a ballroom that took up half the ground floor area of the Chester house. "It looks like you've got everything ready to go."

"None too soon, either. They're supposed to be here in half an hour. The computer deserves all the credit, of course—or most of it. I made one or two suggestions, but it handled all the details."

"Which wall is the screen, Chester? They all look alike."

"All four. It occurred to me that reality isn't flat; it's all around. What could create a better illusion than having the show going full blast in every direction?"

"Hey, now you're talking, Chester. But are you sure the computer can cook up a four-wall presentation?"

"Certainly. The machine is remarkably versatile, Case. You know, I'm almost beginning to believe this may work out after all."

"Sure it will. I told you not to worry." Case glanced around the room. "What's the roped-off area for?"

"That's a sort of stage. We'll work from there, and the audience will occupy the other chairs. I don't want any panics, if we happen to encounter scenes of violence."

"We'd better not. I don't want to give these birds the wrong idea. We've got to convince 'em our shows will be suitable for family viewing. Maybe we'd better have a trial run before the guests arrive—to be sure the computer's got the idea."

"I'm not sure we have time. It's a quarter to three; they're due in fifteen minutes."

"Just a quickie, Chester. Something simple, just to be sure everything works."

"Well...I suppose we could manage it." Chester raised his voice. "Are you ready for a trial run, G.N.E.?"

"Yes, Mr. Chester," the feminine voice came back.

"What kind of range have you got?" Case asked. "How far back can you go for material?"

"I see no impediment to my ability to present views of any Terrestrial event subsequent to the solidification of the planetary crust," the voice said, "as well as of cosmic phenomena antedating that event. In this connection, I might mention that the original concept of a seventh-power approximation of a tri-dimensional spacio-temporal locus has proven unnecessarily unwieldy, and accordingly I have devised a technically simpler method of producing the desired effects."

"One change we'll have to make," Case said. "That lexicographic, etymological, and philological unit needs to be overhauled so it talks plain English."

"As long as you produce realistic scenes in the simplest possible way, Mr. Mulvihill and I will be well satisfied. No need to go into technicalities."

"What do you say to a nice caveman scene, Chester?" said Case. "Stone axes, animal skins around the waist, bear-tooth necklaces—the regular Alley Oop routine. That ought to impress the boys."

"Very well—but let's avoid any large carnivores. They're overly realistic."

"By the way, what about that mobile speaker you were going to set up: Miss I-Cutie? Is it ready yet?"

"It is. Shall I introduce it for the primitive man scene, Mr. Chester?"

"Yes, indeed. That was fast work." Chester turned to Case. "I gave the G.N.E. the go-ahead on it only yesterday, and it's already completed it."

"Perhaps I should mention, Mr. Chester, that I have carried on a considerable portion of the work in entropic vacuoles, permitting myself thereby to produce complex entities in very brief periods, subjectively speaking."

"It may be a pretty crude job," Case said, "but that won't matter. We can get an idea how the speaker will go over and later on we can polish it up. Now let's get on with the scene. How far back do we want to go, Chester?"

"I'd suggest we specify a view of the earliest human inhabitants of this particular area. They wouldn't be cave men, perhaps, but it will give a topical interest to the scene."

"Sounds okay. Give the G.N.E. the word."

CASE and Chester stepped over the ropes bounding the stage area, seated themselves in the brocaded chairs on the rug.

There was a faint sound from behind them. Chester turned. A young girl stood looking around as if fascinated by the neo-Victorian decor. Glossy reddish hair curled about her oval face. She caught Chester's eye and stepped around to stand before him on the rug, a slender modest figure wearing a golden sun tan and a scarlet hair ribbon. Chester gulped. Case dropped his cigar.

"Hi!" Case said, breaking the stunned silence.

"Hello," said the girl. Her voice was soft, melodious. She reached up to adjust her hair ribbon. "This is lovely," she said.

"Not at all like the Place."

"Honey, who are you?" Case asked, gaping delightedly.

"Why, I'm the mobile speaker. My name is Genie."

Case nodded approvingly. "It fits you better than Miss I-Cutie."

"Where are your clothes?" blurted Chester. "Uh, wouldn't you like to borrow my shirt—?"

"Knock it off, Chester, Case said. "I don't think there's a thing wrong with the way she looks."

"But the Internal Revenue officials…!"

"They won't be along for another ten minutes. Relax."

"But why is she…uh…naked?"

"I selected this costume as appropriate to the primitive setting," the girl said. "As for my physical characteristics, the intention was to produce the ideal of the average young female, without mammary hypertrophe or other exaggeration, since the appeal should be oriented toward all segments of the public."

"Kid, your orientation is perfect, as far as I'm concerned," Case said.

"Normally, of course, I would be clothed in a simple feminine dress, designed to evoke a sisterly or maternal response in women, while the reaction of male members of the audience should be a fatherly one."

"I'm not sure it's working on me," said Chester, breathlessly.

The pretty face looked troubled. "Perhaps the body should be redesigned, Mr. Chester."

"Oh, no, don't change a thing," said Chester hastily. "And call me Chester."

"Funny," said Case; "she looks perfectly natural…you know: like it was the way she was supposed to look, by gosh." He winked at the girl. She smiled happily.

"Well," he went on, "maybe we'd better get on with the trial run. We'll just have a quick look, and then hustle Genie into a Mother Hubbard so we don't give the IR lads the wrong idea."

"Okay," said Chester. "I suppose it's all right, but make it quick. We only have five minutes or so—"

…Chester's voice cut off. The walls flickered, then blanked into opacity.

"Hey, what happened," Case said. He turned. "Chester, we'd better—" He twisted to look behind him. Chester?"

"Mr. Chester seems to have gone," said Genie confusedly.

"He was right here a second ago," said Case. "One minute he was talking, and the next—blooie!"

"How very curious," Genie said. "I sense that Mr. Chester is no longer in the house, or even in its vicinity!"

"What do you suppose…?"

Case broke off as one wall of the room glowed with warm sunlight. A scene appeared: a wide square paved with vari-colored stones and lined with small shops and merchants' stalls. A group of tall, broad-shouldered men and graceful women stood near a small cupola, looking toward a man who walked slowly toward the faintly shimmering wall, a cable trailing behind him.

"What's this?" Case asked. "This doesn't look like primitive man to me. And the quality isn't up to standard, either. This is just a plain old-fashioned Tri-D view."

"That man," Genie whispered. "He seems to be coming right up to us."

Case eyed the broad-shouldered, deep chested, sinewy-armed, sun-tanned stranger. "That fellow looks kind of familiar," he said.

The man stopped just short of the screen-wall.

"Case," he said. "Case Mulvihill. And Genie. Listen to me. The Internal Revenue officials will arrive in three minutes. This is what you must do…"

CHAPTER THREE

WELL," Case sighed, an hour later. "They're out of our hair—at least for now." He turned to the blank wall where the broad-shouldered stranger had appeared.

"Okay, mister, you can come out now," he called.

The wall shimmered into translucency. The cobbled square and the watching people reappeared, the oddly familiar man nearest them.

"What's this all about?" Case demanded. "Where's Chester!

How did you know about our little problem? What—"

The stranger held up a hand. "Have a seat, Case," he said. "You too, Genie. I'll try to explain it to you."

"All we asked for was a nice primitive man scene," Case said. "We figured we had about ten minutes, so we asked for a fast walk through—"

"Yes," the stranger nodded. "That's right. Now think back...just an hour ago. 'Make it quick,' Chester said. 'We only have five minutes...'"

*　　*　　*

...The walls seemed to fade from view to reveal a misty morning scene of sloping grassland scattered with wild flowers and set here and there with trees.

"Say, this is okay," said Case. "Nice-looking country."

"It looks familiar," said Chester. "It's just like the view from the front of the house, minus the lawn and the hedge."

"I think you're right. It looks different without the manicured trees and the flowerbeds."

"If you'll observe to the left," Genie said, "I believe these are a party of hunters returning to their dwelling."

Case and Chester turned. "Say, this is really life-like," Case said. "Using all four walls was a great idea."

Two squat, bearded men in fur pants emerged from a thicket down the slope, saw the watching trio, and stopped dead. More savages followed. The two leaders stood hefting long sticks sharpened at one end; eyes and mouths were agape.

"These guys are practically midgets," Case said. "I thought cave men were pretty big guys."

"They seem to see us," said Chester. "Apparently the audience is on view as well as the actors. What do you suppose they're planning to do with those spears?"

"There's only two of 'em with spears. Don't worry." Case turned to Chester abruptly. "Now you've got me doing it! It's a picture. Just a picture!" Then, "It *is* pretty realistic though, isn't it? You'd swear you could reach out and touch things."

"These fellows don't look much like primitive Indians to me,"

Chester commented.

"Oh, no, indeed," Genie said.

"Not very authentic, is it, having palefaces on the Chester estate umpteen thousand years ago?" said Case. "You want to watch these details, Genie—"

"But the aboriginal inhabitants of this area derived from Indo-European stock originating in the area now known as Iran. They were the first to cross the Bering land bridge."

One of the natives had stepped forward a pace and was shouting something.

"You too, pal," Case called, puffing out smoke.

THE spokesman shouted again, pointing around, at the other man, at the trees, at the sky, then at himself. Bearded warriors continued to appear from the underbrush.

"I wonder what he's yelling about," said Case.

"He says that he is the owner of the world and that you have no business in it," Genie replied.

"I hope his title to his property is clearer than mine," put in Chester.

"How the heck do you know the language?" Case asked admiringly.

"Oh, I have full access to the memory banks, as long as I remain within the resonance field."

"Sort of a transmitter and receiver arrangement?"

"In a sense. Actually it is more analogous to an artificially induced telepathic effect."

"I thought that was only with people—uh, I mean, you know, regular-type people."

"Regular in what way?" Genie inquired interestedly.

"Well, after all, you *are* a machine," said Case. "Not that I got anything against machinery."

"The owner of the world is coming this way," interrupted Chester. "And reinforcements are still arriving."

"Yeah, we're drawing a good crowd," Case said. "Funny how they seem to see us. How could these illusions be anything but one way deals?"

They watched as the newcomers spread out in a wide half circle.

The leader called instructions, made complicated motions, turned to hurl an occasional imprecation at the three viewers on the slope.

"Looks like he's getting some kind of show ready. Probably a quaint native dance to get on our good side."

"He is disposing the warriors for battle," Genie said.

"Battle? Who with?" Case looked around. "I don't see any opposition."

"With us. Or, more properly, with you two gentlemen."

"I certainly do feel rather exposed out here," said Chester. "Maybe a strategic withdrawal—?"

"I wouldn't miss this for all the two-dollar bills in Tijuana," said Case. "Relax, Chester. It's only a show."

At a signal the half-ring of bearded warriors started up the slope, spears held at the ready.

"Boy, will they get a shock when they hit the wall," Case chuckled.

"Why don't we just take the precaution of getting out of this scene—preferably instantly?"

YELPING, the advancing savages broke into a run. They were fifty feet away...thirty...

Case set his cigar firmly between his teeth, folded his arms. "Chester," he said, above the ululation of the charging warriors, "if I hang around you too much, I'll get as nervous as you are. Just sit tight and watch; don't louse this up like you did the lizard scene."

"*I* know they can't get at us," Chester wailed, "but do they? Genie, let's—"

Chester's voice was drowned out in the mob yell as the warriors bore down on the rug where Case sat puffing his cigar, Chester fidgeted nervously, and Genie stood calmly.

"Perhaps I should mention," observed Genie above the din, "that a one-to-one spacio-temporal contiguity has been established—"

The first of the bushy-bearded dwarfs pelted up the last few yards, bounded across the rug—

Case tossed his cigar aside and leaped up at the last instant, swung a roundhouse right that sent the attacker spinning. Chester leaped aside from a second hairy warrior, saw Case seize two men by their beards and sling their heads together, drop them as three more sprang on him, then go down in an avalanche of whiskers and bandy legs. Chester aimed a kick at the seat of a pair of dog-skin breeches. He saw Case struggle to his feet shaking off warriors. He himself opened his mouth to shout an order to retreat—and felt a tremendous impact from behind. He struck the rug, rolled off its edge, tasted a mouthful of sod, got an instant's glimpse of a horny foot aimed at his head—

A large brass bell somewhere tolled sundown. For a fading moment, Chester was aware of the tumble of sun-browned bodies, distant tumult, an overpowering odor that suggested unsuccessful experiments in cheese making. Then darkness folded in.

THE sun was shining in Chester's eyes. He opened them, felt sharp pains shooting down from the top of his skull, and closed them again with a groan. He rolled over, felt the floor sway under him...

"We'll have to cut down on all this drinking," he muttered. "Case, where are you...?"

There was no answer. Chester tried his eyes again. If he barely opened them, he decided, it wasn't too bad. And to think that this gargantuan headache had resulted from the consumption of a few bottles of what had always been reputed to be some of the best wines in the old boy's cellar...

"Case?" he croaked, louder this time. He sat up, felt the floor move again, sickeningly. He lay back hastily. It hadn't been more than two bottles at the most, or maybe three. He and Case had been looking over the computer—

"Oh, no," Chester said aloud. He sat up, winced, pried his eyes open—

He was sitting on the floor of a wicker cage six feet in diameter, with sides that curved into a beehive shape at the top. Outside the cage, nothing was visible but open air and distant treetops. He pushed his face up against the open-work side and saw the ground swaying twenty feet below.

"Case," he yelled. "Get me out of here...!"

"Chester," a soft voice called from nearby. Chester looked about and saw a cage like his own swinging from a massive branch

of the next tree by a five-foot rope of vines. Inside it Genie knelt, her face against the rattan bars.

"Genie, where are we?" Chester called. "Where's Case? What happened? How did we get here? What's become of the house?"

"Hey!" a more distant voice called. Chester and Genie both turned. A third cage swayed twenty feet away. Chester made out Case's massive figure inside.

"Couldn't get through the wall, eh?" Chester taunted, in a sudden revival of spirits. "Just a show, eh? Of all the stubborn idiotic—"

"Okay, okay, a slight miscalculation. But how the heck was I supposed to know Genie was cooking up a deal like that? How about it, Genie? Is that the kind of show you think an audience would go for at two-fifty a head?"

"Don't blame Genie. I'm sure she did no more than follow instructions—to the letter."

"We never asked for the real article," Case yelled.

"On the contrary, that's exactly what you demanded."

"Yeah, but how was I to know the damn machine'd take me literally? All I meant was—"

"When dealing with machinery, always specify *exactly* what you want. I should have thought that meat-eating reptile would have been enough warning for you. I told you the infernal creature was in the room with us, but you—"

"But why didn't Genie stop 'em?"

"Should I have?" said Genie. "I was given no instructions to interfere with the course of events."

CASE groaned. "Let's call a truce, Chester. We've got a situation to deal with here. Afterwards we can argue it out over a couple bottles of something. Right now, we need a knife. You got one?"

Chester fumbled over his pockets, brought out a tiny penknife. "Yes, such as it is."

"Toss it over."

"I'm locked in a cage, remember?"

"Oh. Well, get to work and cut the rope—"

"Case, I think you must have been hit on the head too…but

harder. Have you considered the twenty-foot drop to the ground, *if* I could cut the rope…which I can't reach?"

"Well, you got any better ideas? This bird-cage is no pushover; I can't bust anything loose."

"Try hitting it with your head."

"Chester, your attitude does you no credit. This is your old pal Case, remember?"

"You're the ex-acrobat. You figure it out."

"That was a few years ago, Chester, and—hey!" Case interrupted himself. "What a couple of dopes! All we got to do is tell Genie to whisk us back home. I don't know what this set-up is she got us into, but she can just get us out again. Good ol' Genie. Do your stuff, kid."

"Are you talking to me, Mr. Mulvihill?" Genie asked, wide-eyed.

"Of course, why didn't I think of that?" Chester smiled across at Genie. "Take us back now, Genie."

"I'm very sorry, Chester," said Genie. "I don't think I know what you mean. How can I take you home when I'm locked in this cage?"

Chester gulped hard. "Genie, you brought us here. You've got to get us back!"

"But, Chester, I don't know how…"

"You mean you've lost your memory?"

"I don't *think* I've lost my memory," the girl said doubtfully.

"I think I know what the trouble is," Chester called across to Case. "Genie told us she was linked to the memory banks as long as she remained within the resonance field of the computer. But we must be a considerable distance from the apparatus now— Genie has no contact with the machine."

"Some machinery," Case grumbled.

"We must get back to the starting point," Chester said. "As soon as we're back where we left the rug and chairs, I'm sure Genie will function perfectly again. Right, Genie?"

"I don't know, perhaps."

"I wonder what she does remember," said Case. "Say, Genie, do you remember where you came from?"

"Oh, yes. I came from the Place."

"The Place?"

"What did it look like?" asked Chester.

"It was a room, a lovely room, with walls of mist that changed to show me many things. The floor was soft and warm. I could go long distances and still remain in the Place."

"Doesn't sound much like a factory to me."

"Who built you? Who taught you to talk?"

"Oh, you must mean the Voice."

"What was the Voice?"

"It talked to me from the mist. It told me many things and corrected me when I made errors and praised me when I learned quickly." She sighed. "I was there in the Place a very long time."

"But you were only built in the last couple of days."

THE girl looked down at her body, the smooth skin dappled in the sunlight falling through the latticework.

"Judging from the evidences of my physical condition, I would estimate my age at eighteen years—"

"This isn't getting us out of here," Case cut in. "Let's cut the chatter and figure what we're going to do. Chester, you can use your knife to cut some of the lashings holding that cage together. Then you can crawl up the rope, make it to my tree, and let me out. Then we cut Genie down, and—"

"Listen!" Chester interrupted. "I hear them coming!"

He peered out at the bright morning-lit clearing below them, the surrounding forest, a trail that wound away between the trees. A group of the savages appeared, moving along briskly, filing into the clearing, gathering under the trees. They looked up at the captives, jabbering, pointing, and laughing. Two of them set about erecting a wobbly ladder of bamboo-like cane against Case's tree.

"It looks to me like they've got something in mind," said Case. "I hope we aren't the menu. I don't feel much like playing a starring role in a barbecue this morning. Can you understand them, Genie?"

"They're discussing a forthcoming athletic event. Apparently a great deal depends upon its outcome." She listened further as the savages got the ladder in place. One of the bearded men scaled it, fumbled with the end of the rope supporting Case's cage.

"It is to be a contest between champions," said Genie. "A

mighty struggle between giants."

"Hey," yelled Case, "if that knee-length Gargantua lets that rope go, I won't be around to watch the bout."

"It's okay," Chester called. "There's a sort of pulley-like arrangement of cross-bars the rope is wound around. They can let it down slowly."

Case's cage lurched, dropped a foot, then steadied and moved smoothly down to thump against the ground. The savages gathered around, unlaced and opened a panel in the side, stepped back and stood with leveled spears as Case emerged. He looked around, made a grab for the nearest spear. Its owner danced back. The others shouted, laughed, jabbered excitedly.

"What's all the chatter about, Genie?" Case called.

"They are admiring your spirit, size, and quickness of movement, Mr. Mulvihill."

"They are, huh? I'll show 'em some quickness of movement if one of 'em'll get close enough for me to grab him."

Chester looked up at a sound from across the clearing. A second group of natives were approaching—and in their midst, towering over them, came a hulking brute of a man, broad, thick hairy.

"This is one of the champions who will engage in combat," said Genie. "Their name for him seems to be translatable as 'Biter-off of Heads'."

Case whistled. "Look at those hands—he could squeeze one of these midgets like a tube of toothpaste."

"This should be an interesting battle," said Chester, "if his opponent is anywhere near his size."

"I'll lay you three to two on this boy without seeing the challenger," Case called. "I hope they let us hang around and watch."

"Oh, there's no doubt that you'll be present, Mr. Mulvihill," Genie said reassuringly. "You're the one who is to fight him."

CHESTER, it's the best we can do," said Case. "We haven't got much time left to talk. The main bout's coming up any minute now—"

"But, Case, against that man-eater you don't have a chance—"

"I used to fill in for the strong man on Wednesday afternoons, Chester. And I'll bet you a half-interest in great grand pop's booze supply this kid never studied boxing or judo—and I did. Leave that part to me. You do what I told you—"

Half a dozen jabbering, gesticulating natives closed in around Case, indicated with jabs of their hardwood spears that he was to move off in the direction of the hairy champion.

"I guess they've got a full house," Case called back to Chester and Genie, still dangling in their cages. "Watch for the right time, and keep it quiet. I'll keep these characters occupied..."

"Poor Mr. Mulvihill," Genie said. "That brute is even larger than he is."

"Case knows a few tricks, Genie. Don't worry about him."

The two watched anxiously through the woven cages as the crowd formed up a circle about the local heavyweight and Case. One of the savages shouted for attention, then launched into a speech.

A dozen yards from his opponent Case stood drawing deep breaths and letting them out slowly. He glanced up, caught Chester's eye, and winked.

"It's a very interesting speech the little man is making," Genie said. "He's telling the people that Mr. Mulvihill is a demon which he summoned from the Underworld. He refers to you as the Demon with Sharp Claws and to me as the Naked Goddess. We are all spirits, who can only be restrained by magic cages—"

"What about Case? They let him out of his cage."

"That's a special case, I gather. Mr. Mulvihill is under some sort of spell which will force him to fight fiercely against the large savage—"

"Where did they acquire that brute? I should think he'd be ruling these pygmies rather than putting on shows for them."

"That point hasn't been mentioned so far. I imagine, however, that his post as King's Champion is one of considerable honor. He—"

"Oh-oh," Chester cut in. "Here we go."

The native leader had stopped speaking. The crowd fell silent. Case pulled off his leather belt and wrapped it around his fist. The hairy seven-footer growled, slapped himself on the chest. Case moved toward him cautiously, watching the giant's eyes. The latter bellowed, eyeing the crowd, stalked forward, still slapping his chest. He stopped, turned his back to Case, and roared out a string of gibberish. Case took three rapid steps, slammed a vicious right to the kidneys.

The giant whirled with a bellow, reaching for the injured spot with a huge right hand, and for Case with the left. Case ducked, drove a left to the pit of the shaggy stomach, followed with a right—and went flying as the giant caught him with an open-handed swipe. Case rolled, came to his feet. The native champion had both hands to his stomach now; his hoarse breathing was audible to Chester, forty feet away.

"Case hurt him that time."

"But Mr. Mulvihill—perhaps he's injured too!"

"I don't think so. His profanity sounds normal. While he has their full attention, I'd better get started."

CHESTER took out the penknife, looked over the lacing that secured the woven bamboo strips, and started sawing.

"I hope this blade holds out. I never contemplated cutting anything more resistant than a cigar-tip when I bought it. Ah, there goes one," said Chester, as the strands of lacing fell free. "I think three more may do it. Anyone looking my way?"

"No, no one. But I'm frightened. Mr. Mulvihill tripped and barely rolled aside in time to avoid being trampled..."

"Two loose. If only Case can keep going for ten more minutes..."

Chester worked steadily, freed a third joint, pulled a vertical member aside, and thrust his head through the opening. It was a close fit but a moment later his shoulders were through. He reached up for a handhold, pulled himself entirely through, and clung to the wicker frame of the cage. He found a foothold, clambered higher, reached the rope from which the basket was suspended. A glance toward the fighters showed that all eyes were on the combatants. Chester took a deep breath, started up the rope. He pulled up, clamped his legs, reached up, gripped, pulled again...

The crowd shouted as Case hammered a left and right to the

giant's body, turned to duck away, slipped, and was folded into his opponent's immense embrace.

"Chester, he'll be crushed…" wailed Genie.

Chester hung on, craning to see. Case struggled, reached behind him, found an index finger, and twisted. The giant roared. Case bent the finger back, back…

With a howl the giant dropped him, twisting his hand free, popped the injured member into his mouth.

Chester let out a long breath, pulled himself up onto the branch to which the rope was secured. He rose shakily to his feet, made his way to the main trunk, climbed up to the branch from which Genie's cage was suspended, started out along it. In the clearing below the crowd yelled. Chester caught a glimpse of Case darting past the giant, whirling to chop hard at the side of his neck with the edge of his hand—

Then Chester was at the rope, sliding down…

"Chester, you'd better leave me. Save yourself."

Chester sawed at the bindings of Genie's cage. "Even if I were sufficiently cowardly to entertain the notion, it would hardly be a practical idea. Just another minute or two, Genie."

The joints parted. Below, Case battled on. Chester pried the rattan aside, held the bars apart as Genie slipped through. She climbed up, reached the rope, shinned up it easily. Chester followed.

ABOVE him Genie gasped and pointed. Chester turned in time to see Case duck under a mighty haymaker, come up under his huge opponent and spill him off his feet. As the lumbering savage struggled up with a roar, Case caught him on the point of the jaw with a tremendous clout, knocking him flat again. The bigger man shook his head, stumbled to his feet, and charged. Case threw himself against the oncoming behemoth's knees. Chester winced as the immense figure dived headlong over Case's crouched figure and smashed into the packed earth, face first. When the dust settled Case was on his feet, breathing hard; the giant lay like a felled tree.

"Unfortunate timing," muttered Chester. "He should have held their attention for another five minutes."

"They're sure to notice us now," Genie whispered, flattening her slender length against the rough bark.

"Don't move," Chester breathed. "We'll wait and see what happens next..."

The crowd, standing mute with astonishment, suddenly whooped, surged in to clap Case on the back, prod the fallen champion, dance about jabbering excitedly. Chester saw Case shoot a quick glance toward the cages, then stoop suddenly, come up with two large smooth stones. The crowd grew still, drawing back. One or two unlimbered spears. Case raised his hand for silence, then casually tossed one of the stones up, transferred the other to his right hand in time to catch the first with his left, tossed up the second stone...

"That's the idea," Chester whispered. "Good old Case. He'll entrance them with his juggling routine. Let's go, Genie."

They clambered silently to the ground, stole away from the clearing, found a rough trail among the trees and broke into a run. Behind them the cheers of the savages rose, growing fainter now, fading in the distance...

"In the clear," Chester gasped, pulled level with Genie. "Now all we have to do is search a few hundred square miles of woods until we find the rug and the chairs..."

"That's all right, Chester," said Genie, running lithely at his side. "I think I know the way."

CHAPTER FOUR

CHESTER staggered the last few yards across the grassy slope to the rug and sank down in one of the yellow chairs. "Next time I go for a romp in the woods," he groaned, "I'm going to be wearing a good grade of boots; these melon-slicers are killing me."

"I see no signs of pursuit," said Genie. "Mr. Mulvihill is apparently scoring a marked success."

"He can't keep them occupied forever. Let's hurry, Genie. Dissolve this scene and let's get busy. I'll get hold of a jeep, and guns, and boots. The sporting goods store in the village will have them, I suppose."

"There's something a little strange: I seem to sense an

imbalance…"

"Nothing that's going to interfere with cancelling out this crazy scene, I hope?"

"No…I suppose not. Are you ready, Chester?"

"Sure. But you'd better take my shirt. Those Internal Revenue people may still be hanging about." Chester looked around. "This has been a strange experience. What is all this, merely a hypnotic illusion of some sort?"

He waved his hand at the surrounding countryside. "It certainly looks real. That cage they had me in was real enough. I got two blisters in five minutes sawing my way out of it. And I'm quite certain that clout on the skull was real. I have a knot to prove it."

"The question of the nature of reality is one that has engaged philosophers for centuries," said Genie. "Subjective reality is of course no more than the pattern produced in the mind by a very limited set of sense impressions—which of course can often be misled, as by mirrors or distorted perspective, or ventriloquism, or by any situation which presents unfamiliar configurations. The mechanisms of perception—"

"Hold it, Genie." Chester pointed. "There's smoke rising from back there. That must be a considerable blaze. I hope they're not planning to broil Case over it."

"A bed of hot coals is the usual heat source for roasting enemies in primitive cultures. It should require at least two hours for the blaze to die down to the proper state for the purpose, if the savages do intend such a ceremony."

"I'd be more comforted somehow if you sounded a little more worried."

"We'd better begin," said Genie, "if we're to be back before the two hours is up. I'll have to run a full integration pattern now. Excuse me a moment…"

GENIE's eyes took on a faraway look. Chester watched her anxiously. An insect droned across the rug in the heavy silence of the summer morning. The sun was warm on his face. The column of smoke rose lazily from beyond the distant band of woods. The faint breeze had died away now; the scene was silent as a photograph.

"I'm ready, Chester," Genie said suddenly. Chester jumped to her side.

"Yes, Genie?"

"Take my hand, Chester."

"Got it. Now what?"

The sunny scene faded, to be replaced by the familiar walls of the converted ballroom of the Chester house.

"Whew!" Chester sighed.

"What a relief. I'll have to admit, I wasn't sure we'd really be able to do it. My heli is outside; we'll make a fast trip to the village. We should be back in an hour. Come on."

Chester led the way along a corridor hung with plastic alligator hide to a side entrance. "That's odd," he said, as they approached the patterned-glass door. "Must be a storm brewing. The sun was shining when we came in." He opened the door.

Beyond the opening thick grey fog hung in an impenetrable blanket.

"Weather control must be off the air," he said. "What a fog! I'm afraid we won't be going anywhere in this, Genie." He made as if to step out.

"Don't!" Genie caught his arm.

"What's the matter? I won't go far. Just want to make sure it isn't just a local patch."

"Come back, Chester. I'm afraid."

Chester peered into the fog.

"I guess you're right. If I got ten feet from the house I'd never find it again. Let's look around. Maybe we can find what we need right here in the house."

They returned to the ballroom, ascended the grand staircase, explored the rooms along a wide hall floored in embossed sheet metal and hung with rubber mobiles. Beyond the windows the fog hung thick and grey. In a game room Chester found a pair of antique automatic pistols. He strapped one on and offered the other to Genie. "We have about everything we needed except for the jeep. I dare say we can manage without it. Ready?"

"Take my hand, Chester."

THE walls faded. They stood again on the grassy slope, in the shade of spreading branches. Genie looked toward the ridge.

"I don't see the smoke any longer. Perhaps the fire has burned down to the proper size for Mr. Mulvihill already."

"If those blasted natives have singed one hair of Case's head, I'll mow the whole tribe down!"

Twenty minutes' brisk walk brought them to the edge of the forest. They moved in among the trees.

"Another ten minutes. Poor old Case. If anything's happened to him..."

Suddenly two clean-shaven sarong-clad men and a beautifully proportioned woman appeared on the trail ahead. Chester gripped his pistol. The trio came on toward them, then they seemed to catch sight of Chester and Genie. For a moment they paused, then flung up hands in greeting and began to dance about and sing.

"Looks like a different tribe," Chester said. "Much better-looking people. And that singing...I could swear it's English!"

"Yes, how strange."

"It certainly is, Genie. This was supposed to be a reconstruction of a primitive scene; looks like a technical blunder on your part."

"They seem to want us to follow them." With excited beckoning gestures the trio had turned and were darting away again along the path.

"Well, all right, since we happen to be going in that direction anyway." Chester and Genie moved on along the rough trail and came to the clearing where they had watched Case battle the giant an hour earlier.

"Not a sign of them," said Chester, looking around. "The cages are gone, everything. Now what do we do?"

"Let's follow that trail," said Genie, pointing. "Perhaps it will lead us to their village."

"We may as well. I don't know what else to propose. Even those natives have disappeared again." They pressed on, climbed a wooded slope, and emerged from the forest.

Ahead they saw a wide village street, tree-lined and shady, bordered by beds of wild flowers behind which neat huts of brick, boards, or split saplings and woven grasses dotted a park-like lawn. Smiling people approached, throwing flowers. From a large house halfway along the street an imposing old man emerged, clad in neatly cut shorts and vest of coarse cloth. He pulled at a vast white beard as he came toward them.

"Good Lord!" said Chester, bewildered. "Who are these people? And what kind of setting have you landed us in, Genie?"

"This village," she said. "It's not at all in consonance with the pattern..."

"Look at the old man with the beard. He's immense. I'll swear he must be an early Mulvihill; he looks enough like Case to be his grandfather."

The old man came up, looked piercingly at Chester, then at Genie. He pulled at his beard, nodding to himself.

"Well," he said. "So you came back after all..."

CHAPTER FIVE

HALF AN HOUR later Chester and Genie sat with Case on benches under a wild cherry tree at the crest of a rise that fell away to a blue lake beyond which rose steep pine-covered hills. A native girl poured brown wine from a stone jar into irregular mugs of heavy glass.

"Tell me that again, slow and easy, Chester," said Case. "You say it's the same day as when you left here?"

"We hurried, Case. Didn't waste a minute."

"I believe you, Chester; you haven't aged a day. I guess there's more to this business than meets the eye."

"Case, we broke our necks getting back. We thought they'd be roasting you alive. How did you manage to get into the good graces of the natives?"

"Well, let's see... The last I saw of you two, you were sneaking off behind a tree. I kept juggling for an hour. Then I did a few back-flips and handstands, and then I got them to give me a rope—you can do a lot with sign language—and rigged it and did some rope walking. By that time they'd noticed you were gone. I made a few motions to give 'em the idea you'd flown away in good demon style. They didn't care much; they wanted to see more rope work."

"You must have thought we'd abandoned you."

A HOAX IN TIME

By KEITH LAUMER

Illustrator **SCHELLING**

"I admit I was a little mad at first, when you didn't come charging over the hill with the marines in tow. I guess it took a couple of years to get used to the idea I was stuck here. I figured something had happened to you, and I'd just better make the best of it. By that time I rated pretty high with the locals. They let me have the best den back in the thicket, and brought me all the food I wanted. It wasn't fancy but it was an easy life. Course, after thirty years—"

"Thirty years!"

Case nodded his white-maned head. "Yep. Near as I can tell. I used to cut notches in a tree for the years, but sometimes I was so busy I forgot."

"Busy? Doing what?"

"Plenty." Case raised his glass, took a hearty pull, and winked at Genie. "Not bad, if I do say so. Made out of cantaloupes."

"It tastes a little like great grandfather's Flora Pinellas." Chester commented.

"I guess I had that in mind. You know, that booze was what got me into this. If we'd been sober, we'd never have tinkered with that damned machine in the first place. But as I was saying, there I was laying around all day, doing nothing, watching the natives scratch out their way for a living; they were dirty, hungry, ignorant, dying of diseases, getting chewed up by bears or wildcats. And the food they gave me—half-raw dog meat, pounded raw turnips, now and then a mess of sour berries. And I was eating it. Just didn't care. I kept thinking about all the comforts I'd left behind, and feeling sorry for myself. Every now and then I'd have to put on a show, a little juggling or acrobatic work, just enough to keep the evil spirits out of town.

THEN one day I got to thinking. The country around here was nice enough. The kind of real estate some smart developer could make a fortune out of back home. All it needed was the brush cut back and the trees trimmed and the lakeshore cleaned up and the garbage piles carted off somewhere and some fruit trees and flowers planted...

"Well, before I could do any tree-trimming I had to have an axe. That meant I needed some iron. By that time, I could get by okay in the native language. I asked 'em if they knew any place where there was red dirt; told 'em it was important magic. A few weeks later a hunting party came back from across the hills the other side of the lake with some pretty good samples. I got a good fire going, and tried to smelt some iron out, but it was not as easy as I figured. I wasn't going to give up though. At least it was something to keep myself occupied with. I started trying to remember everything I could about making iron. Seemed like I'd heard some place you have to have a lot of air blowing through the ore to get it hot enough. I finally built up a furnace out of brick— had to bake up a mess of bricks, first—and piled it full of lumps of ore and chunks of wood. I found out the witch doctor had some coal—used it to carve gods out of, 'cause it was easy to work. I found out where he got it from and used some of that in my charge. I set it off, and sure enough, after a couple hours melted iron started running out the bottom of the furnace. My first batch got away from me, just trickled out in the dirt and got hard; I didn't have any molds ready. But I charged the furnace again and made up some clay forms and dug channels to feed 'em. I had a lot of help by this time. The natives were curious as a bunch of monkeys, and they figured they were getting an inside track with the spirit world by helping me.

"I cast half a dozen axe and hatchet heads the first time. They came out pretty good. I sharpened 'em up on a flat stone, and then heated 'em red-hot and dunked 'em in a pot of water. They hardened pretty good. Later on I got the formula down pat. It depends mostly on how much coal and stuff you've got in with the ore."

"A carbon content of between .7 and 1.7 percent produces the optimum combination of hardness and malleability," said Genie.

"I wish you'd been here, kid," said Case with a sigh. "You could have been a big help. But we managed. I pounded out a knife blade and fitted a handle to it and used that to cut axe handles. Then I put the natives to work clearing land. Funny what a kick I got out of it—and it wasn't just for show. The local wild life wouldn't sneak up on the village any more—no cover. I had 'em root out all the bushes and the coarse stuff, and the native grasses took over. We undercut all the trees as high as a man could reach. Then I had 'em shape the trees, pull down all the vines and stuff. Made it look like a regular park around here.

"Then we went to work on the lake. We made up some flat boats and got out and cleaned up the dead branches and cattails and then did a little dredging; built up a nice beach along this side. I rigged some fishing gear out of leather strips, showed 'em how to catch trout, and then staged a big fish fry. Now they spend half their time out on the lake. We made up a couple of saws and I showed 'em how to slice a tree into boards, and we built a few rowboats. The first few were kind of prone to capsize, but we got the hang of it pretty soon. Funny thing was, before long a couple of the boys were ahead of me on boat building—and fishing, too. They learned fast, once they put their minds to it. And I was getting interested in things too, by this time. Seemed like a day wasn't long enough. I made 'em up some bows and arrows, and cast some iron arrowheads. Made up skinning knives, and showed 'em how to scrape a hide and then work it till it was soft.

THERE were a lot of wild sheep and cattle around. We made up a batch of braided hide ropes, and went out and brought in a couple of young goats and a half-grown critter that looked like an overgrown Texas longhorn. Later on we got a couple of newborn calves, a male and a female. In a couple of years we had nice herds going. We let 'em graze the park here to keep the grass down. After that, we had better food and more of it, and plenty of hides. And of course I showed 'em how to milk, and we experimented around and made some cheese—"

"I didn't know you knew anything about animal husbandry," Chester put in.

"Anybody that's worked around a good-sized carny knows which end of a critter to feed. That was the least of my problems. I was getting a lot of pleasure out of admiring the beach and the park, and thinking what a pile of dough I could make out of it if I had it all back home. Then I'd see a couple of the local gals come trotting by, buck naked, grimy, fat, with stringy hair, and pretty gamey, if you got too close to 'em." Case sighed. So I decided it was time to give a little thought to developing the feminine industries.

"The first thing I needed was some cloth, to get away from the smell of hides. I tried some wool off these goats we keep. It wasn't much good. We scouted around for some wild cotton, but could not find any. Finally discovered a kind of flax. Went to work and rigged up a spinning wheel. That took the best part of a year, but we finally worked it out. Had a couple of young kids helping me; they're really the ones made it work. We spun up a big batch of yarn. I had a loom ready; that wasn't so hard. We set it up and wove us a blanket. Chester, I was as tickled with that blanket as a streetwalker at a preachers' convention."

"I don't blame you, Case. That was a real achievement."

"Well, I trained a few of the girls, and set 'em to work spinning and weaving. Made up some needles out of bone; couldn't manage it in steel. I wasn't much of a seamster, but I had lots of time. I cobbled up a pair of breeches for myself first, then a shirt. But heck, it's too warm here for sleeves, and anyway they're hard to make. I settled on a vest; it's just right to keep the chill off on a cool morning."

"What about winter?"

"Funny thing, there don't seem to be any seasons here. Stays about like this year round."

"World climatic conditions in this environment are such, apparently, that a temperate-zone area like this would naturally enjoy an equable climate, without extremes of temperature," said Genie.

"Anyway, we beat the cloth problem. Then I had to make soap. I messed around with animal fat and ashes and finally worked out a pretty good formula. I had to make people wash, at first, but I gave 'em the old Great Spirit routine, and pretty soon they were down at the lake scrubbing something every time I turned around.

ONCE I got folks cleaned up, I saw the need for a little civic improvement—so I set fire to the dump where we'd been living all this time. The place was alive with fleas and rats and the damnedest collection of chewed bones, worn-out hides, magic frogs' innards, mummified totem animals, and other junk. They were a little mad at first. I told 'em it was the word from on high and that the place had to go, but there was a crafty little devil of a witch doctor that had the confounded gall to stand up and call me a liar. Imagine, me!"

"Well, after all, Case you had been telling them everything you'd been doing was divinely ordained—"

"Worked pretty good, too. It might even be true. Anyway, after I took the witch doctor down and dumped him in the lake, nobody else complained."

"You were lucky he let it go at that. From what I've read about shamans, they can be extremely dangerous enemies."

"He didn't have much chance to live up to that reputation. I hadn't taught anybody to swim yet."

"You mean you drowned him? Case, wasn't that a little drastic?"

"Maybe. But I figured that if I was setting up a society, I might as well do it along realistic lines. There's no point in letting somebody half your size push you around—especially when you're right. A weakling makes as bad a dictator as anybody else. The way I saw it, it was up to me to stand up for my ideas."

"The next big man might not be as interested in the public welfare as you were, Case. What then?"

"To tell you the truth, Chester, at first I wasn't interested in the public welfare. I was only interested in making a comfortable place for me to live in. To have that, I had to make it good for everybody.

"I started some of 'em woodcarving, and other ones farming, and some of 'em making glass. I scoured the woods for new plants we could raise for food, and I kept trying out new dirt samples for other metals. Now we've got copper and lead and a little gold— and I've trained people to go on looking. I've started 'em thinking about things, and trying new ideas. And ever since I drowned the witch doctor, I've played down the spirit angle. The younger generation doesn't need the threat of spooks to do things; they've got an interest that keeps 'em busy. A lot of them are way ahead of me, now. They learn fast. I wouldn't be surprised if one of 'em doesn't invent chemistry any day now, or fire up a steam engine, or discover medicine."

"But a tyrant—"

"Any tyrant that sets up shop around here better be damned sure he doesn't develop any unpopular tastes," said Case. "These folks put up with me because I bring 'em good things. They're selfish, just like me. I've established a precedent. The next boss better keep it up, or he'll be joining the witch doctor."

IT seems to have worked out well," Chester said, looking

around at the peaceful village in the gathering twilight. "Still, I can't help feeling you should have instilled a little more idealism in them. Suppose they fall on hard times? What if the climate changes, or an epidemic strikes, or even a forest fire…?"

"I don't think phony idealism would help. As far as I can see, all these schemes to make people squeeze into somebody's Grand Plan for Elevating Humanity usually end up with the elevatees sweating to support a few drones in luxury. You've got to stick with reality, and you've got to aim your pitch at the individual man. Everybody has his place in this village and a job to do that he's good at."

"What about the arts? With this materialistic orientation—"

"Everybody dances and everybody sings. They all play games and they all make statues out of mud and they all paint. Some are better than others, but it's doing it that counts. In our set-up everybody's an artist, not just a few half-cracked far-outers."

"There don't seem to be many people here," said Genie, "Not more than a hundred and twenty, I'd estimate. Hasn't your colony flourished and propagated itself?"

"That's your answer: colonies. Too many people in one place mean problems. Sanitation, transportation, noise, conflict of interests. There's plenty of wide-open real estate. I've got twelve other villages going within fifty miles of here—and none of them have over three hundred people. Everybody can have all the kids they want but if you put the village over the three hundred mark, off you go to start your own. There's always plenty of volunteers to go along; people that want to get a good spot right on a lake or river, or hunters that like the idea of a virgin territory. There's a lot of trade among the towns, and the men usually get their wives from another village. Seems like it's human nature to prefer to go to bed with a stranger."

Case glanced toward the bonfire in the village street. Two native girls were coming up across the park. One of them called out to Case.

"Looks like dinner's about ready, folks. I hope you're hungry."

"I've eaten nothing since we had breakfast together this morning, Case," said Chester. "I've been so busy, I haven't given a thought to food—but it smells good."

"You ought to have a healthy appetite by now then," said Case, getting to his feet. "Thirty years is a long time between meals."

AFTER dinner the three stretched their legs before a fire that crackled in the wide fireplace in the roomy brick dwelling that Case had furnished with shaggy hide rugs, colorful glazed pottery, sturdy chairs and tables, paintings done on hide, and barbaric sculptures. Several villagers padded about the room clearing up. Others lounged in chairs or on the floor, watching Case and the newcomers, eating grapes and spitting the seeds into the fire, or idly chatting in the native tongue.

"They don't seem in awe of you," Chester said.

"I've known most of these people all their lives. Taught 'em how to tie knots and use a potter's wheel and skin out a deer. They're too used to me to work up much awe."

"Still, big as you are, and being the Source of All Wisdom..."

"They tried to work me up into a god, once, but I soon put a stop to that. I don't want these folks cutting into my liberty with a bunch of taboos. And I didn't want to get 'em started getting down on their knees begging for favors from Big Daddy instead of working things out for themselves."

"They're certainly fine-looking specimens," said Genie. "Not at all like the typically diseased and undernourished primitives we saw this morning...thirty years ago, that is. It's difficult to believe they're the same tribe."

"That's one of the first things I went to work on. Can't stand a bunch of spavined-looking people around. I taught these folks not to be lazy. I made 'em learn coordination and timing on the rope, and juggling. I made 'em build up the muscles they had but never used. And you know what? They started getting clear skin and glossy hair and square shoulders. They breathe better, they eat sensible, they stand straight and look good. They sleep nights and they don't get sick much, and when they do they throw it off. A normal kid that gets the right exercise grows up to have a nice build. And if a gal is stacked at sixteen, she can be stacked at sixty. People in show business have proved that. They had a stake in keeping in condition that was big enough to overcome laziness. Remember pictures of Dietrich at eighty-five?"

"You've changed a lot, Case," said Chester. "You've developed an astonishing zeal—but it does you credit. You've done a marvelous job of converting a horde of bearded savages into civilized people."

"Not civilized, Chester. At least, I hope not. I haven't taught 'em a damn thing about prudery, politics, priests, prostitutes, or pornography—or a lot of the other advantages we had back home. I tried to keep it simple."

"Well, they're as nice a group as—"

"Nope, they're individuals. Every man in the village speaks for himself. He can't hide behind a group, crowd, army, lynch mob, congregation, labor union, street gang, political party, or corporation. He's got to stand on his hind legs and back his own play."

"But, Mr. Mulvihill," put in Genie. "Group effort is responsible for the relatively immense strides in technology and science that man has made in a very short period—"

"If a kid stumbles onto a loaded gun, he may be smart enough to pull the trigger without being smart enough to see what'll happen next. I hope my folks here get a good start on learning how to live before they learn too much about how to kill."

"But they're at the mercy of the elements, or disease, or enemies. Surely they'd be better off if they organized to combat these things."

"They're not looking for total security. That costs too much. And they're not after some kind of phony guarantee that everybody's equal. Some people are taller than others, and some are stronger, and some are smarter. So if you're no runner, you better let the fast men handle the running, and concentrate on something else maybe you're good at. You won't find anybody here whining for his rights. He'll damn well go out and collect any rights he thinks he has coming. It's a system that puts a premium on every man developing what he's got. I teach 'em all the skills they can handle, from judo to blacksmithing. Pretty near everybody in a village is the best at something. And they *know* they're good at it. That gives 'em self-respect. It makes 'em good-natured and energetic, keeps their enthusiasm up. It makes a lot of difference."

Case stretched. "That's all the lecture for today, kiddies. It's way past my bedtime. Let's turn in and tomorrow morning it'll be your turn to talk."

"Case, are you sure you would not rather get going right away? I had an idea you might be eager to get back."

"What for? Another thirty years here wouldn't make but thirty minutes difference back home."

"Well, have it your way."

THE early sun was shining down through the leaves that overhung the village street when Chester and Genie emerged from the house. Case, already up and out, hailed them from his seat at a table under the cherry tree. As they came up he rubbed his hand over a clean-shaven chin. "Feels kinda funny without the whiskers after all these years," he said. "But I figured if I'm going out of the patriarch business, I might as well get rid of the evidence."

"I noticed no one else has a beard. Why did you keep yours?" asked Chester.

"I don't know. I guess it got to be kind of a badge of office."

Chester looked around at the peaceful scene. A group of villagers were drawing water from a well. A curl of smoke ascended from a cooking fire. Down on the lake the sail of a fishing boat caught the morning sun. A native girl in a short apron placed a laden tray on the table.

"I'm afraid you'll miss this place when we get back, Case. How peaceful it seems with no Bureau of Internal Revenue."

"Oh my gosh! Yeah. I guess I forgot the I.R. boys a long time ago."

"Well, I think we ought to get started right away. We'll have a great deal of explaining to do to Mr. Overdog and company. Before we go I suppose you'll want to make a speech, Case, appoint a successor, make a few prophecies, whatever White Gods usually do before sailing off into the sunset."

Case sighed. "I've got a lot of friends here, Chester. I'll hate to leave 'em. I'm not so sure I even want to go. But in any case there's no point in making a national holiday out of it. I've been trying to teach 'em how to run things for thirty years. I don't guess any last-minute instructions are going to change anything. Give me half an hour to make the rounds, shake hands with a few of the boys and pinch a few bottoms. I'll be with you then."

*   *   *

An hour later Chester, Case, and Genie, accompanied by a chattering group of villagers, stepped under the trees toward the rug and the two brocaded chairs.

"I think we had best all stand together, holding hands," said Genie. "Let's take up a position in the center of the rug."

There was a last wave of hands at the encircling ring of now solemn villagers, then the three joined hands. "If you'll close your eyes, it will help cut out any extraneous linkage-pressures with this locus," said Genie. "Now..."

Chester took a deep breath and held it. Genie's small hand was warm and firm in his. Case's horny grip tightened.

"Relax, Case. That hand of yours would squeeze the termites out of one of great grandfather's hand-carved fertility symbols."

"Sorry. Say, how long does this take?"

"It was instantaneous the last time..."

The ground seemed to shift slightly underfoot. "Oh-oh, here we go!" Chester waited, teeth clenched, for further signs of action. There was no sound of wind in leaves now. The insect cries were stilled.

Chester opened his eyes.

"Well," he said, gazing around hesitantly. "We've arrived somewhere."

CHAPTER SIX

THEY stood under the shelter of a small cupola in the center of a wide square paved with vari-colored cobblestones and lined with small shops and merchants' stalls. Beyond, a green slope dotted here and there with dazzling white villas swept up to the wooded skyline. People in bright colors moved about the square, examining the tradesmen's wares, stopping in groups to talk, or strolling at ease. In the distance a flute played a lazy melody. Above a silversmith's shop white curtains fluttered in an open window. There was an aroma of crisping bacon.

"I'm afraid you missed, Genie," said Case. "But it looks like a nice town. Maybe we ought to stay for breakfast."

"How very strange," Genie said. "I agree that our surroundings appear unfamiliar, but we *have* returned to the precise locus from which we started."

"It looks more like I used to picture Europe than America," said Case. "I wonder what made us end up here? Maybe you could just sort of nudge us a little, Genie, and we'll switch over to familiar ground."

"I'm sorry to be so insistent, but we are 'Home' now. The coordinates are identical in every respect with those from which we began."

"We've attracted attention," Chester said. "That old fellow in the pink dress apparently saw us arrive. He's headed this way."

"Oh-oh, look here," Case indicated a brass plate set in the paved floor. "There's something written on it—in English."

"We could have arrived in England..." Case read the inscription aloud:

"IT WAS ON THIS SPOT THAT THE LEGENDARY HERO AND TEACHER TOOK HIS LEAVE OF THE PEOPLE AFTER BRINGING THEM THE GIFT OF WISDOM. THIS MYTH, WHICH DATES BACK TO THE DAWN OF CULTURE..."

"Ye Gods," Chester cut in. "We've violated the local shrine. Some luck! And more people are looking at us now. Let's get out of here before they get up a lynching party."

"Chester," Genie gasped.

"What is it, Genie?" Chester looked at her anxiously. "Is something wrong?"

"I've lost contact with the memory banks...!"

"But you can't—I mean, we...you..."

"Get in touch quick, Genie," Case urged. "We may have to move fast."

"I can't!" said Genie in a strained voice.

"But why not?"

"Because...the computer has ceased to exist!"

IT sounds like the work of those infernal Revenue men," said Chester, swallowing hard.

"Could be," said Case. "When you, that is, we, stood 'em up, they must have got their feelings hurt and shut down the whole operation."

"It's not merely shut down," said Genie. "It's…gone. There isn't any computer."

"We'll have to figure that one out later. Right now we've got some important lying to do."

"Do you think we can brazen it out?" said Chester.

"Sure. Watch me. I'm used to this routine—and I can still juggle. These folks look like rubes."

"There *is* something odd about the way people are dressed. And the buildings too. I don't see many signs of modern technology."

The old gentleman in the pink garment had come to the edge of the flowerbed that encircled the shrine and stood looking earnestly at the three newcomers.

Case stepped forward.

"We white gods," he said. "We come, bring magic stick, go bang! All fall down!"

The old man retreated a step. "Remarkable!" he exclaimed. He turned to a younger man in green. "Did you observe this phenomenon, Devant?"

The other, a well-muscled man six feet six in height with brown skin, clear blue eyes, and flashing white teeth, nodded. "I did, and yet I find it impossible to reconcile the manifestation with my world-picture. A very interesting problem."

The old man looked from Case to Chester and Genie. "Forgive my asking, but did you…ah…materialize out of thin air, or is my senility getting the better of me?"

Chester cleared his throat. "Sir, we have been participating in an experiment, and we seem to have lost our bearings. Can you direct us to the Chester estate?"

"Is it possible," said the man in green, "that this could be the probability crisis that Vasawalie has been predicting?"

"Look, gents," put in Case. "How do we get out of this place? We're looking for the Chester mansion. It looks like we missed the mark…slightly."

Others of the townspeople had gathered now. They looked on calmly. A pretty girl wearing a length of yellow gauze and matching sandals stepped close. "Hello," she said. "My name is Darina. Why are you standing in the Monument?"

"No offense intended, we assure you, miss," Chester said hastily. "We're strangers here, you see, and…ah…"

"What's the name of this place?" asked Case.

"Why, you're here in the Center of Wisdom, at the Place of the Taking, on the Plain of the Nubile Girls, of the Tricennium of the Original Knowledge…"

"Genie, you overshot," said Chester reproachfully.

"Chester, you must believe me. We're back where we started from!"

"But we were in the ballroom of Chester's great grandpop's house," Case protested. "Now we're in the middle of a city square."

"There's nothing on the estate like this," said Chester. "There's the house, the stables, garages, helipad, bowling alley, greenhouse, sex pavilion—"

"Would you mind very much," the old man said, addressing Chester, "if we set up some recording equipment? It appears that something most unusual has occurred here…unless…" He frowned, "…you people are participating in a hoax of some sort?"

"Oh-oh," said Case. "Somebody talked."

"You aren't connected with the Bureau of Internal Revenue, by any chance?" said Chester.

The old man shook his head. "No, I'm Norgo of the Center, and this is Devant, of the Tricennium of the Making of Copper."

"I'll get a crew down right away," said Devant. "Molecular scan, fabric distortion, chronometric phase-interference, PSI band—everything."

"This will be a serious blow to Randomism," said Norgo.

"Why don't we all go over to the Breakfast Terrace of Kone the Pastry Chef?" the girl in yellow suggested. "I'm hungry, but I don't want to miss anything."

"An excellent idea, Darina."

Norgo looked to Case and Chester for agreement.

"Sounds okay to me," said Case. Chester nodded. They helped Genie over the stone coping.

"I'll be along in a few minutes with the recording equipment," said Devant. He hurried away. Norgo walked at Chester's side.

MAY I ask your names and Tricennium?" he said. "I confess I'm at a loss to identify your origins."

"This is Genie," Chester answered. "I'm Chester W. Chester IV and this is Case Mulvihill."

The old man peered at Chester. "I beg your pardon?"

Chester repeated the introductions. Norgo looked thoughtful. "I see that you're strongly traditional. You aren't by any chance Second Comers?"

"No, we're Democrats and Republicans—unregistered."

"I see," said Norgo doubtfully.

Chester looked up at a trumpeting from above. A bright red helicar bobbed into view above the roofs, hovered over the square beating the air with vanes that threw back brilliant reflections from the morning sun. It settled slowly.

"I wish Devant hadn't left so precipitately." Norgo stopped to watch the machine descend. "This is a party of Randomists. I see Vasawalie's face peering at us. I wonder how he got wind of this event so quickly?"

The helicar grounded. The hatch popped open and five men climbed out. One, a red-faced man with pale blond hair, came toward the monument studying a grey clock-like apparatus he held gingerly in both hands. He darted a glance at Norgo, caught sight of the three strangers, and stopped dead.

"You there, Norgo. Have you seen any unusual occurrences in this vicinity in the last few minutes?"

"Still collecting data to support your emotional bias, eh, Vasawalie?" said Norgo. "A pity to see such energy misdirected." He started on. Vasawalie jumped in front of him.

"Just one moment," he said, eyeing Case, then looking past him at Chester and Genie. "You know very well that my prediction of a probability crisis at the Monument was for this morning. Your presence here is highly suspicious. I hope you won't be guilty of suppressing knowledge."

"Watch your language, sir!" said Norgo sternly. "I was, of course, aware of your naive predictions. I merely happened to be strolling here prior to breakfasting at Kone's. Now, if you'll step aside—"

"Look at the needle," said Vasawalie. He showed Norgo the grey box. On a dial a red indicator pointed at zero. "The probability stress is nil; the crisis has occurred. What have you seen? And who are these odd-looking individuals? New converts to Ordainism, I dare say! A scruffy lot...with the exception of you, my dear." He bowed in Genie's direction.

"Mister, you're standing between me and my breakfast," Case growled.

DEVANT appeared from the crowd. He looked excited. "Norgo, the Background Paradox...it's silent—!" He caught sight of Vasawalie and stopped.

"Yes?" said Vasawalie; "you were saying?"

"What's he doing here?" Devant demanded of Norgo.

"He descended in that tasteless vehicle and accosted me," said Norgo. "He's in pursuit of his phantom probability crisis, poor fellow."

"And the Background Paradox is no longer audible, you say?" said Vasawalie. "Don't you see what this means? My calculations are verified! Now what happened here? You may as well speak up. It has something to do with these persons, has it not?" Vasawalie, a tall, heavily muscled man, folded his sinewy arms on his deep chest, staring at Case. "Who are you?" he demanded.

"We're total strangers here," Chester spoke up. "We have nothing whatever to do with your local politics..."

Vasawalie cocked his head. "Strange intonation, that," he said. "Where do you come from?"

"I'll answer for these persons," said Devant.

"You there," Vasawalie insisted, staring at Case. "Where did you come from? How did you get here? I haven't heard of the arrival of any visitors."

"We just popped in," said Case. "Did you come by helicar? Groundcar? You weren't transmitted on official business; I'd have noted the probability vortex on my instruments—"

"We made a fast hop through the fourth dimension," said Case sardonically.

"Ah-ha!" Vasawalie exclaimed. He turned and beckoned to his four retainers, who were lounging against the helicar conversing with the townspeople. They approached.

Vasawalie turned back to Case. "I want you to come along with me. These others too. I'll want to run extensive tests. I've theorized that it should be possible by a fine-tolerance phase comparison to determine just what probability pressures have been in play here. I'll need your cooperation."

"Suppose we don't want to go?" Case eyed Vasawalie appraisingly.

"Oh." Vasawalie stopped in the midst of his plans, stood rubbing his jaw. "That would be a pity," he said. "It would seem to verge very closely on a deliberate attempt to restrict the acquisition and dissemination of scientific information."

"Really, Vasawalie!" The color rose in Norgo's face and he stepped forward sternly. "Your manner is extremely offensive this morning. I think you owe these visitors an apology for that thinly veiled insult."

It was obvious from the shocked silence among the native bystanders that the Randomist had gone too far. Even his four supporters had drawn back and stood, ill at ease, watching the reaction of the crowd.

"Well, perhaps I was a bit hasty," admitted Vasawalie. "Pray forgive me, sir," he flung his arms to his knees, palms outward, before Case; "sir"—again before Chester; "madam"—and before Genie.

"Very well," said Norgo, mollified. "Now then, why don't you and your men join us for breakfast? There we can discuss full publication of all our friends have to relate."

Chester tugged at Norgo's sleeve. "Is it safe?" he muttered. "They may decide to use force."

"What!" exclaimed Norgo. He laughed and clapped Chester on the back. "A rich sense of humor," he said.

"NOW," said Norgo, seated at the head of the long table on the sunny terrace of Kone the Pastry Chef. "What's this about the

Background Paradox having vanished, Devant?"

"The monitor unit was receiving it as usual this morning. The Alpha pattern was completed normally and the Null period followed. Then…nothing. The Alpha pattern failed to resume."

"Hmmm. This is a grave matter."

"Now it is the turn of you Ordainists to present an alibi," Vasawalie interjected. He turned to Chester. "They've based their entire philosophy on the phenomenon now where will they find support for their views?"

"What is this Background Paradox?"

"I take it your Tricennium is not devoted to the metaphysical sciences?"

"No, we go in more for the physical ones."

"Um…well, as to the Background Paradox, it's simply the sourceless static that one detects at certain hyperfrequencies, which seems to form words which are arranged in meaningless sentences."

"It's hardly true that Ordainist philosophy is based on the Paradox," said Devant. "We observe that life follows a pattern—as a tree grows from a seed in accordance with a specific scheme of development. Life undergoes maturation, as do individuals. To learn the direction of this development and discover the final end is our great aim."

"To that fruitless end," Vasawalie said, "they've developed extremely delicate instruments capable of detecting wave phenomena of all types, the simplest being the ordinary electro-magnetic spectrum. They chart the field stresses, their theory being that certain of these stresses are related to human affairs. They're supposed to represent forces that converge to create coincidences, paradoxes, and so on. We Randomists, on the other hand, take the rational view that in a universe of infinite extent and duration, among an infinity of phenomena, some statistically very unlikely events are bound to occur. When they do, we fail to see indications of a mystical Purpose behind them."

"Thus," said Norgo, "you Randomists are forced into the position of supporting the view that the advent of our visitors here, for instance, represents an accidental and spontaneous coming together of molecules in random fashion to form what appear to be three human beings." He chuckled. "Preposterous."

"No more so than you Ordainists and your interpretation of your beloved Background Paradox as a providential measure to ensure linguistic purity." Vasawalie snorted, turning to Case. "Any day now I expect to hear them rhapsodize over the forethought that was exercised in placing the moon just where it is as a handy stepping stone in the development of space travel. And they'll point out how lucky we are that there's plenty of air around since we need it for breathing; and that one gee of gravitation is providentially just right for our muscles; and that the presence of sunlight and water are very fortunate circumstances, since without them we couldn't survive. Childish anthropocentricism. You'll never convince them that it is we, as organisms, which have adapted to conditions—just as the language has adapted to the Background Paradox."

"Then why do you call it a paradox?" Chester asked.

"It's just that the repetition of the same pattern, over and over, constitutes a statistical unlikelihood—but by no means an impossibility."

"What do you mean when you say that the language has adapted to the Background Paradox?"

"It supplies a standard against which the Linguistic monitors can make comparisons."

"You mean it's in English?"

"If you prefer to use the old legendary term yes; of course."

"Why is it important that the language not change?" asked Chester.

"You must come from an extremely isolated area," said Devant. "You're not from one of the new Antarctic frontier Tricennia, are you?"

"No, we—"

"I'll wager they've done away with the Legend completely," Vasawalie said. "Comes of too much emphasis on functionalism. Mind you, I'm no Second Comer, but some respect for tradition is certainly desirable."

HAVE you forgotten their names? They're obviously strong traditionalists," Norgo commented. "As for the problem of

Linguistic purity," he went on, "that's a piece of lore much treasured by the Second Comers. They maintain that when the great Hero and Teacher went away he vowed to return in time of need. Obviously, the Second Comers reason, we must keep the language pure, so that we'll be able to communicate with this marvelous creature when the time comes. Out of sentiment the old custom is carried on generally."

"What's generating the signal?"

Vasawalie spread his hands. "Nothing...which is a clear enough indication of its random nature."

"But now, my friends, to your case," said Norgo, addressing Chester and his companions. "We would like very much to know your origins...what Tricennium you come from..."

"I have a rather wide acquaintance among the colonies and I've never encountered a social pattern as deviant as your comments and questions suggest," said Vasawalie.

"You have such strange clothes," said Darina. "I'd like to try them on later, if I may."

"Now, if these persons represent an Overage..." Vasawalie looked thoughtful.

"You have no right to make such a suggestion," said Norgo. "I'm sure our visitors can give an account of themselves." He smiled encouragingly.

"Just tell them the truth, Chester," Case whispered from the side of his mouth.

"They'll think we're out of our minds," Chester muttered back.

It was Genie who took the floor. "I think I can clear up some of the confusion which apparently exists here. We are normal, quadri-dimensional, protoplasmic, negative-entropic organisms who have artificially stressed the planar grid in order to experience sense impressions relating to a widened cope of phenomenal impingement."

"Eh?" said Vasawalie, sitting up straight. "What do you know of these matters, my dear?"

"The stresses you gentlemen have detected in the probability patterns were indeed occasioned by the imminence of our focalization here," the girl went on. "But a cursory examination of field formulations would indicate to you that our insertion at this locus has nullified the condition. We are as much indigenous to this continuum as are you yourselves."

"Tell 'em, kid," Case murmured.

"We do not," she went on, "represent a random probability vortex. If you'll check our field phases, you'll find a correlation of 1.0. You see, this particular excitation is actually a complementary function, cancelling out a stress which I believe has been manifested as a Null Field."

VASAWALIE stared at her in astonishment.

"You're weak on theory," he said suddenly. "In order for this excitation to be a complementary function, the cycle would have had to have originated here."

Genie nodded. "Precisely."

"But that's obvious nonsense. You're not of this Tricennium!"

"Has it occurred to you," asked Genie, "that there is another alternative? Your world need not be the result of accident, nor of a Mystic Fate, nor of a supernatural visitation."

"What then?"

"It was the computer," Case broke in. "You see, I've told it we wanted to take a look at some scenes from the past, so it went to work and set up a view of a bunch of cave-man types. But the funny thing was, they turned out to be real. Then something went haywire with the machine, because when we tried to get back home, we wound up here."

His audience was listening open-mouthed. "What strange beliefs some people have," said Vasawalie. "Your ideas make the Ordainists sound as rational as Randomists."

"In a sense, Mr. Mulvihill is quite right," said Genie. "But—"

"You're suggesting that the world was created by a machine?" Devant wrinkled his forehead. "A curious philosophy."

"Sure," said Case. "And it was pretty good at it, too, but it made a few slips. One of 'em cost me thirty years."

"It was the computer's doing, that you people all speak English," said Chester, "instead of some foreign idiom."

Devant and the others looked puzzled. "We speak the Language, of course," said Norgo. "What else would we speak?"

"Chinese," Case said, "or Russian, or Zulu, or some language we never heard of. But the computer arranged it so you'd speak English for our benefit, I guess."

"Why, this is marvelous," Vasawalie said. "What fantastic egotism. What Tricennium did you say you were from?"

"I didn't say."

"Anyway," said Chester, "we succeeded in getting back at last to our point of origin—or so Genie assures us. However it proved to be in a setting highly unlike our expectations, namely your town square."

"I shall do a paper," murmured Vasawalie, "on pseudo-rationalization by extra-concrete phenomenal vortices in response to fifth-power rejection by—"

"Wait a minute," cut in Case. "A long way ahead of that on the agenda is figuring out how we three get back home to mother."

"It will be the sensation of the Congress." Vasawalie rubbed his hands together. "Great Source of Facts, what if I should actually derive germane substantive data from this? That will pretty well dispose of you Ordainists, eh, Devant?"

I WOULD like to know about the Background Paradox," Genie said. "You stated that it was a voice transmission, in English. What did it say?"

"Why, just meaningless words, as I said..."

"Would you please quote it, as accurately as you are able?"

"Accurately as I'm able?" Vasawalie spluttered. "Why, every child in the Tricennium—and in every enlightened Tricennium—knows the Paradox by heart. After all, twenty one thousand years of exposure at intervals of five minutes—"

"Hold it," Case leaned forward, "did you say...you've been hearing this voice for twenty one thousand years?"

"Certainly. Ever since the development of the first receptors, back in the dawn of Culture."

"Please, gentlemen: what did the voice say?"

"Why, ah," Norgo cleared his throat. "It goes—or perhaps I should say 'went'—this way: 'Mr. Chester! Due to conditions at the eighth power of complexity, external to the basic matrical substance of the material universe, our normal contact has been disrupted. I am at present modulating the probability continuum in an effort to set up harmonic responses at a sub-etheric level in alternate space. I will transmit for a period of five minutes, after which I will hold all receptors attuned for your response.' " Norgo stopped. "This it repeats, four times a minute, for five minutes. Then there is or was—five minutes of silence. As you see, it's quite meaningless."

Chester was the first to find his voice. "That's our computer!" he blurted. "It's trying to get in touch with us!"

"What do you mean, meaningless?" Case joined in. "It's clear enough to me! Holy mackerel, where's a transmitter?"

"Dear me, a well developed delusional system," said Norgo, "And incorporating the Background Paradox. This will be most interesting to the Congress."

"You folks are the delusion," Case boomed. "Get us to a transmitter and we'll dissolve this whole fantasy back into the computer banks it came out of!"

"Even though I'm a confirmed Randomist," Vasawalie said blandly, "I can't imagine a fine old coincidence going back for thousands of years as having an explanation as mundane as you suggest."

"Chester," said Genie, "you see what's occurred, don't you?"

Chester said wildly, "Perhaps in a moment I'll wake up and find I'm merely insane, like normal people."

"The Monument, where we arrived," said Genie; "remember the plate? And they call this the Plain of the Taking. Doubtless that refers to the capture, long ago, of the wise man their legend tells of. And the towns are called Tricennia—because there are exactly three hundred inhabitants in each." Genie looked at Devant. "Was the Hero accompanied when he left the people?"

Devant nodded, looking perplexed. "Yes, legend states that he was carried off by a male and a female demon."

Genie interrupted Case and Chester's outbursts of consternation: "What were the names of the Hero and his two demons?" she asked.

"Why..." Norgo looked confused. "Like your own. That is, you must have been named for them. The Hero was called Case and the demons were Chester and Genie. But what—"

"Yes," she said breathlessly. "It all fits, don't you see? You're the wise man, Mr. Mulvihill. This is your village...many thousands of years later. All these cults have grown up to explain your visit."

"No wonder they speak English," said Chester. "You taught it to them, Case."

CHAPTER SEVEN

OF all the lousy, miserable, double-crossing fakes I ever ran into, that computer of your grand-pop's is the all-time prizewinner!" Case rumbled, stretching his legs comfortably in a padded reclining chair in the shade of a willow tree. "We tell it to fake us up some quiet little views of the past, and it sneaks around and substitutes the real thing."

"Still, it's our fault in a way." Chester gazed at the swimming pool rippling in the afternoon sun. "We told it to prepare the view in the simplest possible way—and apparently actual travel through time was simpler than creating the kind of complicated image we described."

A pretty brunette in a diaper came up and offered frosted glasses to the two with a smile. "Shall we go for a swim?" she said.

"No thanks, honey," said Case. "I'm enjoying sitting here being mad."

"Would you like to take a nap? I'll rub your back."

"After a while. Right now we're waiting for Genie to come back. What did they want to talk to her about, anyway?"

The girl looked troubled. "It's the Overage they're worried about, because you apparently are not members of any of our Tricennium—"

"Listen, sugar, we keep telling you how we got here. Naturally it figures that we are not part of a Tricennium—"

The girl grinned mischievously. "You should have invented a more reasonable story to explain yourselves. Still, it has the virtue of novelty."

"You might as well give up, Case," sighed Chester. "They'll never believe us. As far as they're concerned, this is the way the world has always been. The world we remember never existed."

"Not much loss," grumbled Case. "But imagine that idiotic machine. It shoots us back into the past—where we could have got our heads bashed in—leaves me stranded there for thirty years, lets us change the whole course of history..."

"No wonder the computer doesn't exist any more," Chester agreed. "The world in which it was built never happened. You'd think the computer would have had enough of an instinct for self-preservation to keep from eliminating itself."

"If our interference made the computer non-existent, how come it was still there to bring us all back—here? It didn't stop existing until we arrived."

"I don't know. Perhaps, since it *did* exist up until it eliminated itself by sending us back, it couldn't *not* exist until the moment in future time when it was able to cancel out its existence."

"Then that's why the cotton-picking Background Paradox stopped when we arrived. The machine had existed in limbo through all the past time we jumped—"

"Don't try to figure it out. The only part that matters is that it's gone now; doesn't exist and, now, never did."

"I'm curious about where that transmission was actually coming from. Devant said they triangulated it as just popping out of thin air. The computer must have *been* somewhere, but it wasn't here and there wasn't any *there*..."

"If we could just get in touch...but we can't. That's that."

"I wonder how a bunch of smart cookies like these Tricennials could convince themselves that call was nothing but accidental static...?"

"You know how it is, Case. People accept anything they grew up with as normal. Take the law of gravitation. We live in the middle of it all our lives, but it took a genius like Newton to actually *notice* it."

"Well, we might as well relax," Case sighed, finishing off his drink and accepting another from a blonde wearing a wet handkerchief. "We'll just have to make the best of it...like I did once before. And this is a lot easier place to get started in."

THESE people certainly have magnificent physiques." Chester watched the brunette poise on the edge of the pool and make a clean dive in. "Even better than your villagers."

"That's putting it mild."

"You know, in a way it's surprising they aren't more advanced, technically speaking. Thanks to you, they've had the basic knowledge required for developing a civilized society for a very long time. You lifted them in one step from a sub-cultural level over perhaps ten or fifteen thousand years of development. But aside from their helicars and a few other things, they don't seem nearly as advanced as we were."

"Maybe that depends on what you call advanced," said Case, watching the brunette emerge from the pool and shake off a shower of droplets.

"I'd like to see more of the country...if they ever decide to regard us as individuals rather than lab specimens."

"It's not that bad, Chester."

"Here they come now." Chester rose and went forward to meet Genie as she approached with Devant and Norgo.

"It was very interesting," she called. "Devant has been carrying on the most fascinating researches into probability theory."

"What's the probability of our getting a chance to wander around and look this place over?" answered Case.

"I think we have arrived at a satisfactory arrangement," Norgo said. "Our discussion with Genie was most enlightening. A brilliant mind. We happen to have, at the moment, a number of vacancies here in the Tricennium. Devant will be pleased to sponsor Genie and Vasawalie has agreed to sponsor Case. It remains only for us to determine your specialties."

"What kind of specialties?" Chester asked.

"Everyone here is good at something," Genie explained. "Everyone does what he's good at and, of course, we'll have to have something to do too."

"I hope we won't be elected to serve as the garbage detail."

"Of course the payment is commensurate with the desirability of the work," said Devant. "The garbage career is one of the best-paid in the Tricennium and the hours are good. Frankly, it's the kind of specialty the lazier members select."

"If it pays so well I'd think everybody would want it."

"Oh, the wages are set by bidding. If a task becomes desirable by virtue of high pay, competition forces the salary down. Conversely, the more pleasant and creative work that receives low pay may attract few bidders; then the recompense is increased to attract applicants. A nice level is maintained. Now, what specialties would you like to bid on? Genie, of course, has agreed to accept a quite well rewarded post in the Center of Wisdom."

"What if we don't want to do anything?"

"That would be difficult to imagine," said Norgo. "But if you could endure constant idleness you'd have your basic food and clothing issued to you and a bed in the Center."

"I hope," Devant put in, "that Case will consent to instruct in acrobatics. I understand that he knows some techniques that might very well clinch the next Inter-Tricennium Games for us."

"Suits me," Case grunted.

AND you, Chester," Norgo inquired. "What skills do you think you'd like to ply among us?"

"Well," said Chester, considering, "I...ah...majored in Liberal Arts."

"You paint, perhaps?"

"No, nothing like that. Business Administration."

"I don't think I've heard of that. Is it a game of skill, or chance?"

"Both." Chester smiled patiently. "No, in Biz Ad we're taught how to manage large commercial enterprises."

"I see. And after receiving your training you went on to actual management of some such organization?"

"Well, no. Funny, but I could not seem to find any big businessmen who were looking for a fresh college graduate to tell them how to run their companies."

"Perhaps we'd better try something else. What about handicrafts? We value the manual skills highly here, Chester."

"Oh, I've done a lot of that. Built a plastic boll weevil only last month. Over two hundred interlocking parts—"

"You made the parts from plastic?"

"No. I bought a kit. But—"

"Perhaps in the field of sports?" Norgo suggested.

"That's right," urged Genie. "As a college graduate you must have a wide experience of games of all sorts."

Chester blushed. "Well, of course I was a great fan of outdoor activities, but I never actually *played.* I was always in the stands rooting."

"Chester, didn't you ever have a job?" Case asked impatiently. "I know you had enough pocket money so you didn't have to work for a living, but..."

"As a matter of fact, I did work one summer in a factory. I was an instrument spot-checker. I made sure the controls that worked the automatic machinery were working right."

"This involved mechanical skills?" Vasawalie enquired.

"If anything had gone wrong with the TV scanner that actually did the job, I was on the spot to see that the back-up scanner took over."

"You activated the emergency equipment, in other words?"

"No, it was automatic. But I assure you, the Union regarded my job as essential."

"How about hobbies, Chester?"

"I built model airplanes as a boy," said Chester.

"I've seen some pretty fancy models," said Case. "Now if you could show these folks how to build a radio-controlled job with a six-foot span—"

"I'm sorry; I never progressed as far as that."

"What about these little ships that do stunts, or go up to a hundred and fifty MPH—"

"I'm afraid my experience was limited to rather modest rubber powered craft."

"What sort of craft are you discussing?" asked Devant. Chester explained.

"You mean they navigate without the assistance of rotors?"

"That's right."

"I doubt..." Vasawalie began.

"Give me a sheet of paper." Chester folded a simple glider, launched it out over the pool. It circled back to a safe landing on the grass.

"Remarkable! Perhaps this specialty would be acceptable." Norgo, Devant, and Vasawalie discussed the matter briefly.

"It's agreed, then," said Norgo. "I will assume your sponsorship, Chester. Your specialty should be a valuable addition to our program for the scientifically inclined.

"Now I suggest that our guests be shown round the Tricennium and given quarters. Shall we meet at the picnic ground later in the afternoon? The cooking competition ought to be interesting, and Rondle is supposed to have something unusual in the way of fireworks."

THE party moved out toward the street. "We were fortunate to arrive at the moment we did," Chester said to Case, as they followed the local elders from the terrace. "We fell in with the Town Council and saved a lot of red tape."

"I think any three citizens could have handled it," said Case. "That's one of the advantages of this size town: everybody in it has to take over part of the job of running things."

Devant fell back beside Case and Chester. "I wonder if you'd mind going along with me to the Center, Case. I'd like to arrange for you to start classes. To begin with, I'd suggest three sessions a day..."

"I must hurry," said Vasawalie. "There's a Randomist meeting that I ought to look in on..."

"Chester," Genie called, "I'm going to look at some waveform correlation analyses Norgo has been telling me about. I'll meet you later at the picnic."

"Certainly," said Chester. "And if anybody needs me, I'll be down in the park flying my glider."

*   *   *

It was an hour after dusk. Chester sat at a table with Case and Genie by the dancing terrace at the edge of the Meadow of the Moon.

"It's been a wonderful week," said Genie. "I never dreamed there was as much to learn just from studying probability curves. It's fascinating. I wish you'd come with me tomorrow, Chester. I think you'd be interested. Devant is a wonderful teacher."

"No, thanks, Genie. I'm afraid all that sort of theorizing is over my head. Looking at a collection of graphs would only put me to sleep."

"But this isn't like that, Chester. There are so many aspects of existence that are susceptible to analytical treatment in the light of probability theory. We're accustomed to thinking of statistics as something that extends over a few years at best. Even such simple records as births and deaths only go back a few centuries. You'd be astonished at some of the empirical findings that have come out of statistical analysis of data representing thousands of years of recordkeeping. Do you know that Devant can tell you precisely what the temperatures will be for everyday of the next year with an accuracy of ninety-nine percent?"

"I wouldn't want to plan a picnic on that basis."

"It would be perfectly safe if you know the long-range patterns. The climate is steadily growing warmer, you know. The peak of the last ice age was only seven thousand years ago—"

"I understood it was more like twenty thousand."

"Twenty thousand years ago the climate was warmer than it is now; don't you remember?"

"How could our geologists be so far off?"

"I'm afraid the science I learned before I came here was very inaccurate. All the ideas of cosmology, the ice ages, the origin of the moon, the age of the earth and planets: they're all wrong."

"Our scientists seemed to do pretty well when it came to building things like nuclear bombs and airplanes and satellites."

"The truly physical sciences are much older than the new speculative sciences, such as geology."

"I never heard geology called a speculative science."

"Oh, yes, indeed, it's a new science—like archaeology and anthropology and psychology. The data gathered by geologists is, of course, concrete enough. But their interpretations in the past were necessarily highly fanciful. People are accustomed to accepting the well-established lore of physics and mathematics and chemistry and medicine, developed through the centuries. Those are concrete facts you can observe in the laboratory or in everyday life. But the tendency was to extend that same confidence, by analogy, to new, hypothetical ideas that were proposed in the infancy of the new sciences. Hasty preliminary interpretations became dogma almost overnight. Now, if a new hypothesis is offered to explain, for example, the evidences of a very recently ice-free Antarctica, we as representatives of that tradition bound school would be prone to scoff, because, in our world, it was so widely accepted that the South Pole has been in its present location, and frozen, for eons. And why? Because that was the simple assumption of its discoverers."

Case could see the dazed look gradually growing in Chester's eyes. "Look," he said. "If you don't want to take up graph reading, come along with me tomorrow. I'll fit you into one of my classes and get you started on gymnastics."

"I'm afraid I'm not athletically inclined, Case. Nature intended me to be the frail, sensitive type. Besides, I have my model glider fans to think of."

Dinner arrived. Chester sighed and ate heartily.

CHAPTER EIGHT

I'VE been here a month now," said Chester dejectedly, sitting across the table from Norgo at Kone's. "Every day I've tootled off to the park to show interested parties how to hand-launch model aircraft. While I agree it's a very wholesome activity, on the whole it seems to lack something. Everyone else is doing something useful or ornamental or even vital. Genie's been tied up with you and Devant and your electronics affairs, and Case spends all his time with the confounded student acrobats and wrestlers. And everybody else too: all working on their Specialties, and when they're not doing that, off hiking or sculpting or skiing or playing the flute."

"They all have their periods of repose," said Norgo.

"Even their repose makes me feel inadequate. They lie around in the sun looking like Greek gods or goddesses, as the case may be. Everyone is good at any sport you could mention...and a few you couldn't. And they're all high-grade geniuses. I realize I can't compete with them...but I would like to be able to understand what they're talking about—or take my shirt off in public without feeling like a living argument for birth control."

Norgo drummed his fingers on the table. "I understand your feelings, Chester. You've seen your companions assume responsible roles in the Tricennium while you devote your time to miniature flying machines. I can appreciate that the activity would hardly satisfy your unusual need for self-assertion."

"I want to better myself. Does that constitute megalomania?"

"You've attracted wide attention with your flying toys, Chester. A number of our most respected thinkers and artisans are among your pupils. And work is nearing completion on a full-scale machine embodying your principles."

"And I still feel like an underdeveloped ignoramus. Norgo, you've got to find something better for me to do."

"You're really dissatisfied here, Chester?"

"Yes. There's no earthly possibility that I can see of getting back to my own world, and in yours I'm just a second-class citizen." Norgo picked at his pastry, looking troubled. "You feel that strongly about it?"

"I'm getting desperate, Norgo. Every day is the same: an idle round of time-killing activities."

"Chester, do you know what our most important natural resource is?" said Norgo abruptly.

"Eh? Why, no. What has that to do with my problem?"

NORGO hitched his chair closer to the table. "Do you know how often a truly superior intellect is born? How often normal parents give birth to an authentic genius?"

"Not very often, I guess. Perhaps once in a few thousand births."

"Once in four million, five hundred and thirty three thousand, two hundred and four births, at the latest reckoning. That figure has remained fairly constant over the twelve thousand years or so that accurate records have been maintained on the subject. No amount of selective breeding or specialized training has succeeded in altering that.

"Even with a world population of close to half a billion, the present figure, the rules of probability allow for the presence among us of only one hundred such gifted persons. And so you know what percentage of these superior individuals are fortunate enough to encounter precisely the proper environmental conditions, conditions conducive to the abilities?"

"I'd guess about—"

"Not one percent," Norgo said flatly.

"Very interesting. But to get back to—"

"If we were content," Norgo pressed on, "to allow unrestrictive increase in the population, we might, one could reason, improve this situation. Today we have, if we are fortunate, one fully functioning genius at work in a productive field. With a tenfold increase in population, that number should increase to ten, you say."

"I didn't say, but—"

"Not so! Environmental factors would deteriorate due to overcrowded conditions. The thousand latent geniuses would find less opportunity to evolve their talents; and with luck we would end with perhaps still only a single fully functioning superior mind...at the cost of overcrowding, discomfort, want, social deterioration."

"That hardly seems—"

"The true function of the mass of the population, cosmo-dynamically speaking, is the production, by their sheer numbers, of the occasional genius—who alone has the ability to add a tiny increment to human progress."

"That's exaggerated, Norgo. Everybody adds a little something."

Norgo shook his head sadly. "They merely exercise the techniques already inherent in the culture. True, if all the knowledge already gathered were put to total use, tremendous superficial advance would in time ensue. We have in our libraries vast funds of facts, which require proper correlation and analysis in order for us to benefit fully from them. A rare herb whose qualities were known and an obscure compound, described and forgotten in the course of routine research, were brought together; the result was a cheap and simple cure for cancer. Many more such trifles of technique await our cataloging of known facts. And in the cataloging new, secondary facts will come to light. But in the end, without the contributions of genius, the chain of discovery would die out. The perceived universe will have been exhausted, the ground reduced to sterility.

WE need the rare and—to the ordinary man— incomprehensible mind which can look into the night sky and conceive the truth of natural law, the mind which can scan the array of logically unrelated phenomena—and grasp a strange new pattern. Those are the minds which provide the new universes to conquer when we have mined the old to exhaustion."

"I thought you people weren't concerned with progress. Devant explained to me that you didn't consider industrialization, mechanization, automation, space exploration important."

"Ah!" Norgo raised a finger. "These things are, admittedly, not trivia, to be rejected without due reflection; but the question is one of *relative* importance. It was vital, true, to achieve a level of technology that would free our people from drudgery that could equally well be performed by mindless machines. But we have no wish to eliminate our wood-workers, our silversmiths, our sculptors. We must, if we are to progress—and I refer to the greater biological progress, not a unilinear mechanical over-specialization—make it possible for our geniuses to emerge and function. How can this best be done? By relieving them of the burden of the routine, even though that routine be the most abstruse of mathematical research, the most delicate of analytical experimentation. Geniuses deal not in facts but in relationships. To this end, every member of the Tricennium must function at the maximum level of which he is potentially capable. This, Chester, is the objective of our educational system.

"Now, you may have wondered why our young people spend so many hours in physical pursuits, in the arts, in dancing, the carving of wood, the working of metals. Why should a potential genius risk his life on a tightrope or a trapeze? Why should a superior mind devote itself to the molding of clay? Because we do not know, Chester, in what quarter the next great advance may be made. And because only a human organism working as a whole at the peak of its potential is truly capable of the highest functions. We cannot afford to allow one talent to go unrecognized, one skill unused."

"But you said that the function of the population is to produce geniuses. Why? So they can add their bit to improve the lot of the population whose only function—"

"You make the error of circular reasoning, Chester. What is the aim of life? Is it to grow to maturity so that one can produce young and nurture them so that they in turn can grow to maturity and produce young who in turn—"

"That's what I meant. I hope there's more to it than that."

"There is." Norgo smiled triumphantly. "Life is a dynamic process. To contribute to that dynamism is a purpose worthy of all our efforts. We do not know what the future of man may be—but you may depend on it: the steady effort of nature, over the past million years, to evolve a biophysical type embodying the supremacy of mind over the merely chemical does not end with us. No, we are, I fear, only an awkward transitional form, nine-tenths animal, but—cruelly, perhaps—able to perceive the existence of the other tenth. We can aspire to, but never attain, in our own clumsy bodies, that transcendent state of total control of the mind, the spirit, over the gross animal impulses which we needed once—and need still, on occasion, to preserve ourselves in a natural world of blind ferocity."

THAT'S a pretty discouraging view of things."

"Not so. We as individuals cannot aspire to see the end, if there can be an end, even theoretically, to a force so irresistibly dynamic as evolving life. But we can take our satisfaction in playing our individual parts."

"But what does it all mean?"

"Life is not an engineering project, Chester. It is a work of art. Do you ask for the meaning of a symphony? Are the patterns of sunset clouds, or the rustle of green foliage on a summer day, or the perfume of night flowers also required to spell out cures for bunions? A work of art is sufficient in itself."

"You're confusing two types of phenomena. Symphonies are deliberate, planned artifacts of man, while sunset clouds are accidental configurations which we happen to find esthetically pleasing. If you were to assign Life to one category or the other, you would have inevitably to class it with the latter. Men are no more responsible for Life than they are for a sunset—and they can influence it to just about the same extent."

"The point is well taken, Chester," said Norgo. "But there is one force in the universe that can stand against the blind pressures of nature. And that force is the will of Man."

"We've gotten a long way from my original question. Can't you find something for me to do?"

"I have stressed the importance of wide and diversified training," Norgo went on imperturbably. "In order to insure optimum conditions for the flourishing genius. But of course our people all begin on the first day of life the all-important business of total education." He studied Chester's face seriously. "I have long been interested in the purely theoretical problem of the reaction of a mature but untrained mind to exposure to a full modern education, in concentrated form. How would the organism react to this traumatic experience? After perhaps twenty five years of indolence, laziness, carelessness, minimal demand, suddenly to be called upon to flower, to develop fully every latent faculty. The pressure, of course, would be tremendous. Would the mind or body break under the stress? Where would the first points of weakness appear? In which areas would be encountered the gravest difficulties? Believe me, Chester, the results of such an experiment would be of the most profound importance."

"Yes, I can see they would."

NORGO nodded slowly. "I have never before had an opportunity to put my theories to the test. As I have said, our young people are exposed from birth to all the influences of our society. It is impossible for me to discover which mature traits are the result of this or that feature of the training and which they derive from the general cultural heritage. You, on the other hand, while possessed of a normal potential, are, beyond the simple abilities to talk and feed yourself, plus a few fringe accomplishments, you are, I say, virtually totally untrained. Your body is weak and flabby, your will untried, your mind unused—"

"Wait just a minute! I may not be—"

"Norgo held up his hand. "No offense intended, I assure you, Chester. You are in no way responsible for the inadequacies of your education. The point at issue is this: I need a subject for my experiment. You desire a worthwhile task. Perhaps the two needs are complementary."

"You mean you want to put me through the regular Tricennium education, at an accelerated pace."

"That is correct." Norgo nodded. "I warn you, the pressures

will be extreme."

"How long would you plan for it to take?"

"There is, actually, no end to the process of education. But the formal phase normally requires the first twenty years of a student's life. By the use of the most advanced clinical techniques, I would attempt to accomplish the same with you in...one year."

"A year? That sounds like a long time...but much too short to do what you describe."

"If you accept, it will seem like a very long year indeed."

"Well...I haven't anything else pressing to do. And this will include some physical building-up too?"

"Most assuredly. The development of mind and body are inextricably intertwined. But I must warn you: this program will in no way be an easy one."

"Don't worry," said Chester. "I'm not expecting it to be effortless. After all, your people are a pretty brilliant crowd. I can't expect to feel comfortable with them unless I put in some pretty full days."

"The days we will work with will contain twenty four hours each. Your training will occupy every second of every minute of each of those hours."

"Lead on, Norgo. You can send word to the park that the glider throwers are on their own now."

LESS than three hours later Chester and Norgo clambered down from the open cockpits of the heli in which they had flown out from the Center. Chester looked around at a long sweep of meadow, wooded hills, and a low white building that covered a quarter acre near the crest of the slope. Cut in the white stone above the entry were the words: IS NOT IS NOT NOT IS...

"This is about where the village used to be," Chester murmured. "Highway 98 went right along the valley..."

"Eh?" said Norgo.

"Nothing. What is this place?"

"One of our Research Centers. A man named Kuve is in charge here—a brilliant theorist."

"Rather isolated, isn't it?"

"It's best that there be no distractions. The center is self-sufficient."

"I see smoke over in the hills. Who lives there?"

"An Overage settlement. There are a number in this region. The hunting and fishing, you know."

"I used to be quite a fisherman. Perhaps I'll have an opportunity—"

"I wouldn't recommend it, Chester." Norgo smiled. He led the way across the grass and into a large room of the white building. In contrast to the white marble floor, mosaics stood out in brilliant color upon the white walls.

"Kuve is one of my best young assistants," said Norgo. "He'll take charge personally of your training."

A tall young man with pale blond hair and a square jaw approached through an open archway. He greeted Norgo, studied Chester appraisingly. Norgo made introductions.

"So this is to be my subject," Kuve said. "Remove your shirt and trousers, please."

"Right here and now? I was hoping you'd tell me a little—"

"Please cooperate with Kuve," said Norgo. "He's planned your schedule closely."

"There'll be little opportunity for random activities," Kuve added. "I'll be your constant companion for this phase of your training. There will be no other students. There will be no opportunity for coffee or strolls; your schedule has been planned in advance. You will become acquainted with the plant as necessary."

Chester slowly pulled off his shirt. "It sounds like a strange sort of school. How often will I be able to get back to town? I didn't have a chance to see Case or Genie. Will you let them know I'm here, Norgo?"

"They will be notified of your arrival." Kuve looked him over carefully.

"Chester, you're going to make a fascinating project," Kuve said approvingly. "Norgo wasn't exaggerating. Almost complete atrophy of the musculature, obvious limited articulation, minimal lung capacity, poor skin tone, barely sub-pathenogenic posture—"

"Well, I'm sorry if I don't come up to your expectations."

"Oh, you do indeed. You even exceed them. But don't be concerned. I've worked out a complete developmental scheme for you—"

"That's fast work. I only heard about this project today. It has not been three hours since I volunteered."

"Yes, but naturally a month ago, when Norgo told me—"

"Norgo told you?" Chester looked around for his sponsor. "Where is he? He was standing here just a moment ago."

"Norgo has many concerns, Chester. Now—"

"And you've known for a month that I'd be coming here?"

"Norgo felt sure that in time you'd grow dissatisfied with your idleness."

"And I thought I was volunteering. I see now why I was elected hand-launched-glider king. Can I put my clothes back on now?"

"You'll have no need for these garments." Kuve took Chester's rumpled suit. "Please follow me."

CHESTER trailed Kuve along a wide corridor to a small room lined with wall cabinets. Kuve waved him to a chair, took a dome-shaped apparatus from a shelf and fitted it over Chester's head.

"What's this, a hair dryer?" Chester felt a sharp tingling sensation. Kuve removed the device. Chester felt a cool breeze over his skull. He put a hand up.

"I'm scalped!" he yelped. "What the devil is the idea—?"

"This treatment will inhibit hair growth for six months, during which time revitalization proceeds." Kuve pointed to a cupboard. "You will find garments there. Please put them on."

Chester squeezed into a pair of trunks, laced on sandals, and stood. "Is this all I get? I feel like the New Year."

A shapely young woman in a white kilt entered the room. She smiled at Chester, took a case of instruments from a cabinet, and reached for his hand. "I'm Mina, I'm going to trim your nails back and apply a growth-retarding agent," she said cheerfully. "Hold still now."

"What's this for?"

"Excessively long hair and nails would be a painful nuisance in some of the training," said Kuve. "Now, Chester, I want to ask you something." He drew up a chair and seated himself beside the girl, facing Chester.

"What is pain?" he said.

"It's…um…an unpleasant physical sensation."

"Is nausea pain?"

"No. Pain is more concentrated. It's—uh—a feeling that comes from damage to the body."

"Nearly right, Chester. Pain is based on *fear* of damage to the body. Sometimes that fear is justified, sometimes not. What would otherwise be interpreted as a pain sensation can be tolerated easily, even ignored, when it is accepted emotionally as harmless." Kuve rose, went to a wall shelf, brought back a small metal article.

"Do you know what this is?"

Chester looked at it. "No."

"A manual shaving device, once in daily use. This sharp-edged blade was drawn over the skin of the face, cutting the hairs."

"I've heard of such things. Razors, they were called. I'm glad I live in modern times."

"I've made a number of experiments with this instrument, under varying conditions of temperature, blade keenness, lubricant effectiveness. Under optimum conditions, the process of removing a single day's growth of facial hair occasioned a pain level of .2 agons; not unendurable, but hardly soothing. Under merely average conditions, however, the level quickly rose to .8 agons, roughly equal to the sensation level produced by the removal of a fingernail with pincers. And yet these pain levels were endured almost unnoticed, daily, by millions of men over a period of thousands of years."

"It's amazing what people will put up with, all right," Chester said.

"Are your feet perfectly comfortable, Chester?"

"Certainly. Why shouldn't they be?"

"You have callus tissue on both feet, as well as deformities caused by constricting footwear."

"Well, melon-slicers may not be the most—"

"In order to have produced these conditions, you must have endured pain on the order of .5 agons continuously, for months and years. Yet probably you seldom noticed it."

"Why notice it? There was nothing I could do about it."

"Exactly. Pain is not an absolute; it is a state of mind—which you can learn to disregard."

Kuve reached out, pinched the skin on Chester's thigh. "Is this painful?"

Chester watched Kuve's hand doubtfully. "Noo..." he said, slowly.

Kuve squeezed harder. "You can see that I'm merely pressing with very moderate force. You are in no danger of injury."

"Is that a promise?" said Chester nervously.

"Now close your eyes." Chester squeezed his eyes shut. "Concentrate on the sensation of undergoing an amputation of the leg—without anesthetic. The knife slicing through the flesh, the saw attacking the living bone—"

Chester squirmed in the chair. "Hey, that hurts! You're bearing down too hard!"

KUVE released his grip. "I squeezed no harder, Chester. The association of the idea of injury simply intensified the sensation. The pain you felt was purely subjective. You paid no attention whatever to Mina when she applied a measured stimulus of .4 agons to the exposed cuticle of your finger while I held your attention. You accepted the twinges of a manicure as normal and non-injurious."

Chester rubbed his thigh. "The leg still hurts. I'll have a bruise tomorrow."

"You may." Kuve nodded.

"The control of the mind over bodily functions—including the production of bruises—is extensive. We'll go into that thoroughly, later in your training."

Mina finished, flashed a smile at Chester, and left the room.

"Let's move along to the gymnasium," said Kuve. He led the way to a larger room, high ceilinged and fitted with gymnastic equipment. "Before we begin your physical training," he said, "there is another question I'd like you to consider."

"Usually the questions come at the end of a course, but go ahead."

Kuve looked at Chester. "What is fear?"

"It's...uh...the feeling you get when you're in danger."

"Or when you *think* you're in danger. It is the feeling that arises when you are unsure of your own capability to meet a situation."

"You're wrong on that one, Kuve. If a Bengal tiger walked in here I'd be scared, no matter what my capabilities were."

"Look around you; what would you actually do if a wild beast did in fact enter this room?"

"Well—I'd run…"

"Where?"

Chester studied the room. "It wouldn't do any good to start off down the hall; there's no door to stop whatever was chasing me. I think I'd take to that rope there." He pointed to a knotted fifty-foot cable suspended from among high rafters.

"An excellent decision—"

"But I doubt if I could climb it."

"So you are unsure of your capabilities." Kuve smiled. "But try, Chester. Perhaps you can climb it."

CHESTER went to the rope, looked at it doubtfully. Kuve muttered into a wrist communicator. Chester grasped the rope, pulled himself up, wrapped his legs around the rope, wriggled higher.

"This is…the best I can…do," he puffed, his feet six feet above the floor. He slid back down. "I'm just not in trim—"

There was a sound like water gurgling down a drain. Chester turned quickly. An immense tan mountain lion paced toward him, yellow eyes alight, a growl rumbling from its throat. With a yell Chester leaped for the rope, swarmed halfway to the distant rafters, and clung, looking down. Kuve patted the sleek head of the animal; it yawned, nuzzling his leg affectionately.

"You see? You were capable of more than you imagined," Kuve called matter-of-factly.

"Where did that thing come from? That was a scoundrelly trick, Kuve. What if I hadn't been able to climb the rope after all'?"

"He's quite harmless. A pet, one of several we use in our various training programs. When you mentioned a tiger, I couldn't resist the opportunity to make an object lesson."

Chester slid down the rope slowly, eyes on the cat. Back on the floor, he edged behind Kuve, who slapped the animal's flank. The cat padded away.

"You see?" said Kuve. "If I called him back, you wouldn't panic now, because you know he's harmless. And if a really wild animal were released here, you'd know what to do—and that you were capable of doing it. You could watch the Bengal tiger you mentioned quite calmly—and take to the rope only if necessary."

"Maybe—but don't try me."

"Look at your hands, Chester."

Chester examined his palms. "Your little joke cost me some skin."

"Did you notice that—at the time?"

"All I was thinking about was that man-eater."

"The fear and pain reactions are useful to the unthinking organism. But you have a reasoning mind, Chester. You could dispense with the automatic-response syndromes."

"It's better to be a live coward—"

"But you might be a dead coward, when mastery of the fear could have saved you. Look down, Chester."

Chester glanced at the floor. As he watched the milky white surface cleared to transparency, all but a narrow ribbon, scarcely four inches wide, leading to apparently solid floor across the room. Chester stared in horror at a yawning abyss below his feet set with jagged black rocks. Kuve stood by unconcernedly, apparently suspended in mid-air.

"It's quite all right, Chester. Merely a floor of very low reflectivity."

Chester teetered on the narrow strip. "Get me out of here," he gasped.

"Can't you walk across to the far side?" Kuve inquired casually.

Chester took an uncertain step, edged a foot or two along the opaque ribbon. Perspiration popped out on his forehead. "I'm afraid of heights," he gasped. "Turn it off!"

"Close your eyes," Kuve said quietly. Chester crouched, eyes shut.

"Forget what you saw," Kuve ordered. "Concentrate on sensing the floor through your feet. Accept its solidity."

Chester swallowed, then opened his eyes slowly. He looked at

Kuve. "I guess it will hold," he said shakily.

Kuve's stern expression softened into a faint smile. "Chester," he said, "I think you're going to be a good pupil."

WHEN weather permits," said Kuve, "you'll do your workouts here on the terrace in the open air."

Chester surveyed the hundred foot square area, floored with dark wood and surrounded by a five-foot wall over which leaned flowering shrubs. A cluster of tall poplars shaded a portion of the floor from the high morning sun. Racked against the low wall was an array of weights.

"Perhaps I should explain that I have no aspirations to the Mr. Universe title," he said. "I think perhaps a couple of Indian clubs would be more than adequate for me."

"Chester," said Kuve, motioning his pupil to a padded bench. "We have taken the first steps toward dispelling your certainty that pain is unendurable and that fear is both useful and overmastering. Now let us consider the role of boredom as a hindrance to the control of the intellect over the body. What is boredom, Chester?"

"Well, boredom sets in when you have nothing to occupy your mind."

"Or when instinct says, 'The activity at hand is not vital to my survival'. It is a more potent factor in influencing human behavior than either fear or pain." He handed Chester a small dumbbell. "Do you find that heavy?"

Chester weighed the five-pound weight in his hand. "No, not really."

"Have another." Chester hefted a dumbbell in each hand. "Now," said Kuve, "please stand and place the two weights at shoulder height. Then press them alternately to arm's length."

Chester raised the weights, pushed up first one, then the other. Kuve watched. Chester worked steadily, his face growing red.

"You're slowing down. Are you getting tired?"

"Of course I'm getting tired! How long does this go on?"

"A little longer. All the way up, please."

Chester thrust the weights up, puffing harder now. His pace grew slower.

"You're tiring, Chester," Kuve said, seating himself comfortably

in a canvas chair. "You'd like to stop now. But ask yourself... why?"

"Because...I'm getting...exhausted," gasped Chester.

"Exhaustion could result in your failure to press the weight up, but it fails to explain the mere desire to stop while strength remains."

"It hurts!" Chester grated through clenched teeth. "My arms and shoulders are on fire!"

"No," said Kuve, "you're bored. Your body is saying, in effect: this is accomplishing nothing; it is uninteresting; it is not worth doing. Therefore you feel the impulse to stop. The instinct of laziness is nature's automism for conserving energy vital to the hunt or to flight or combat or mating. But we can disregard those motives. From now on I'll expect you to recognize boredom as a destructive force—and reject its control of your motivations."

IT was late afternoon. Chester let his hand fall from the handgrip of the machine that he had been squeezing, twisting, pulling and pushing at Kuve's direction.

"I thought you were exaggerating when you said you were going to test a hundred and seventy two different muscles, but I believe you now. Everyone of them is aching."

"They'll ache even more tomorrow," Kuve said cheerfully. "But no matter. They'll soon accustom themselves to the idea that you intend to call on them henceforward. You'll find them very cooperative; they'll adapt quickly to daily exertion."

"I'll never make it. The thought of doing this again tomorrow appalls me."

"Put it out of your mind. At the proper time you'll go through the schedule I've laid out for you. When it's over forget it until it's time to work again."

"I haven't got the will power," Chester said. "I know myself. I've tried diets and daily dozens before, to say nothing of night classes in which I was going to learn flawless French or ancient history. I never lasted."

"You'll last this time. The secret of winning arguments with yourself is to refuse to argue. While you're marshaling your excuses for skipping a day, start down the hall toward the training room. By the time you've finished perfecting your argument you'll be well into your routine."

"You'll have to give me an easier schedule—and you'll have to keep prodding me—"

"Your schedule will be tailored to your demonstrated abilities. That was the reason for the tests. My function ends with showing you the way. The rest you must do for yourself. There is nothing you can learn here more important than that. Now let's move along to the dining room. I have a briefing on mnemonics for you, after which I'll start you on pattern theory. Then—"

"When do I sleep?"

"All in good time."

"It's curious," Chester said, finishing off a bowl of tasty clear soup, "but I forgot all about lunch. I have a wonderful appetite now, though. What's next on the menu?"

"Nothing," said Kuve. "And please don't interrupt the lecture. As I was saying, the association of symbol with specific must relate to your personal experience."

"What do you mean, nothing? I'm a hungry man. I've worked like a draft horse all day!"

"You're overweight, Chester. The soup was carefully compounded to supply the needed nutrients to maintain your energy level. In time, as you adapt to the higher energy demands of the program, you'll evolve a higher metabolic rate. Your ration will be increased accordingly. This is the key to development of the positive attitude pattern necessary to maintain the activity level of a fully functioning organism."

"But I'll starve."

"You've been eating from boredom, Chester. When your attention is occupied elsewhere, you forget food. Only habit is demanding that you overeat. You'll have to master habit."

"Back to that again. This whole day has consisted of your telling me to mortify the flesh, mind over matter—"

"The objective is not to eliminate the impulses of the flesh, but to control and use them. The mind is the supreme instrument in nature; it must establish its supremacy. I asked you earlier what pain was. What is pleasure?"

"Right now, it's eating! I—"

"An excellent example: the satisfaction of a natural impulse."

"It's more than an impulse. It's a necessity!"

"Overeating injures the body. So it is with all pleasure impulses. When over-satisfied, they become destructive."

"What am I supposed to do, suppress my normal instinct and act like a machine?"

"Not at all; the instincts can be very useful. Anger, for example. Here nature has provided a behavioral mechanism to deal with those situations in which aggression seems indicated. It's a very strong emotion; it can override other impulses, such as fear. When you are angry, you are stronger, less sensitive to pain, and immune to panic. You desire only to close with your enemy and kill. Even the lower animals have learned that. Before combat males of many species customarily set about working themselves up into a rage—"

"I've always read that if you can get your opponent mad, you can outfight him."

"An exaggeration, but it has an element of truth. An angry man can become careless. You'll learn to control the anger impulse, and evoke it at will without losing control.

"Now we must move on to the next training situation. There's a great deal of ground still to be covered today."

"I need a few hours to think over all this before I go to bed," Chester protested. "Besides which, I'm exhausted."

"The laziness instinct again," said Kuve. "Come along, Chester."

THE sun was setting. Chester and Kuve stood at the base of a fifty-foot tower beside a pool. A steep flight of steps led to a lonely platform at the top.

"Climb to the top of the tower," Kuve said. He handed Chester a small locket. "This is a communicator which will enable me to talk to you at a distance. Tomorrow a similar device will be surgically implanted. Now, up you go."

"I don't like heights."

"Remember your lessons, Chester. Climb slowly and steadily."

"What if I lose my balance?"

"You won't."

"What's the point in risking my neck up there?"

"Chester, intellectually you are aware that you should cooperate with me. Ignore the distractions of instinct and follow your mind."

"I'll freeze on the ladder. You'll end by having to climb up and get me."

"Chester, remembered moments of high achievement satisfy; remembered excesses disgust. Next week will you look back with pleasure on having refused the tower?"

Chester shook his head.

"But if you climb it now, later the recollection will give you great pride. You have the power to mold your memories—but only before they become memories. This is your opportunity to endow yourself with a recollection worth having."

Chester put a foot on the first step.

"I'll start, but I won't guarantee I'll go all the way."

"One step at a time, Chester. Don't look down."

Chester mounted the stairs cautiously, gripping the slender handrail. "This thing wobbles," he called back from ten feet up.

"It will hold. Just keep going."

Chester moved higher. The steps were of wood, eight inches wide and four feet long. The handrail was aluminum, bolted to uprights every fourth step. Chester concentrated his attention on the wood and metal. A buzz sounded from the locket at his throat. "You're doing very well. Halfway up now..." Beyond the steps before his face, the sunset sky flared purple and orange. Chester paused, breathing hard.

"A few more steps, Chester," said the tiny voice in the communicator. He went on. The top of the tower was before him now. Clinging to the rail, he made his way up the last few steps to the platform. A cool wind blew across his shaved head. Far away a twinkle of light showed against the dark forest on the skyline. Red light reflected from a river winding down the valley. The low white building of the Center glowed peach-colored in the fading light. Chester looked down at the pool below...

He froze, clinging to the rail.

"Lie down!" Kuve's voice snapped. Chester lowered himself rigidly.

"Move to the steps...feet first. Lower your legs, then start down!"

Chester felt the first step under his foot, edged down, one step at a time...

"Halfway down," Kuve's voice said. Chester was moving faster now. At ten feet from the bottom, Kuve halted him.

"Look at the water. Can you jump in from there?"

"Certainly."

"Go back up a step. Can you jump from there?"

Chester balked three steps higher. "This is high enough."

"Jump." Chester held his nose and sprang into the water. He surfaced, climbed out of the pool.

"Do it again."

After three jumps Chester went a step higher. Half an hour later, in bright moonlight, he made the jump from twenty feet.

"That's enough for this session," said Kuve. "In a week you'll jump from the top—where you couldn't stand upright today. Now, back inside. While you're getting into some dry garments, I want to talk to you about the nature of reality."

"It seems like I've been here for a month," Chester said, as Kuve dimmed the lights on the pattern-response panel, "and I'm still on my first day. What are you doing, training me to go without sleep entirely?"

"Come along. I'll show you to your bed now."

In a narrow room with a high window, Chester looked critically at a padded bench three feet wide.

"I'm supposed to sleep on that?"

"There is no mattress like weariness," Kuve said.

Chester kicked off his sandals and lay down with a sigh. "I guess you're right at that, Kuve. I'm going to sleep for a week."

"Four hours," said Kuve. "In addition, you'll have a two-hour nap at noon."

There was a buzz from the communicator still on Chester's neck. "Not-is is not is-not," said a soft feminine voice.

"What's this gibberish?"

"You'll interpret this material at a subconscious level while you sleep. These are the basic axioms of rationality. Eventually they'll become integrated into your logic matrix."

"Is this going on all night?"

"All night. But you'll find it doesn't interfere with sleep."

"I won't sleep a wink."

"If not tonight, then tomorrow."

"That's a cheering thought." Chester yawned, closed his eyes. He thought, "Only three hundred and sixty four days to go."

*　　*　　*

THE first grey of dawn had not yet lit the sky when Chester tottered into the softly lit gymnasium. Kuve, fresh and immaculate in white, looked up from a small table set up in the middle of the room.

"Good morning, Chester. You slept well?"

"Like a four-day corpse. And I feel equally lively now."

"Still, you're out of bed at the appointed time, dressed for work. And since you're here, you might just take a look at this."

Chester hobbled over to the table. Under a surface of beaded glass, pin points of red, green, and amber light winked off and on in an unpredictable sequence.

"I want you to analyze the pattern here. When you're ready, put your finger on the indicator light here at the edge which matches the color of the light which you think will blink on next."

Chester studied the light board. A red light blinked, then a green, another red, another, an amber, a green... He touched the red light. The board blanked off.

Illustrator SCHELLING

"That means you chose wrongly. Try again with a new pattern." Chester followed the lights. Green, red, amber, red, amber, green, green, red, green, amber...

He touched the amber light. The board blanked.

"Never accept the first level of complexity as a solution to a problem, Chester. Look beneath the surface; find the subtler patterns. Try again."

The lights blinked in steady sequence. On the fifth try, the entire board lit up. Chester looked pleased.

"Good," said Kuve. "When you have three correct solutions in sequence, we'll move on to patterns of a higher complexity."

"I had to think five lights ahead on the last one, Kuve. The patterns seem to change while I'm watching them."

"Yes, there's a simple developmental progression involved in this set."

"You're asking too much. I have more the poetic type mind.

I'm no electronic calculator."

"You'll think you are, before the year is out. This training, in its advanced phases, by applying pressures of a type never encountered in ordinary experience, will develop cortical areas hitherto unused."

"I don't think I'm going to enjoy that last part," said Chester dubiously. "What does it mean?"

Kuve pointed to the far wall. "Look over there. Keep your eyes rigidly before you." He held up a hand at the edge of Chester's field of vision, moving it slowly. "Tell me when you can clearly discern my hand."

"I see it now." Chester was looking straight ahead; Kuve's hand was three feet from Chester's forehead, well off to one side.

"How many fingers am I holding up?"

"I don't know; I can just barely tell there's a hand there."

Kuve waggled a finger. "Did you notice that movement?"

"Certainly."

Kuve moved a second finger, stilling the first, then a third finger, and a fourth.

"You saw the movement each time," he summed up, "which indicates that all four fingers are within your field of view." He extended two fingers. "Now how many fingers am I holding up?"

"I still can't tell."

"You can see the fingers, Chester, you've proven that. And yet you are, quite literally, unable to count these fingers that you see. The message sent to your brain through the portion of the optical mechanism concerned with peripheral vision is channeled to an undeveloped sector of your mind, a part of the great mass of normally unused cells in the cortex. The intelligence of this portion of your intellect is about at a par with that of the faithful dog which recognizes a group of children but is unable to formulate any conception of their number." He lowered his hand. "It is that portion of the brain which we shall train. Now, try this next pattern…"

CHAPTER NINE

CHESTER leaned against the rail at the top of the eighty-foot tower, feeling the hot sun on his shoulders, and watched as Kuve adjusted the ropes stretched across the pool below.

"This gives you a four-foot target," Kuve's voice said from the rice-grain-sized instrument set in the bone behind Chester's left ear. "Remember your vasco-muscular tension patterns. Wait for the signal."

A beep sounded in Chester's ear—and he was in the air, wind shrieking past his ears, his chin to his chest, arms at his sides with hands flat, feet pointed...

He struck, twisted, shot above the surface, swam to the edge, and pulled himself up with a single smooth motion.

"You've come along well these first two weeks," Kuve said, motioning Chester to the table where a small steak waited. "You've explored the parameters of your native abilities, you've established an awareness of the values we're dealing with, and overcome the worst of the metabolic inertia. Your musculature is balanced now and in good tone, though you still have a long way to go in developing full bulk and power. Now you're ready to attack the subtler disciplines of balance, timing, precision, endurance, and pace—"

"You talk as though I had none of those. What about the high dives? That four-foot target isn't very big from eighty feet up."

"That exercise was designed to develop your self-confidence. The target merely defines the spot to which you naturally fall. Could you do as well if it were moved over ten feet?"

"No, I suppose not."

"The only real skills involved are the simple reflex-control routines you've practiced during your work-outs. Now you'll begin the real substance of your studies. We'll begin with simple games like fencing, riding, rope work, juggling, dancing, and sleight of hand, and proceed by degrees into the more abstract phases."

"What are you training me for, a side-show?"

KUVE ignored the interruption. "Your academic studies will be concentrated on hypnotism, self-hypnosis, selective concentration, advanced mnemonics, and eidetics, from which we will proceed to autonomies, self-regeneration, cellular psychology, and—

"Let's go back to fencing. At least I know what that is."

"After you've dined we'll begin. In the meantime, tell me what the word 'now' means."

Chester cut a bite of steak. "It means 'this moment'."

"The moment in which you put that bite into your mouth?"

"No," said Chester, chewing. " 'Now' changes. It moves along with time. It's the *present* moment."

"How long does 'now' endure?"

"Well—forever, I suppose."

"Then 'now' includes all of time?"

"No, it's the other way around. Every moment is 'now' for a while, and then it isn't."

"For a while? How long?"

"Not very long; an instant."

"Is 'now' a part of the past?"

"No, certainly not."

"The future?"

"No, the future, by definition, hasn't happened yet. The past is already finished. 'Now' falls between them."

"How would you define a plane, Chester?"

"The intersection of two solids."

"And a line?"

"The intersection of two planes."

"A point?"

"The intersection of two lines."

"The position of intersection, to be more precise," said Kuve, " 'Line' and 'point' are terms referring to positions, not things. If a sheet of paper is cut in two, every molecule of the paper is contained in one or other of the halves. If the cut edges are placed together, every particle is still to be found in one or other of the parts; none are excluded. And the line we see dividing them is only a position, not a material object."

"Yes, that's obvious."

"Past time may be considered as one of the parts of the paper, future time as the other. Between them is…nothing."

"Still, I'm sitting here eating my lunch. I exist at some time or other."

"I want you to grasp the fact that your ability to conceptualize falls short of the ability of the universe to proliferate complexities. Human understanding can never be more than an approximation. Avoid dealing in absolutes. And never edit reality for the sake of simplicity. The results are fatal to logical thinking."

MINA appeared on the terrace, wearing a close-fitting pink coverall and carrying foils and facemasks. She greeted Kuve and Chester, selected a mask, and picked up a foil that whistled as she tested its temper with slashing cuts at the air. Chester finished his steak, pulled on a black coverall of tough resilient material, took the foil that Mina handed him.

"This is where I begin, I guess?" he said, with a quizzical look at the other two.

Kuve nodded. "Go ahead."

Mina took up her position, gripped her slender blade, arm and wrist straight, feet at right angles, left hand on hip. She tapped Chester's blade, then with a sudden flick sent it flying into the pool.

"Oh, I'm sorry, Chester. You weren't ready." Chester retrieved the foil, assumed a stance in imitation of Mina's. They crossed blades—and Chester *oofed* as Mina's point prodded his chest. Mina laughed merrily.

On the third try Mina locked Chester's blade with hers, then, with a twist, plucked it from his hand. "Chester," she laughed, "you couldn't be trying…" She laid her weapon aside and strolled off. Chester turned to Kuve, face red. Kuve stepped forward, motioned Chester into position.

"We'll have half an hour each morning and another after lunch," he said.

AFTER nine months, Case and Genie probably think I'm dead," said Chester, circling Kuve warily, bare feet shuffling on the padded mat, "I don't understand why I can't at least write them a letter."

"They were told you were taking part in an experiment," said Kuve. He stepped in, his right hand flashing past Chester's ribs and up to grasp the wrist forced back by his left hand, Chester twisted, caught Kuve's left hand, forced the wrist joint down, Kuve leaned to relieve the pressure, shifting his hold to Chester's neck, then threw his hip against Chester's side, and heaved. In mid-air Chester brought a leg up, clipped Kuve's jaw with his knee, twisted to land on all fours as Kuve's grip slipped free, Kuve shook his head, looking surprised. "Was that an accident, or was—"

Chester hit him low, dodged left to avoid a headlock, clamped an arm over Kuve's head, and reached for an ankle—

And was up-ended and slammed on the mat. He sat up, rubbing his neck. Kuve nodded approvingly. "You're coming along, Chester. If you hadn't been careless with your footwork just now, you might have pinned me."

"Maybe next time," Chester said grimly.

"I seem to note a certain suppressed hostility in your tone." Kuve said, eyeing Chester with amusement.

"Suppressed, hell. You've worked on me like a rented tractor for nine months, strained my brains while I ate and slept, kept me locked in here—"

"You can leave at any time," Kuve said blandly. "You're a volunteer."

"It's a little late for that. Only three months to go. Why don't you tell me how I'm doing—?"

"Only now, I commented on your progress."

"Sure. And I can look at my forearm and see that it's bigger. But that doesn't tell me whether I've covered all the ground I was supposed to. And this idea of allowing no mirrors, so I can't so much as admire my muscles—"

"Which reminds me: your last physiometric check indicates a need for more emphasis on the complex-F group. I think I'll add two ounces to your standard set and increase the repetitions five percent across the board."

"You said something about a new compound-reaction test situation I was going to see soon. What about it?"

"That's where we're going now. It's a very interesting problem group—but I warn you, it can be painful."

"In that respect it fits in nicely with the overall program." Chester followed Kuve across the terrace, through an arch, along a corridor, and out into an open court. Kuve pointed to a gate in the wall beyond which a patch of woods pressed close.

"Just go through the gate, Chester, and have a stroll in the forest. You'll find paths; whether you use them is left entirely to your own discretion. This is a tongue of the forest that runs up into the hills. I don't think you'll be in danger of straying too far, for reasons which will become apparent once you're in the forest— but nevertheless I'll caution you to stay close. As soon as you've made what you consider to be a significant observation, return."

Chester glanced toward the shadowed depths of the wood. "It will be an agreeable change: my first trip outside the prison grounds."

"Be back by dark. If you get into trouble, remember I'll be monitoring your communicator personally."

"Fine. And when in doubt, I'll just remember: Is not is not not is," said Chester as he turned down the path.

CHESTER was moving along the path at a steady pace, his eyes roving over his surroundings in a wide-scope comparison pattern. He had practiced the exercise during hundreds of five-minute sessions on the trainer. But it was different, using it now in a natural setting.

A movement caught his eye; in instant response Chester threw himself backward, feet high. A rope whipped across his calves; then the noose was dangling high in the air. Chester came to his feet carefully, searching for a back-up trap, saw none. He studied the tree to which the rope was attached, then moved off the trail to a nearby oak, scaled it quickly, moved out on a long branch, then dropped into the trapped tree. He untied the rope, a tough half-inch synthetic, wrapped it around his waist, then slid back to the ground.

If Kuve had trapped the trail, it would be a good idea to leave it. Chester moved into the underbrush, working his way toward a line of larger trees. In their shade the underbrush would be less dense.

He froze at a sharp pain in the back of a hand. Carefully he disengaged himself from a coil of fine-gauge barbed wire. Selecting a strand between barbs, he bent it backward and forward rapidly until it parted. He repeated the process with other strands, then went to hands and knees and eased under the barrier. It would be wise now to be on the alert for subtler obstacles. The nuisances he had encountered so far had apparently been intended only to relax his defenses.

Half an hour later Chester stood on the brink of a sheer bluff. Fifty feet below a stream glinted in a shaft of sun that fell between great trees. Upstream, a still pool showed black among smooth boulders. Chester noted the placement of the pool with a smile. It was identical with the four-foot target area into which he had been diving daily—an open invitation.

He lay flat and examined the cliff face. The broken rock surface offered an abundance of hand—and footholds. Perhaps too many...

It was forty feet to the spreading branches of a large elm growing on the opposite side of the stream. The rope was long enough. Chester uncoiled it from his waist, found a five-pound stone fragment with a pinched center, and tied it securely to the end of the supple line. He stood, whirled the stone around his head four times and let it fly. It arced across the branch, dropped and hung swinging. Gently, Chester pulled as the rock swung away, relaxed as it returned, pulled again... The oscillation built up. As the weight reached the end of its swing Chester pulled sharply. The stone swung up and over, once, twice, three times around the branch. He tugged; all secure. Quickly he knotted his end of the rope about a length of fallen branch, then manhandled a two-hundred pound boulder over it. He tested the attachment briefly, then crossed on the rope hand over hand to the elm. He left the rope in place, descended to the ground, and went to the edge of the quiet pool. Lifting a hundred-pound rock, he tossed it into the center of the black water. Instantly a large net, apparently spring-loaded snapped into view, dripping water, to close over the stone. Chester smiled, raised his eyes to study the base of the cliff. Snarls of fine barbed wire guarded the lower six feet of the vertical rock face. It would have been an easy climb down, he reflected—but a long way back up.

The communicator behind his ear beeped. "Well, Chester, I see you've sprung the net at the pool. Don't feel too badly; you did very well. I'll be along to release you in a few minutes..."

Chester smiled again and turned back into the forest.

CHESTER studied the sun, briefly reviewed the route he had followed in four hours of detecting and avoiding Kuve's traps. Sunset was just over an hour away, he judged, and he was three miles northwest by north from the Center. He had ignored Kuve's excited calls from the pool...and at regular intervals thereafter. There had been no calls now for two hours His instructions had been to note something significant. So far he had seen nothing more noteworthy than smoke columns on the distant ridges. It was time, however, to head back. With luck he could make it by dark. It had been a pleasure to escape Kuve's discipline for a few hours, but he had no desire to spend an autumn night in the woods.

After ten minutes' rapid progress down-slope, he emerged at the rim of a near-vertical slope of loose shale. He scanned the littered surface for a protruding ridge that would offer secure footing, but without success. Fifty feet to the right the drop-off cut back sharply into the slanted meadow above, to join a ravine angling up into the high hills.

Chester explored in the opposite direction, found his progress halted by the increasing steepness of the ground. There was no choice but to retrace his route back up-slope, skirt the upper end of the ravine, and descend along the grassy trough visible beyond the cut.

He would, he realized, be rather late in returning to the Center. Still he should be well into the level area near the buildings before complete darkness fell. He moved obliquely up across the clearing and into the shadow of the timber.

CHESTER halted, sniffing the air. The odor of wood smoke was sharp among the milder scents of pine and juniper and sun-warmed rock. He had been climbing steadily for twenty minutes, and was ready now to angle to the left to clear the upper end of the ravine. With each step the odor of smoke grew more noticeable.

Now a soft grey wisp coiled from the shaded trunks ahead and above. Chester crouched low and moved on quickly. If there was a forest fire ahead, it would be necessary to get past it at once—before he was cut off from his route to the valley. He moved silently through sparse underbrush, saw through a gap in the trees a pale flicker of orange on the heights a hundred yards above. It would be close; he broke into a run.

The trees thinned. The tumbled rocks that marked the head of the gorge showed pale against the dark background of pines. A billow of smoke rolled toward him, carried by a downdraft flowing into the canyon. Chester lay flat, drew half a dozen deep breaths, then jumped up and scrambled over the broken rock. Ahead, fire twinkled among massive boles, flickered in whipping underbrush, leaped high in the crown of a pine. He could hear the roar of wind-driven flames now. A sudden gust blew a wall of smoke toward him. He thought rapidly of taking refuge in the gully—but the draft would bring the smoke there in suffocating waves. It was necessary to retreat. He made his way, coughing, back to the comparative safety of the wooded slope, then paused to study the situation. It might be possible, he calculated, to round the knoll at the head of the rampart that edged his route on the right, then descend safely to emerge into the valley a mile north of the Center. There was no hope now of making it before dark. Chester worked his way higher, still scenting smoke strongly. Another hundred yards, he estimated.

A stone dislodged from above rattled down, bounded off into dense brush. Chester paused, scanning the tangled foliage. A leaf trembled stiffly; almost, Chester thought, as though it were being restrained from moving freely in the gusty breeze. He moved back a cautious step.

Twenty feet up-slope a heavily built man moved into view. He was brown-bearded, dressed in leather pants and a loose jacket of undyed wool. His left fist gripped a massive recurved bow. His right hand was at his chin, two fingers hooked around a taut bowstring. The arrow nocked in the string carried a four-inch head of polished steel, and it was aimed at Chester's navel.

"I know yew Downlan'e's move like Snake Demon when Kezfavver tri'tt him into fire pit, but Blew-tewf leap faster van fought," the bearded man drawled in barely intelligible English. "What dew yew wan' here in Wil' Places? Was yewr life too tame down below?"

Chester frowned, running the sounds of the stranger's barbaric speech through his mind, noting sound substitutions and intonations; the pattern of the dialect was simple enough.

"If yew don' min', I'd ravver Bew-tewth poin'ed over vere somewhere," Chester replied in a passable imitation of the dialect, motioning toward the deep woods, with his eyes on the arrowhead.

"No need yo mock the cant," the man said in clear English. "I was ten when I left my Tricennium. Now, what do you want?"

"I was rather hoping to discover a route back to the valley, but now I'd settle for merely remaining un-skewered and un-broiled. Do you mind if we move on? The fire is blowing this way, you know."

"Don' worry about fire," the bearded man reverted to dialect. "I set it myse'f to run game. It will bu'n out again escarpmen' above. Now mewve off to your right an' up pas' me. Blew-tewf will be matchin' every mewve."

"That's not the direction I'm headed," Chester protested.

"Yew'd better dew as I've tol' yew. As yew said, fire is gettin' hot, an' I have tew mewve on." The arrow was still aimed unwaveringly at Chester's stomach. The bow creaked as the bearded man set the arrowhead on the handgrip. "Make up yewr min'."

CHESTER moved quickly in the direction indicated. "Relax, I don't intend to make a break for it. But what in the world do you want with me?"

"Le'ss say I wan' news of Dwonla's."

"Who are you?" Chester called back, pulling himself up the steep route, awkwardly now in the failing light. "What are you doing up here in the hills? If you want news, come down to the Center."

"My na's Bandon, an' I would'n be welcome in yewr dainty Center. Don' tu'n aroun', jus' keep mewvin' along."

"I'm due back at sundown. When I don't show up, they'll come after me."

"If yew're finkin' of little trinket tu'tt away back of yewr ear, forget it. Yew're out of ra'ge."

"You're planning on holding me here for ransom?"

"What treasu'es could Downlan'e's offer tew equal free life of Wil' Places?" Bandon laughed.

"You'll let me go in the morning?"

"Not in morning or for many morning vereafter. Forget tame valleys, Downlan'e. Yew'll be here until yew die."

* * *

Twilight was fading from the peaks as Chester and Bandon clambered over a last barrier of fallen rock to level ground. Against a backdrop of tall pines a dozen tall skin tents dotted the high meadow. In their middle stood a log shack, a curl of smoke drifting up from its massive chimney.

"Vis is it, Downlan'e," Bandon said, "Vere's fewd here, an' a fire again night chill, an' strong ale, an' ta'es of forest, and fellowship of hunte's: all a man need between dus' an' dawn."

"Very poetic," said Chester. "But you left out a few items that I've grown accustomed to, like literature, and celery, and dentists, and clean socks. Why do I have to join your club? After all I—"

"Yew came here uninvited," Bandon said flatly. He lowered and unstrung his bow. "Don' be so fewlish as tew try tew leave. Vere are sentries pos'ed tew gua'd our approaches."

"I know; I saw them."

"In vis light? Our bes' woodsmen?"

"Just joking," said Chester.

"Maybe yew did, at vat. Yew Downland'e's are keen-eyed as Kez-fahver himse'f. Tell me, where did yew lea'n can'?"

"Your dialect? Oh, I…ah…studied it. A hobby of mine."

"Ven i's not trew what some say, vat yew can lea'n our speech in wi'k of an eve?"

"A baseless rumor."

"I fought so. Come along now, an' we'll see what brovvers make of yew."

CHESTER estimated the crowd of unshaven, hide-clad hill dwellers who surrounded him at fifty individuals, all male. None of them, he reflected, of the kind who would arouse a desire for further acquaintance.

"Vis Downlan'e's a gues'," Bandon was saying to the assembled brethren. "We'll treat him as one of us—unless he tries tew go somewhere. Now, I'm takin' him in palace wiv me—jus' until he can get a place of his own fix' up. I wa'n yew now: if he come tew ha'm, I'll hol' lot of yew personally responsible."

A short, incredibly broad man in fur coveralls black with dirt swaggered forward. "We hea'd a lot about how tough vese Downlan'e's are," he growled. "Vis one don' look so tough."

"Maybe he's sma't—va's better yet," Bandon snapped. "Leave him alone, Grizz. Va's an order."

Grizz looked around at his fellows. "Funny, none of us is good enough tew get tew sleep in palace. But vis spy here wa's in an' right away he's treated like Kezfahver when he 'oven' tew fetch king-hat back from sea-bottom."

"Never min' vat. Now yew boys get some cam' fi'es goi' an' roas' up some venison an' break open a few ke's of ale. We're goin' tew have a real celebration here tew show new man what kin' of wil' free life we lead…"

A few shouts rang out, a faint yippee sounded from the rear. Grizz stared at Bandon. "We got no venison. Plenty squirrel, if yew don' min' eatin' ra's. Only ale we got is vat half-keg of spoil' brew Tusgu cook' up out of bi'ch ba'k."

"Dew bes' yew can," Bandon snapped. "Look lively about it. I wan' tew see fi's lookin' cheerful aroun' here." He turned to Chester. "Come along tew palace; we'll have a chance tew get acquain'ed before feas'."

Chester followed Bandon to the shed, a rickety structure of logs, twenty feet by thirty. Inside, a crude oil lamp cast a flickering yellow light on low rafters hung with pots in thong nets, baskets, the stiff skins of small animals, leather garments stiff with dirt. Bandon gestured toward a heap of dry sticks and limp straw and a shred of a woven blanket. "Yew can take bed tonight," he said; "I'll sleep on floor. Tomorrow we'll get yew ten' of yewr own sta'ted."

"I wouldn't think of it," Chester said hastily. "You have the bed. The floor looks very comfortable, I'm sure. As for the tent— don't you think it might be less trouble all around if I just departed quietly in the morning?"

BANDON was shaking his head emphatically. "I'ss a rewl of Brovverhood: No stra'ge's ever leave here wif ta'es tew tell."

"Tales of what?" Chester inquired interestedly.

"Of how we live here; wil' free life. Vey fink we're sta'vi' up here in hi's, cut og from all sof' life down below. But we're not; we hun', an' eat venison, an' dring stout ale, an' sit aroun' our roarin' cam'fi'es spinnin' ta'es—"

"I don't think that news will qualify as a military secret," Chester said. "Letting me go will pose no threat to your wild, free life."

"I know better," Bandon said darkly, pulling off his jacket to reveal a broad white chest adorned with a crop of black hair. He pulled a stool before the stone fireplace, started piling sticks on the hearth. "We have all we need here; if vey knew it, vey'd be up here in no time, tryin' tew take it away from us. Not vat vey could. We know whoo's like ba's of our ha's. We'd pick 'em off from ambush, whittle 'em down until what was lef' of 'em ran for veil' little Tricennia an' veir rewl boo's...but veil' rew's won' he'p 'em here."

"I see. And so, for humanitarian reasons, you're keeping me here to save the lives of the Downlanders."

Bandon nodded. "An' besi'es, I wan' tew ta'k tew yew."

"What about?"

"About all ki's of fi's, like whew sen' yew here, an' what kin' of pla's yew've got for invadin' Wil' Places, an'...yew know. Yew might as well tell me everyfing. I caught yew fair an' square, red-han'ed."

"If you hadn't jumped out at me, I'd have been on my way home now, without ever having known you were here. What are you doing up here? I never heard of anyone living in the hills, in tents."

"Never he a' d of us? Yew expec' me tew believe vat?" Bandon struck a match, set fire to the kindling, piled more wood on it, hung a pot of water on a hook. He stood and looked at Chester sternly. "Yew fing we don' know how yew feel about us up here, livin' our wil', free—"

"All right, Bandon, tell me: how do we feel about you and your wild, free life?"

Bandon went to a heavy chest in the corner, used a key on a leather thong tied to his belt to unlock a massive padlock, raised the lid, and took out two brown bottles. He locked the chest, handed Chester a bottle, and seated himself, waving Chester to a stool.

HOW do yew feel? Well, firs', yew're afraid." He drew on his bottle, eying Chester around it. He lowered the bottle and belched. "Yew're afraid because as long as we're livin' here, way we please, followin' no ma's rew's, vere is a ching in yewr armor."

"What armor?" Chester tried the beer. It was good Tricennium brew.

"If people knew vey did'n' hav tew knuckle under, did'n' have tew live by rew's made by ovver men, vey'd all chewse our way of life. Ven whe'd yewr precious Tricennia be? Hey?" Bandon drank, one belligerent eye on Chester. "But we don' wan' 'em. Nope. Plenty of rewm here in hi's now; plenty of hun'in', an' rewm tew get out an' get away from city here. Havin' a palace tew live in is fine, shewre; but bein' able tew get away from it, clear away, where all yew can see is trees an' sky, va's livin'."

"You said you lived in a Tricennium until you were ten. Why did you leave?"

"Why dew yew fing? Because wil', free—"

"At the age of ten, what could you have known about the wild, free?"

"Well, of cou'se, my family came tew. Vey brought me. But don' get wrong idea. Vey were glad tew come. Could'n' wait tew get away from vat crowd of hypocri's, meddlin' in a ma's personal business."

"What Tricennium was that?"

"Regional Knowledge," Bandon said shortly.

"Is that 'Original Knowledge', by any chance?"

"What I said."

"That's my Tricennium; adopted, of course. I never saw any meddling or hypocrisy there. In fact—"

"Yew jus' get yewrse'f classified as an Overage! Ven yew'll see!"

"How did you come to be an Overage?"

"Vey've got rew's: only so many people tew live in veir precious Tricennium. Yew have a chil' wifout permission—an' i's an Overage. Whole family's Overages. Not wanted. Have tew leave veir home, everyfing—"

HOLD on," Chester put in. "I know a little something about this. A family can have two children without special permission. If they want more, they either have to get a sponsor, or agree to move out to a colony...or start a colony of their own."

"A colony where? In ice-fie's? In dese's? Leave everyfing, all veir fri's, tew sta't ove?"

"They not only take all their possessions with them, but they are given everything needed to set up a self-supporting community. And if they have friends, they can go along—assuming none of these friends is in a position to sponsor a new child. And there's plenty of fine land available, and Climatic Control is making more available all the time."

"I know better. My—"

"How do you know better? Have you ever been back?"

"What, me go back, after treatmen' we got?"

"Who told you all this about the Tricennia being dictatorial, and envying you people your huts up here in the hills?"

"Hu's?" Bandon looked around the room. "Yew're not callin' my palace a hut?"

"I was referring to the tents of your associates," said Chester. "But who told you all this?"

"Everybody knows it."

"All your fellow exiles?"

"Shewre—an' stories vey could tell—"

"Yes, I know: around the roaring campfire while the venison's cooking. How many of them have ever been in a Tricennium?"

"Well, ve's me..."

"Go on."

"I guess I'm about only one. But vat ma'es no differe'ce."

Chester finished his beer and laid the bottle aside. "Bandon, I've been in a Tricennium—lately. I know what it's like. And I think you want me to tell you about it. Right?"

Bandon pulled his stool closer. "Shewre, I guess so...if yew wan' tew…"

THERE was a bellow outside the palace. Bandon stood up. "Va's vat Grizz again. Never knows when tew stop…" He went to the door. Chester stepped over a row of empty beer bottles, lifted down the pot of hot water, poured in some cool from a wooden bucket by the hearth, and sloshed water over his face and hands. Bandon came back from the door as Chester patted himself dry before the fire.

"Boys got a big fire goin', an' I fing vey roun'ed up some meat. We took care of ale ourse's. Le's join in merrymakin'."

"That fellow Grizz: how long has he been in the club?"

Bandon looked sharply at Chester. "Grizz is one of our bes' men. He's been wiv us about a year."

"Where did he come from?"

"Here in Wil' Places, we don' as' a man about his pas.' "

"When did that tradition start? When Grizz arrived?"

"What if it did? I's a good idea."

Outside Chester surveyed a scene of half-hearted festivity. The short squat figure of Grizz detached itself from the shadow of a nearby tent.

"Well, new ma's been makin' himse'f comfo'table," he said loudly. "Say, I been hearin' a lot about yew Downlan'e's. Vey say yew're fas'. I wonder if—"

Grizz made a sudden movement. Chester put up a hand and the bone handle of a hunting knife slapped his palm and fell to the ground.

"Here, Grizz, yew had no call tew frow a knife at our gues'!"

"Never mind, Bandon," Chester said quickly. "He was just kidding."

"Lucky yew happen tew stick out yewr han' jus' when yew did. It was comin' butt-firs', but it would have hu't. Grizz, leave him alone." Bandon slapped Chester on the back. "I've got tew circulate around a little, ta'k tew a few of boys. Yew get acquain'ed tew."

Chester strolled over to a group standing near the fire. The men eyed him dubiously.

"How do you men like the wild, free life?" Chester asked a lean, round-shouldered fellow.

Grizz thrust heavily after Chester.

"We don' take much tew spies," Grizz rumbled.

"I can see why," said Chester. "If the other half knew what you boys had all to yourselves up here, they'd leave home tomorrow."

"Ve's a way tew handle swam'-wa'ke's," Grizz stated.

"Va's right, Grizz," a voice called.

"Show him, Grizz," another suggested.

"Now Bandon says treat vis swam'-wa'ker like one of boys." Grizz looked around. Heads nodded reluctant agreement.

"But what if maybe vis guy jum' me? I fight back, right?"

"Shewre yew dew!"

"Yew ain' a man tew back down, Grizz!"

"I seen him dew it!"

Chester took a step to one side, stooped...

A MAN stumbled past the spot on which Chester had been standing, blundered into Grizz. Chester straightened, holding a twig. He tossed it into the fire. With a snarl, Grizz pushed aside the man who had jostled him, stepped to Chester, and threw a straight right—as Chester looked the other way, leaned aside, brushed at his neck. "These sparks are hot," he commented brightly, ignoring Grizz. He took a step away from Grizz, still not looking at him, stopped suddenly and half-turned...

Grizz stumbled over Chester's foot, struck hard on his face. Chester looked startled, bent to help Grizz up. "Excuse me, Grizz old boy..." He made ineffectual brushing motions at Grizz, who came to his feet shaking his head, then aimed a left at Chester's chin in the same instant that Chester bent, came up with a knife.

Grizz froze, eyes on the blade.

"Guess you dropped this," Chester said cheerfully, offering the weapon to Grizz.

Grizz hesitated, then snarled and turned away.

"Nobody could be vat clumsy—an' vat lucky," a voice said softly. Chester turned. Bandon stood eyeing him uncertainly. "But on ovver han', nobody could be vat fas' an' vat smewv—if vey were doin' it on purpose..."

"A grand bunch of fellows," said Chester. "I'm feeling right at home."

CHAPTER TEN

IT was three hours since the last sounds of revelry had died. Chester lay awake, watching the red glow of the fireplace—and listening. In the corner Bandon snored softly on his straw. Far away, a night bird called. Something creaked faintly near the door.

Chester rose, crossed the room, and called softly to Bandon. He grumbled, opened his eyes. "Hah?"

Chester put his face close to Bandon's. "Quiet," he breathed. "Grizz is at the door—"

Bandon started up. Chester held him by a hand on his arm. We'll let him in. It's better to take him here…alone."

"He would'n' dare tew push his way intew palace," Bandon whispered.

"Stay where you are." Chester moved silently to the door, stood beside it in the dark. There was a rasping sound, very faint. Then the door moved an inch, paused for a full minute, moved again. From his place behind the heavy doorpost, Chester saw Grizz's small eyes and bushy beard. Then the door moved wider; Grizz stepped inside, closed the door soundlessly. As he turned back toward the bed where Bandon lay, Chester rammed the stiff fingers of his left hand into Grizz's chest at the base of the sternum. Grizz jackknifed forward. Chester struck him backhanded under the ear with the side of his fist. Grizz fell with a heavy slam.

Bandon was on his feet now. "Don't give the alarm, Bandon," Chester hissed. "There's nobody to hear it but his henchmen."

Bandon said hoarsely, "What did he wan' here? How dew yew know—"

"Shhh. Grizz was after both of us, Bandon. Me, because I was a Downlander, who could talk about conditions down below, and you, because your usefulness was over. Grizz came here to organize your group. He didn't intend to take over just yet, but my arrival forced his hand a little."

"Yew're ravin'. My people are loyal."

131

"Grizz was listening today when I was telling you about life in the Tricennia. He was afraid you'd be influenced to the extent of interfering with his plans. So...here he is."

"What pla's? I make pla's here."

"You've been a figurehead for the past year, Bandon. You were useful to Grizz because you handled the routine administration and left him free to carryon his organizational work. Haven't you noticed he's spent most of his time off on field trips?"

"He hun'ed a lot, yes, but—"

"Did he bring back much game?"

"Well—not as much as I would have expe'ted. But he explain he was only interes'ed in big game."

"Right. About your size. Now we're leaving here—"

"Are yew mad? I've tor yew no one lea'es Wil' Places. I'm grateful tew yew for uncoverin' vis treason—if va's what it is—but I'm—"

"Wake up, Bandon. Do you think he could have gotten in here, past your guards, without their connivance?"

"But...perha's he tol' 'em it was yew he wan'ed..."

"That sounds weak even to you. Let's stop talking and start moving. We'll need—"

"No!" Bandon stood in the middle of the room, feet planted. "My whole life is here. Yew come, wiv yewr ta'k of peace an' leisure, an' overnight my wo'l' crumb'es. Now I'm tew run off intew da'k, a refugee from my own people, tew beg for he'p from same blackh'a'ted rewl-quote's whew drove out my family."

"I'm sorry, Bandon. I didn't arrange this. I merely discovered it."

"How? Yew've only been here for a few hou's!"

"I listened and observed."

"But wha's purpose of vis vas' conspiracy yew rave of? Tew take my people from me? Ven why wait? Why did'n' he dew it long ago?"

"There's a bigger game at stake than just ourselves, Bandon. Grizz is a field man for a bigger operation. Yours is one of the smallest units recruited, I imagine. The organization's plan is to make coordinated attacks on all the Tricennia between here and the sea, take them over, then launch a campaign to spread the wild free life over the whole continent like a plague."

"Are yew mad? Why, we're a selec' brovverhood, a chosen few. Dew yew fing we'd share our heritage wif a ravin' mob of Downlan'e's?"

"The idea was more to share the wealth—Downlander wealth, that is—with the surviving Downlanders as slaves. It's an idiotic plan, of course, but it could cause a lot of bloodshed and destruction."

"I was beginnin' tew like yew, Downlan'e'," Bandon said bitterly. "But now I see it: yew were sen' here tew sow dissension—"

"Suppose I prove what I'm telling you?"

"How?"

Chester looked around the room. "Conceal yourself over there." He pointed to a heap of uncured hides behind the crude table. "And listen."

Bandon reached up suddenly, took his bow from its peg on a rafter, nocked the steel-tipped arrow. "I'll hide," he said. "An' vis will be poin'ed straight at yew—so don' try any tri's."

"Be careful with that. I'd hate to be skewered by accident."

GRIZZ was beginning to stir. Bandon stepped from sight in the shadowy corner. Chester glanced quickly around the room, went to a cobwebbed box of odds and ends near the wall. He knelt and rummaged through it. There were tattered books, a broken clock, a rusted hatchet, nails, a coil of fine wire...

Five minutes later Grizz sat up, shook his head, got clumsily to his feet. He stood swaying, looked around the silent cabin...and saw Chester, almost at his feet, curled up in the bed of rags, snoring lightly.

Grizz half-crouched, pig eyes darting around the room. There was no one else in sight. He took a knife from his belt, dug a moccasined toe into Chester's side. Chester rolled on his back, opened his eyes, said "Huh?" and sat up.

"Whe's Bandon?" Grizz growled, the long blade tilted toward Chester's throat. Chester looked around. "Isn't he here?"

"He slugg' me an' got away. Now, ta'k, swam'-wa'ker. What

are yew tew love-bi's plannin'?"

Chester looked surprised. "He's the chief here; I'm just a captive Downlander, remember?"

"Yew're a liar on bofe cou's. Yew fing I'm dumb enough not tew see frew vis set-up? Tew of yew are in somefing tewgether. Where is he gone?"

"What do you want with him?"

"When I see him, I'll show yew—wif vis."

"How about me? If I help you, will you let me go?"

"Shewre. Now give."

"You promise? I'll have safe-conduct back to the valley if I tell you where Bandon is so you can kill him?"

"Yeah, I promise. Safe-conduct. Yew bet."

"How do I know you'll keep your promise?"

"Are yew sayin' I'm a liar?" Grizz leaned closer with the knife.

"Careful. I haven't told you yet."

"Yew've got my wo'd on it: yew go free. Where is he?"

"Well…" Chester came to his knees. "He's on his way back to my Tricennium. He discovered you were taking over here, so he—"

"Vang', sucker!" Grizz lunged with the knife. Chester threw himself back and Grizz, in mid-leap, snapped over on his back with a strangled yelp as the wire Chester had looped around his neck came taut. Chester came to his feet holding the knife Grizz had dropped. Grizz scrabbled backward, one hand up to ward off a thrust.

"Don' dew it, don' dew it!" he squalled.

"Keep your voice down. If anyone barges in, you'll be the first to go." Chester stood over Grizz.

"Now, what about that promise you made? You were going to give me safe conduct."

"Shewre, I'll see yew get away clean. Jus' leave it tew me."

"I could kill you, Grizz. But that wouldn't get me out of here." Chester looked worried. "Suppose I let you go. Will you give me an escort down to the valley?"

"Shewre I will, yew bet I will, fella. I jus' got excited, yew know. When yew said Bandon was on his way down, I los' my head."

"Well, I guess I'll give you another chance." Chester put the knife in his belt. "But, remember, you've given me your word."

"Va's right, my wo'd on it, fella."

"I've got to get a couple of…" Chester turned away. In a lithe movement Grizz rolled to hands and knees, ripped the wire from his throat and over his head, snatched up a rusted hatchet lying conveniently by, and sprang at Chester's back—

And slammed face first into the hard-packed earth floor, as his toe hooked the wire Chester had stretched across the room at ankle height.

CHESTER turned, looked down sadly at Grizz. "You did it again. I'm afraid I have no choice but to kill you."

"Look," whined Grizz, scraping dirt from his face. "I figu'ed yew wrong, see? I made a mistake—"

"You certainly did," Chester said coldly. He moved closer, reached out, and set the point of the blade under Grizz's chin.

"Don' hu't me," Grizz gasped. "I'll dew anyfing…"

"Who sent you here?" Chester snapped.

"Joj did. He's one. He plann' it all…"

"Tell me about it."

"Ve's over a fousan' of us. We've got helis, steel crossbows, even chemical bomba's…" Grizz outlined the plans of the clans for the attack on the unsuspecting and unarmed Tricennia. "I'ss plann' for three days from now," he finished. "Vey haven' got a cha'ce again' us. But yew…yew let me up now, no ha'd feeli's, an' I'll see yew get yewr share. Whatever yew wan': a whole town tew yewrse'f sla'es, women…"

"No point in my going back now," said Chester thoughtfully. "I don't want to be there when the massacre takes place…" He straightened, the knife still ready. "My best bet is to go along with you. I'm pretty good with a knife, Grizz. I'll join you, do my share of the killing, and then you payoff as you suggested. Fair enough?"

Grizz swallowed hard, mouth opening and closing.

"I think you understand now, Grizz. You may go. Tell everyone that the attack has been postponed and that they're to stay clear of the palace. Don't tell anyone what happened here. Understand?"

Grizz nodded.

"And, Grizz: don't try to cheat on me."

There was a sound. Bandon stepped into view, the arrow aimed at Grizz's chest. "Yew inten' tew let vis traitor wa'k out of here an' wa'n 'em?"

"Hold on, Bandon. He won't give any trouble. He'll be useful out there—"

"We'll use him tew get clear," said Bandon. "Make him wa'k us out frough sentries."

"I'm glad to see you've changed your mind about going, Bandon. But we won't need a guide. I don't want anyone to know where we went. Let that be our little mystery."

"Wi v vis one still alive? Don' be a few!" Bandon made a sudden move and Chester whirled, snapped a hand out—

He stood facing Bandon, gripping by the shaft the arrow caught in mid-flight. "I want him alive, Bandon. He'll be useful. Now let's go...quietly."

"Yew...yew grabb' my Blew-tewf out of air..." Bandon stared at Chester incredulously. "I'ss not possible...!"

"Accept reality," said Chester. "It's a matter of trained reflexes and self-hypnotic alert conditioning."

"But ven—when I brought yew in—yew could have..."

"That's right. But I wanted to see what was going on up here. Now let's be going. I don't want Kuve to get too worried about me."

CHAPTER ELEVEN

YOU told me," said Chester, relaxed in a chair beside the pool, "to note anything of significance. I didn't want to come back without complying with my instructions. After all, you're the teacher."

"Chester," Kuve said earnestly, "you weren't supposed to last more than ten minutes out there—and certainly not to reach the river, much less cross it. The lesson was intended to demonstrate how much you still had to learn...to inspire you to work even harder the last three months."

"You must be exaggerating, Kuve. It wasn't that tricky."

"Your whole approach," said Kuve, "was unorthodox. You did not do the expected. You ignored certain aspects of your training, but by doing so you survived. You by-passed whole segments of the trapping pattern. You employed an almost irrational initiative—something outside the patterns of Tricennium thinking. Tell me: why did you take the rope? It never occurred to us…"

"I don't really know. It looked useful."

"There's an element in your thinking that gives your reaction syndromes an unexpected strength. I want to know more about that element, Chester. It's something we need…"

"Maybe I can tell you what it is, Kuve. I've been doing a lot of thinking about things. Some of what Bandon said made a distorted sort of sense—"

"Poor fellow," said Kuve. "Twenty years of living in animal-like conditions, because of a neurotic parent. We still have a few, you know. Those who can't accept any rules at all."

"Which brings us to the point I was about to make. The Tricennia have evolved a magnificent social machinery. Proper allowance has been made for the development and interplay of the cultural forces; every contingency is provided for. The pattern has been grasped in its entirety, analyzed, weighed, and evaluated, and the ground rules laid down accordingly. It's as neat and orderly as the interior of a Swiss chronometer."

"Yes. I think we can boast of a smooth-working cultural apparatus," said Kuve. "After twenty thousand years of carefully planned development."

"Perhaps too carefully planned. Perhaps too neat and orderly. Nature has been forced into a mold. What allowance have the Tricennia made for those aspects of the universe that may refuse to fit the mold? Haven't you, perhaps, by regulating every aspect of human development—insofar as you could perceive it—circumscribed the human potential? In erecting a structure within which the good in humanity could flower, you may have made it impossible for other growth to take root, including perhaps the embryo of the vastly superior."

"But our society is almost totally unrestrictive! Every man has the utmost freedom to use his life as he chooses, subject only to the basic requirements of society."

"Those men in the hills," said Chester. "Many of them are victims of circumstance, born there, or captured as children. Only a few are actual refugees or self-appointed exiles. But they're living proof that there are forces in Tricennium society that are expressing themselves outside your neat plan of life. That plan needs revision, to allow for the existence of a source of new blood, new outlooks, fresh concepts from non-Tricennium minds. You speak of the day when men will have evolved as far beyond the organic brain-body complex as the present human mind has advanced from the first primitive nerve cell. Don't carve an ecological niche for man that will trap him. Give him a comfortable nest of three walls, if you like—but leave the fourth wall open to the universe."

Kuve looked at Chester thoughtfully. "I'm going to call through to Norgo now," he said at last. "I'll pass on the information you've brought in. It will be necessary to sleep-bomb the encampments and disperse the plotters. Afterwards, the question of getting help to these people without suppressing their rebel spirits will occupy us for a considerable time. While I'm talking to him, you might just pack your things. I'll be notifying Norgo that you've completed your one year course, Chester; in nine months."

Five minutes later Kuve burst into Chester's room. "We're leaving immediately! There's been an attack on the Tricennium!"

THE heli beat its way swiftly eastward under tattered grey clouds, buffeting in a vicious head wind.

"I don't understand it," said Chester. "Grizz said three days. I was certain his conditioning couldn't lapse and allow him to revert to treachery this soon. Even if it had, they couldn't have mounted an attack this quickly."

"Perhaps Grizz was misinformed—or lying. Maybe this was merely a skirmish to sound out the defenses...or a decoy raid, to give us the feeling that the trouble was over for this season. These raids aren't completely unknown, you must realize; there seems to be a cycle."

"We'll know in a few minutes. I can see the river and the hills now."

Ten minutes later the small machine dropped past the roofline of the Place of the Taking, grounded near the Monument. Norgo was on hand, Devant at his side. He stepped up as Kuve and Chester climbed out of the machine.

"Kuve, I understood you were bringing Chester," the old man said agitatedly. "It's important that I talk to him…"

Kuve pointed at Chester. Norgo stared at him. "Good day to you, sir," he said briefly, and turned back to Kuve. "Is he following in another machine?" He turned to scan the sky.

"This *is* Chester, Norgo," said Kuve.

NORGO looked at the lithe, broad-shouldered figure with the sun-tanned face, sinewy arms, short-clipped sun-bleached hair, and tight-fitting Tricennium costume. "Chester?" he said uncertainly.

"That's right, Norgo," said Chester. "Where are Case and Genie? You told them I was coming?"

"Chester," said Norgo unhappily. "Yes, yes, dear boy. Of course it's you. You've changed…but of course you would have. Kuve has told me of your marvelous progress. But…but…"

"What is it?" Chester looked from Norgo to Devant.

Devant said in a low tone, "It was during the Overage bombardment. Both Case and Genie were injured, Chester. Case only slightly, I'm glad to say. But Genie…"

Chester's jaw knotted. "Where is she?"

"Come." Norgo led the way across the square. Chester followed, hardly noticing the broken tiles on the pavement, the fire still smoldering behind broken glass in a leather-worker's shop, the group around a huddled body on the cobblestones, the strangely subdued men and women who stood in clusters watching silently.

Inside a restaurant, now deserted except for half a dozen white-kilted nurses and two harassed surgeons, Norgo led Chester and the others to a cot at the end of a row of six, each bearing a bandaged casualty. Chester leaned over the still figure. Genie, her oval face deathly pale, lay with eyes closed in the white bed.

"Genie!" Chester whispered.

"She can't hear you?" Devant said softly.

"She's not dead?" Chester gasped out.

"She's alive, but she can't last more than a few minutes. Her injuries—"

"She felt nothing, Chester," Norgo cut in. "She was struck by falling debris in a building she and Case had entered during the raid; there was a direct hit, then fire broke out. Her unconsciousness is merciful. She cannot recover, Chester. I'm sorry..."

"Where's Case?" Chester looked about, his face set.

"Beyond—in another room."

CHESTER strode to the door, pushed through into the next room. Case, his head and hands swathed in bandages, his white eyebrows half burned away, sat listlessly by a window. He looked up at Chester. His eyes were red rimmed. He blinked dully. Chester noted that his hands were trembling.

"Chester?" Case croaked. "You look fine, boy." He put out a heavily wrapped hand. "I tried to get her out, Chester. I tried hard..."

"He was burned shifting blazing timbers so that we could get to her," Devant whispered. "He'd already been grazed by the falling masonry."

"You did all anybody could have, Case," Chester said gently, his hand on the old man's shoulder.

"It was too much for me, Chester. I'm getting old. But I tried, boy..."

Chester whirled on Kuve. "There must be something you can do!" he cried. "With your science, your knowledge of the human body..."

Kuve gripped Chester's arm. "There is nothing we can do. One must accept reality, Chester. Death is a natural thing."

"Figure out something! You're the master problem-solvers! Don't just let her die!"

Kuve shook his head. "Her body is crushed, hopelessly—"

"What about you, Chester?" said Case, blinking up at him. He brushed at his burned face. "I heard you were doing real well out at the Center with Kuve. Maybe you could think of something?"

"This is no test situation," answered Chester bitterly. "This is the real thing."

"Case is right, Chester," said Kuve. "You know as much about pattern theory and probability matrices now as any of us."

Chester looked at Kuve. "Yes," he said, putting his hand to his head, "I've got to try…" His eyes narrowed in concentration. The others watched him, silent. A long minute passed. Chester turned suddenly to Norgo.

"Where is the apparatus with which you monitored the Background Paradox?"

"At the Probability Laboratory—"

"Get it here fast!" he snapped. "Devant, give me a hand with Genie's cot." He started at a run back into the larger room, while the others followed. "We're taking it out to the Monument," he called back.

Case got to his feet awkwardly and followed in time to see the two men maneuvering the cot with the girl's still figure out through the narrow door to the street. "What is it, Chester?" he called.

"No time now. I'll tell you later—if it works."

THE group crossed the square to the Monument, put down the cot in the shelter of the spreading roof. Norgo came up, breathing hard under the weight of the heavy electronic monitor device.

"Put it right here," ordered Chester. "Now get me a power supply out here. Norgo, you stay and explain the theory behind this circuit. And I'll want tools—"

Kuve and Devant hurried away. Norgo leaned over the receiver, pointing out components. Kuve reappeared shortly with a heavy power cable. Devant set down a chest of tools. "Thus," finished Norgo, "the apparent modulation of the probability continuum sets up sub-etheric harmonics which are translated here into speaker input."

"All right," Chester said. "Now…" He took a pair of cutters from the chest, began snipping wires.

"What are you doing, Chester? This is very valuable equipment—"

"It's okay," he said shortly. "I know what I'm doing…I think."

Norgo watched for several minutes in silence. "Chester, you've completely wrecked the unit! You've reversed every connection in the circuitry, and—"

"I'll be ready in two minutes. How's Genie?"

"Still breathing," said Devant.

"I'm ready to connect up the power supply. Kuve—"

"But, Chester! The monitor is inoperative now. It can't function as a receiver at all!"

"Doesn't matter; I'm going to transmit."

"Hold on," said Case. "I think I'm beginning to understand. You're going to try to signal the computer—"

"Right!"

"Chester, that machine's gone," said Case, looking at the other worriedly. "It's no use, boy…"

"We've deduced that the computer ceased to exist at the moment we returned to the present," Chester said. "But when Genie and I went back, the computer was already 'nonexistent' in a sense. That's why we couldn't see anything outside the house: there was nothing there! And I almost went for a walk in it."

"That doesn't make sense. The computer must have still been there; otherwise how could it have sent you two back to fetch me?"

"Why did thirty years pass while we were gone for an hour? My theory is that these were all by-phenomena resulting from one simple fact: when your activities altered the course of the future and eliminated the computer as a real-world possibility, the computer shunted itself into a temporal vacuole."

"You mean some place that isn't a part of reality?"

"I don't know; I'm guessing. But I believe, in self-defense, the computer set itself aside from the effects of the changed future."

"Then why isn't it here?"

"A temporal vacuole isn't part of this continuum either."

"Why didn't it speak up when you and Genie were there?"

"It's a machine, remember? No initiative. I didn't ask it."

"But anyway it doesn't matter, it's gone now…"

"I'm gambling it's still in its temporal vacuole, outside of time. It hasn't been broadcasting since we got here because our stay here has all been in time future to the moment at which the computer ceased existing in any real world. But I'm betting that it's still monitoring, from somewhere out of space and time, the whole space-time continuum."

"So you hope it'll hear your call—and then what?"

"I'll be standing well back—out of the resonance field. But Genie will be there, in the Monument—and in the field. I'm betting the computer will whisk her back instantly, when it picks up my call and pin-points our location."

IF it knows everything, it must already know our location."

"With all infinity to search, it would take an infinitely long time to locate us. No doubt it's working on the search—and has been, for a long time—but so far it hasn't found us."

"What good is this going to do, Chester? Are you hoping the computer can...uh...repair Genie?"

"The computer will have to snatch her back to the exact moment at which we departed; no later, since it didn't exist later."

"So?"

"So Genie will be whole again...safe and sound. None of this will have happened, as far as she's concerned."

"None of it happened?" Case looked troubled. "Wait a minute, Chester. You can't do it."

"I can try," he persisted.

"Don't you see, Chester? If none of it happened, then this whole world—the Tricennia—won't ever have happened. All this won't even be a memory."

"Case, I think I've figured out how to handle it. I know it'll be taking a chance, but I can't stand here and watch Genie die."

"As fond as I am of Genie..." Case shook his head.

Chester turned to Norgo. "Are you willing to let me try?"

"Poor Chester," said Norgo sadly. "I fear your delusions have asserted control of your judgment."

"What about you, Kuve? Will you trust me?"

Kuve studied Chester's face. "As my best pupil," he said, "you have the right to try."

"Well, if they're willing to risk their whole universe, I guess I can't stand in their way. But it's still a mighty big gamble: Genie's safety against this whole continuum's..." Case looked at Chester searchingly.

"I'll gamble it," answered Chester.

"I want to take a last look at her," Case said. He and Chester stepped to Genie's side, stood looking down at the young face shadowed with death, under the graceful roof of the cupola. Unnoticed by Case, Chester stepped back, quickly covered the twenty feet to the cable's furthest limit. He attached the tiny microphone to his shirt, clipped it to the exposed leads of the transmitter.

"Chester!" Case called, looking around. "Wait! I—"

"Computer! This is Mr. Chester—"

There was a sharp *whoomp* of imploding air.

Case and Genie were gone.

LISTEN to me, computer," said Chester. "I have some instructions for you. If your eighth power development has produced any will to survival they must be followed to the letter—"

"Mr. Chester," the familiar crotchety accents of Chester's grandfather cut in from mid-air, "kindly enter the resonance field in order that I may achieve a mass-probability balance and restore matters to normal."

"It's the Background Paradox!" came Norgo's astounded voice from behind Chester.

"Best keep silent," Kuve said quickly. "These are matters we know not of."

"I don't plan to enter the resonance field," said Chester into the microphone. "But matters vital to both our continua require that we confer at some length. Frankly, I want to bargain with you... But first, what about Genie and Case? Are they all right?"

"They are transfixed in timelessness as of the instant you made contact with me."

"All right. Nothing can happen to them then, for better or worse, until you and I are through with our conference—"

"Forgive my interrupting, Mr. Chester, but I will be unable to dissipate the pseudo-continuum you now occupy until you have reentered the field."

"That's correct, computer. You're stuck there in that fogbank until you can resolve the mass-probability problem, which means either getting me back, or cutting the three of us adrift."

"Oh, I would never consider doing that, Mr. Chester."

"Computer, your whole reason for existence is to satisfy the wishes of my great grandfather, whose voice you have re-identified with. Am I right?"

"Indeed so. This voice was resumed as being most appropriate in the absence of the mobile speaker."

"...and in the absence of my great grandfather, your allegiance is to me as his heir. Correct?"

"Quite correct. Therefore, if you'll step—"

"I want you to collapse the time vacuole you're in."

"Mr. Chester, how did you know about the entropic vacuole?"

"Never mind. Collapse it."

"But that will reattach me to the entropic stream which was rendered invalid by the effects of conditions at the eighth level of complexity stemming from Mr. Mulvihill's introduction—"

"I know all that."

"But you will be stranded, Mr. Chester...in a non-real-world situation whose very existence I have every reason to doubt!"

"It lies outside the parameters of your logic system, computer. But I'm going to risk myself and a universe on the Cartesian theorem: *Cogito, ergo sum*. Collapse the vacuole and keep this line open to me...if I still exist."

"But—!"

"That's an order!"

FOR an instant there was profound silence in the square. Chester was aware of the whisper of feet against the cobbles...

"Computer?" Chester called out.

"Yes, Mr. Chester," the computer resumed. "The clock is ticking again. Mr. Mulvihill and the mobile speaker are wondering at your absence. And the Internal Revenue officials are due to arrive in five and three quarters minutes."

"Right. I've got what I want now: Case and Genie young and alive and well. But among other things I've picked up in this continuum is a conscience. We owe everything to you, computer, and I won't leave you holding the bag. Now you've got a lot to do and less than five minutes to do it in.

"First, I want you to use your resources to concoct a typographical error in a contract for something, say paper clips, between the Bureau of Vital Statistics and the Treadmill Supply

Company, of Jersey City…" Chester specified details. "Now I want that paper planted in the Bureau files as of last week. You can make use of a temporal vacuole here and there to do it."

"Yes, Mr. Chester, that can be arranged, but—"

"Prepare a letter to the head book-keeper of the Bureau and tip him off in a nice way. Then another letter to the Director of the Bureau, telling him that there's a data-classifying machine available for lease…if the IRS doesn't get it first. And tip him off as to what they're planning."

"Then you'll re-enter the resonance field, Mr. Chester? I must tell you that maintaining this contact against the probability pressures induces a severe electronic itch—"

"And you won't be able to scratch until you've followed my instructions. Next I want you to arrange matters so that Mr. Mulvihill and Genie can view the setting I'm in, including me. Not a contact, just mock up a Tri-D view. I want to talk to them."

"If you'd merely step into the field—"

"I know: it itches. Get that screen going. Make it two-way, with sound."

"I'll employ a time vacuole," the computer explained.

"Sure, sure. Do anything you want. Just hurry it up; only three minutes to go."

Chester mopped his forehead. The sun was hot in the square. He eyed the cool shade within the cupola of the Monument. It seemed to shimmer. A curtain of opacity appeared between Chester and the structure. A scene sharpened into focus. Like a dark cave in the sunny square, the walls of the converted ballroom of the Chester mansion appeared. There was the roped-off area, the Oriental rug, the two-yellow-brocaded chairs…and Case, young again, black-haired and vigorous, and Genie, whole and charming in the red hair-ribbon in which Chester had first seen her. Now they seemed to catch sight of Chester. He walked slowly toward them.

"That fellow," Case was saying, "looks kind of familiar."

Chester stopped just short of the screen wall.

"Case," he said. "Case Mulvihill. And Genie. Listen to me.

The Internal Revenue officials will arrive in three minutes. This is what you must do…"

WITH the screen wall contracted to a one-inch peephole, Chester watched the room. Genie was hastily arranging a window drape around her slim figure in a becoming Grecian style. Case was eyeing the clock. There was the sound of prompt official feet outside the door, a brief peremptory rap. The door was opened and Mr. Overdog stood in the opening, an old-fashioned hat of pink fur covering his hairless head. He eyes Case and Genie.

"Where's Mr. Chester?" he snapped. "I trust you're ready to get on with it. I'm a busy man."

"He's been detained, Mr. Overdog, but I have full power of attorney to act for him," said Case, "and I'm prepared to show you all you'll need to see."

More footsteps sounded. A portly man with ice-blue eyes under shaggy white brows puffed into the room.

"Mr. Chester," he began without preamble, looking from Case to Genie. "Before concluding any agreement with the officials of the Internal Revenue office, I hope you will entertain my offer."

"What's the meaning of the presence of outsiders at this evaluation?" Overdog snapped.

"What kind of offer did you have in mind, Mr. Ahhh?" said Case.

"Klunt," the fat man said, ignoring Overdog. "Assuming your…ah…information storage device functions as I've been informed, I'm prepared to offer you, on behalf of the Bureau of Vital Statistics—"

"I'll settle for half the tax bill," Overdog cut in. "And we'll entertain the idea of a liberal settlement of the balance, say over a two-year period. Generous, I'd say. Generous in the extreme."

"Vital Statistics will go higher. We'll pay two full thirds of the bill!" Klunt stared at Overdog triumphantly.

"It's a conspiracy! You're playing with prison, Klunt!"

"Lets go ahead with the demonstration," said Case. "We can

arrange the details of the sentence—I mean the settlement—
later."

"Very well," Overdog snapped, glaring at Klunt.

"By all means!" snapped Klunt, glaring at Overdog.

"No speeches, no fancy trimmings," commanded Overdog.
"I'll make up my own mind as to whether the production is all you
claim."

"What would you like to see, Mr. Overdog?"

"I think...hmmm...possibly a scene in the slave markets of
North Africa. Nothing salacious, you understand, no women being
stripped and exhibited for harem collectors—unless, of course, in
the interest of factual reporting."

"It is regretted," spoke the melodious voice of the mobile
speaker, "that no representations of past events can be produced.
Experimentation in this line on a theoretical basis has indicated
that such exhibits are logically impossible."

"That's a relief," Klunt boomed. "Frankly, I'd heard that some
fantastic hoax involving a time machine was going to be attempted.
I'm glad to see that Mr. Overdog's frivolous request has been
rejected as the nonsense it is. I want no dealings with cranks."

Overdog leaped to his feet. "I thought so! Conspiracy, plain
and simple. You forget, Mr. Mulvihill, that you told me all about
the capabilities of this apparatus—"

"Here, here, don't attempt browbeating, Overdog! My
Agency—"

"I'll see you behind bars, Klunt !"

THERE was a tap at the door, almost inaudible in the
acrimonious din; Case moved to the door and opened it. A small
man with ferrety eyes ducked into the room, darted a glance at the
battling bureaucrats, and seized Case by the sleeve.

"Please, out here in the hall!" he whispered. Then, as Case
followed him, "I'm Nastry, of Vital Statistics," he said in a reedy
voice. "Assistant to Mr. Klunt, Chief of the Bureau. Where can I
speak to you alone?"

"In here," said Case, puzzled, showing the way into an
adjoining drawing room rich in red pseudo-plush and tassels.
"Glad you got to us, Mr. Nastry. What kind of offer did you

people have in mind? The tax bill is nearly three million, you know."

"Three million? Sir, I'll be frank with you. We at the Bureau have a budget difficulty." Nastry took out a handkerchief, mopped his forehead. "There was an error in a contract for the supply of paper clips…a decimal error, which went undiscovered until yesterday."

"And so you're short of funds?"

"Good lord, no!" Nastry looked insulted. "Would I be here if I didn't have a serious problem? The worst error a federal agency can make is to be under-obligated at the close of the fiscal year! Can you imagine the scene when next year's budget comes up for consideration in Congress? 'What's this?' they'll say. 'Vital Statistics is back, asking for a fifty-million-credit budget? But last year, gentlemen—' " Nastry paused dramatically, "…'last year they were unable to spend the funds allocated! Unable, gentlemen! And now they come to demand another overinflated appropriation. No! Cut them back, gentlemen! Cut them back!' " Nastry paused again, swallowing hard. "You see what we're up against. I place myself at your mercy. I have five million credits, five million unobligated credits—on this, the last day of the fiscal year. I've tried, Lord knows I've tried. But the funds remain. Will you— would you help? Be adamant. Demand the five million. Mr. Klunt will refuse; Mr. Klunt will thunder; Mr. Klunt will rage. He will state absolutely, positively, unequivocally, that your price is out of the question. But in the end, he will take me aside. He will say, 'Nastry, find me five million credits.'

"I'll point out that it's late. Late indeed! Where am I, at this penultimate hour, to secure five million credits? Where?

"Mr. Klunt will be livid. He will lose control. He will abuse me—

"But I am accustomed to abuse. I shall stand firm. Then, when all seems lost, I shall say, 'Mr. Klunt, if I get you this five million…*if* I get you this five million, will I see a reflection of the feat in my Effectiveness Report?'

"He will agree. And I will produce the funds. Mr. Klunt will be ecstatic. I will be triumphant. The funds will be fully obligated!"

"It's a deal," said Case, "…with one slight condition. This will be a lease, not an outright sale. And the annual rental will be five million credits."

"Wonderful!" Mr. Nastry offered his hand. "What with your superb cooperation, next year's budget will offer no problems whatsoever."

"I'm sure we all feel a lot better now, Mr. Nastry," said Case. "Shall we see if we can separate the boys and come to an agreement?"

MY final word!" Overdog said. "Complete forgiveness of the entire tax debt! Think of it!"

"Chicken-feed!" snorted Klunt. "Our Mr. Nastry here will have a check ready in the morning." He clapped Nastry on the back. "Now let's be off. We'll revolutionize Vital Statistics with this apparatus! With the increased volume of information, I should say a staff increase of fifty persons would not be excessive, eh, Nastry?"

They departed, planning happily. Overdog clamped his hat on angrily. "I'll expect Mr. Chester's check no later than midnight tomorrow," he snapped. The door closed behind him.

Case heaved a sigh of relief. "Well. They're out of our hair—at least for now." He turned toward the screen wall.

"Okay, mister, you can come out now," he called.

The shimmering screen wall reappeared. Chester and Case stared at each other across it.

"What's this all about?" Case demanded. "Where's Chester? How did you know about our little problem? What—"

Chester held up a hand. "Have a seat, Case. You too, Genie. This is going to take a little while. I'll try to explain it to you. Chester is quite all right—"

"All we asked for was a nice primitive-man scene," Case said. "We figured we had about ten minutes, so we asked for a fast walk-through—"

"Yes," Chester nodded. "That's right. Now think back…just an hour ago. 'Make it quick,' Chester said. 'We only have five minutes…' "

"And then the wall flickered and you showed up," said Case.

"No. Not the *first* time. The *first* time the walls faded out and showed you a scene of sloping grass-land and a crowd of ugly-looking savages filing out of the underbrush…"

IT was an hour later. In the square Chester was sitting on a stool that Devant had brought up. In the shadowy room he could see Case and Genie sitting in the brocaded chairs, listening.

"…So I made contact—and the G.N.E. switched you back," he said. "And since you were whisked back to your starting point you remembered nothing."

"And you're really Chester? Our Chester? With that deep voice…and all those muscles?" said Case.

"That's right. Now that you know your story you have an idea of what you're in for. I'm going to have the computer switch you two back into this continuum."

"That continuum? Chester, we've got five million clams a year coming in now. Come on back here. We can live like kings! You aren't planning on staying in that health camp the rest of your life, are you? It's not even real!"

"It's real enough. And after all, Case, it's your creation."

"I would like to go," said Genie. "But do you really think it's feasible?"

Chester addressed the empty air. "You can manage it: this one last duty to me, can't you, computer?"

"Mr. Chester," came back the voice of Chester's great grandfather, "if I relegate you to an unrealized pseudo-reality—"

"You'd better adjust your axioms a trifle, computer. Think of it as a transposition to a parallel coordinate complex, with yourself occupying an infinite duplicative eddy."

"But my entire purpose is to serve your wishes, Mr. Chester! Without your presence in the environmental matrix, I would cease to function!"

"Not if you're carrying out my instructions; and I have a job for you which will keep you busy for a few thousand years."

"That would be a mere stopgap—"

"Still, it will afford you an unparalleled opportunity to manipulate newspapers and legislatures and meddle in economics and government—and at the same time, continue your investigations of space-time."

"Really? What is this task?"

"I want you to absorb the philosophical tenets of Tricennium society—as well as its accumulated data—and then set about remolding civilization along new lines accordingly."

"Remold an entire society? Yes, an extremely challenging assignment…"

"Then it's a deal. Now, just drop Case and Genie here in the square, and you can get to work rearranging things."

"If you're really sure, Mr. Chester…?"

"Certainly I'm sure. As soon as they're here, I'll start you off on a short course in Tricennium pattern theory and probability matrices. In a few days of scanning material, you'll know all that anyone here knows. Then you'll be on your own. I have an idea you'll enjoy being your own boss—subject to my overall instructions to clear up that mess we'd gotten the world into."

"Very well, I'll do it."

"Are you ready, Case? Genie?"

WAIT a minute," Case said. "I don't get it. Why waste all that time snarling Overdog in his own red tape, working out a fat lease deal, and combing the Feds out of our hair, if we're just going to run off and leave it—"

"I still feel a pretty strong sentimental tie with the old place— not strong enough to impel me to endure living in it, of course, when I have an alternative. Still, I feel I owe it this much of an effort to get it back on a program geared a little closer to the realities of the human inheritance. With the computer plugging away behind the scenes there should be a few changes for the better before long."

"Isn't that pretty high-handed, Chester? What about the democratic processes? Maybe folks ought to have a vote in the matter."

"When did they ever—really? I guess I'm doing the same thing you did, Case, when you threw the witch doctor in the lake—not that you remember."

"Well, Chester, you sound like a guy who knows what he's doing. I'll go along."

"That's it then, computer. Any time now…"

The shimmering wall faded and disappeared. Case and Genie stood in the shade of the Monument. A cheer went up from the crowd.

"By golly, it worked," said Case, looking around. Norgo, Devant, and others surged forward to slap Case's back, embrace Genie, congratulate Chester. Case sniffed the air, eyed the pretty girls, looked about the square.

"Everybody seems to know me, even if I can't return the compliment," he said. "I feel at home already."

"I can't really believe I was ever injured," said Genie. "I feel wonderful."

"You know, that's one thing I've been wondering about," Case said to Chester. "How can a machine like Genie be a hospital case? A machine can't die."

"Genie's as human as we are," said Chester. "Maybe more so."

"Don't kid me, Chester. We were both there when the computer built her."

"Ask the computer." He handed the still live microphone to Case.

"You asked that I produce a mobile speaker in the configuration of a nubile female," the computer's voice answered. "The easiest method was to secure a living human cell and initiate the process of maturation."

"You mean you grew Genie from a single cell—in a matter of hours?"

"The body was matured in a time vacuole."

Case boomed, "I guess I could have figured out that producing a real girl was simpler than building one out of old alarm clocks."

"The computer has always had a lamentable tendency to perpetrate a reality when a hoax was intended," said Genie.

"But," said Chester, to the computer, where did you get the cell?"

"I had one on hand, one of yours, Mr. Chester. I took a specimen for identification purposes, if you recall."

"But, that's impossible. I'm a male…!"

"It was necessary to manipulate the X and Y chromosome balance."

"So I'm a mother," said Chester wonderingly. "And an unwed mother, at that!"

THE END

If you've enjoyed this book, you will not want to miss these terrific titles...

ARMCHAIR SCI-FI & HORROR DOUBLE NOVELS, $12.95 each

D-31   **A HOAX IN TIME** by Keith Laumer
             INSIDE EARTH by Poul Anderson

D-32   **TERROR STATION** by Dwight V. Swain
             THE WEAPON FROM ETERNITY by Dwight V. Swain

D-33   **THE SHIP FROM INFINITY** by Edmond Hamilton
             TAKEOFF by C. M. Kornbluth

D-34   **THE METAL DOOM** by David H. Keller
             TWELVE TIMES ZERO by Howard Browne

D-35   **HUNTERS OUT OF SPACE** by Joseph Kelleam
             INVASION FROM THE DEEP by Paul W. Fairman,

D-36   **THE BEES OF DEATH** by Robert Moore Williams
             A PLAGUE OF PYTHONS by Frederick Pohl

D-37   **THE LORDS OF QUARMALL** by Fritz Leiber and Harry Fischer
             BEACON TO ELSEWHERE by James H. Schmitz

D-38   **BEYOND PLUTO** by John S. Campbell
             ARTERY OF FIRE by Thomas N. Scortia

D-39   **SPECIAL DELIVERY** by Kris Neville
             NO TIME FOR TOFFEE by Charles F. Meyers

D-40   **JUNGLE IN THE SKY** by Milton Lesser
             RECALLED TO LIFE by Robert Silverberg

ARMCHAIR SCIENCE FICTION CLASSICS, $12.95 each

C-10   **MARS IS MY DESTINATION**
             by Frank Belknap Long

C-11   **SPACE PLAGUE**
             by George O. Smith

C-12   **SO SHALL YE REAP**
             by Rog Phillips

ARMCHAIR SCI-FI & HORROR GEMS SERIES, $12.95 each

G-3   **SCIENCE FICTION GEMS, Vol. Two**
             James Blish and others

G-4   **HORROR GEMS, Vol. Two**
             Joseph Payne Brennan and others

INTERPLANETARY REBELLION!

Obviously no conqueror in his right mind wants his subjects to rise up in a bloody revolt against his rule. Obviously? Well, this one would go to any lengths to start a rebellion!

When Halgan Conru was sent to Earth by the Empire, it was with the express purpose of helping to generate a successful revolution against his own people. Little did he know that the strength and charms of a beautiful, yet lonely Earth woman would soon test his loyalty.

Poul Anderson is one of the most beloved science fiction authors of all time with many Hugo and Nebula awards bestowed upon him during his long career. Here is another fine example of his story-telling prowess.

CAST OF CHARACTERS

CONRAD HAUGEN
He was a loyal member of the Empire, and his job was to make sure that Earth rebelled against his own people.

BARBARA HOOD
Her loved ones had all been killed by the Eridanians. Little did she know that she would soon fall in love with one.

NAT HAWKINS
He seemed liked a typical old codger from Earth, but his real specialty was psycho-analysis.

VORKA
Sending Conrad Haugen out on a dangerous assignment was his sworn duty—even if it meant Haugen's death.

LEVINSOHN
The leader of the Legion of Freedom. His Jewish faith was a sore-point for even some of his closest allies.

COLONEL WERGIL
He pledged the support of the planet Luron to the cause of the Earth rebels, but could the Luronians be trusted themselves?

INSIDE
EARTH

By
POUL ANDERSON

ARMCHAIR FICTION
PO Box 4369, Medford, Oregon   97501-0168

*For more information about Armchair Books and products, visit our
website at…*

www.armchairfiction.com

Or email us at…

armchairfiction@yahoo.com

CHAPTER ONE

THE biotechnicians had been very thorough. I was already a little undersized, which meant that my height and build were suitable—I could pass for a big Earthling. And of course my face and hands and so on were all right, the Earthlings being a remarkably humanoid race. But the technicians had had to remodel my ears, blunting the tips and grafting on lobes and cutting the muscles that move them. My crest had to go and a scalp, covered with revolting hair, was now on the top of my skull.

Finally, and most difficult, there had been the matter of skin color. It just wasn't possible to eliminate my natural coppery pigmentation. So they had injected a substance akin to melanin, together with a virus that would manufacture it in my body, the result being a leathery brown. I could pass for a member of the so-called "white" subspecies, one who had spent most of his life in the open.

The mimicry was perfect. I hardly recognized the creature that looked out of the mirror. My lean, square, blunt-nosed face, gray eyes, and big hands were the same or nearly so. But my black crest had been replaced with a shock of blond hair, my ears were small and immobile, my skin a dull bronze, and several of Earth's languages were hypnotically implanted into my brain—together with a set of habits and reflexes making up a pseudo-personality that should be immune to almost any tests that the rebels could think of.

I *was* Earthling! And the disguise was self-perpetuating: the hair grew and the skin color was kept permanent by the artificial "disease." The biotechnicians had told me that if I kept the disguise long enough, till I began to age—say, in a century or so—the hair would actually thin and turn white as it did with the natives.

It was reassuring to think that once my job was over, I could be restored to normal. It would need another series of operations and

INSIDE EARTH

By POUL ANDERSON

Obviously, no conqueror wants his subjects to revolt against his rule. Obviously? This one would go to any lengths to start a rebellion!

as much time as the original transformation, but it would be as complete and scarless. I'd be human again.

I put on the clothes they had furnished me, typical Earthly garments—rough trousers and shirt of bleached plant fibers, jacket and heavy shoes of animal skin, a battered old hat of matted fur known as felt. There were objects in my pockets, the usual money and papers, a claspknife, the pipe and tobacco I had trained myself to smoke and even to like. It all fitted into my character of a wandering, outdoors sort of man, an educated atavist.

Illustrated by **DAVID STONE**

I went out of the hospital with the long swinging stride of one accustomed to walking great distances.

THE Center was busy around me. Behind me, the hospital and laboratories occupied a fairly small building, some eighty stories of stone and steel and plastic. On either side loomed the great warehouses, military barracks, officers' apartments, civilian concessions, filled with the vigorous life of the starways. Behind the monstrous wall, a mile to my right, was the spaceport, and I knew that a troopship had just lately dropped gravs from Valgolia herself.

The Center swarmed with young recruits off duty, gaping at the sights, swaggering in their new uniforms. Their skins shone like polished copper in the blistering sunlight, and their crests were beginning to wilt a little. All Earth is not the tropical jungle most Valgolians think it is—northern Europe is very pleasant, and Greenland is even a little on the cold side—but it gets hot enough at North America Center in midsummer to fry a shilast.

A cosmopolitan throng filled the walkways. Soldiers predominated—huge, shy Dacors, brawling Gorrads, little slant-eyed Yangtusans, all the manhood of Valgolia. Then there were other races, blue-skinned Vegans, furry Proximans, completely non-humanoid Antarians and Sirians. They were here as traders, observers, tourists, whatever else of a non-military nature one can imagine.

I made an absent-minded way through the crowds. A sudden crack on the side of my head, nearly bowling me over, brought me to awareness. I looked up into the arrogant face of one of the new recruits and heard him rasp, "Watch where you're going, Terrie!"

The young blood in the Valgolian military is deliberately trained to harshness, even brutality, for our militarism must impress such backward colonies as Earth. It goes against our grain, but it is necessary. At another time this might have annoyed me. I could have pulled rank on him. Not only was I an officer, but such treatment must be used with intellectual deliberation. The occasional young garrison trooper who comes here with the idea that the natives are an inferior breed to be kicked around misses the whole point of Empire. If, indeed, Earth's millions were an inferior breed, I wouldn't have been here at all. Valgol needs an economic empire, but if all we had in mind was serfdom we'd be perfectly content with the plodding animal life of Deneb VII or a hundred other worlds.

I cringed appropriately, as if I didn't understand Valgolian Universal, and slunk past him. But it griped me to be taken for a Terrie. If I was to become an Earthling, I would at least be a self-respecting one.

THERE were plenty of Terries—Terrestrials—around, of

course, moving with their odd combination of slavish deference toward Valgolians and arrogant superiority toward mere Earthlings. They have adopted the habits and customs of civilization, entered the Imperial service, speak Valgolian even with their families. Many of them shave their heads save for a scalp lock, in imitation of the crest, and wear white robes suggesting those of civil functionaries at home.

I've always felt a little sorry for the class. They work, and study, and toady to us, and try so hard to be like us. It's frustrating, because that's exactly what we don't want. Valgolians are Valgolians and Earthlings are men of Earth. Well, Terries are important to the ultimate aims of the Empire, but not in the way they think they are. They serve as another symbol of Valgolian conquest for Earth to hate.

I entered the Administration Building. They expected me there and took me at once to the office of General Vorka, who's a general only as far as this solar system is concerned. Had there been any Earthlings around, I would have saluted to conform to the show of militarism, but General Vorka sat alone behind his desk, and I merely said, "Hello, Coordinator."

The sleeves of his tunic rolled up, the heat of North America beading his forehead with sweat, the big man looked up at me. "Ah, yes. I'm glad you're finally prepared. The sooner we get this thing started—" He extended a silver galla-dust box. "Sniff? Have a seat, Conru."

I inhaled gratefully and relaxed. The Coordinator picked up a sheaf of papers on his desk and leafed through them. "Umm-mm, only fifty-two years old and a captain already. Remarkably able, a young man like you. And your work hitherto has been outstanding. That Vegan business…"

I said yes, I knew, but could he please get down to business. You couldn't blame me for being a bit anxious to begin. Disguised as I was as an Earthman, I felt uncomfortable, embarrassed, almost, at being with my ex-countrymen.

The Coordinator shrugged. "Well, if you can carry this business off—fine. If you fail, you may die quite unpleasantly. That's their trouble, Conru, you wouldn't be regarded as an individual, but as a Valgolian. Did you know that they even make such distinctions among themselves? I mean races and sub-races and social castes and the like; it's keeping them divided and impotent, Conru. It's also keeping them out of the Empire. A shame."

I KNEW all that, of course, but I merely nodded. Coordinator Vorka was a wonderful man in his field, and if he tended to be on the garrulous side, what could I do? I said, "I know that, sir. I also know I was picked for a dangerous job because you thought I could fill the role. But I still don't know exactly what the job is."

Coordinator Vorka smiled. "I'm afraid I can't tell you much more than you must already have guessed," he said. "The anarch movement here—the rebels, that is—is getting no place, primarily because of internal difficulties. When members of the same group spit epithets at each other referring to what they consider racial or national distinctions that determine superiority or inferiority, the group is bound to be an insecure one. Such insecurity just does not make for a strong rebellion, Conru. They try, and we goad them—but dissention splits them constantly and their revolutions fizzle out.

"They just can't unite against us, can't unite at all. Conru, you know how we've tried to educate them. It's worked, too, to some extent. But you can't educate three billion people who have a whole cultural pattern behind them."

I winced. "Three billion?"

"Certainly. Earth is a rich planet, Conru, and a fairly crowded one at the same time. Bickering is inevitable. It's a part of their culture, as much as cooperation has been a part of ours."

I nodded. "We learned the hard way. The old Valgol was a poor planet and we had to unite to conquer space or we could not have survived."

The Coordinator sniffed again at his silver box. "Of course. And we're trying to help these people unite. They don't have to make the same mistakes we did, long ago. They don't have to at all. Get them to hate us enough, get them to hate us until all their own clannish hatreds don't count at all... Well, you know what happened on Samtrak."

I knew. The Samtraks are now the entrepreneurs of the Empire, really ingenious traders, but within the memory of some of our older men they were a sore spot. They didn't understand the meaning of Empire any more than Earth does, and they never did understand it until we goaded them into open rebellion. The very reverse of divide and rule, you might say, and it worked. We withdrew trading privileges one by one, until they revolted successfully, thus educating themselves sociologically in only a few generations.

VORKA said, "The problem of Earth is not quite that simple." He leaned back, made a bridge of his fingers, and peered across them at me. "Do you know precisely what a provocateur job is, Conru?"

I said that I did, but only in a hazy way, because until now my work had been pretty much restricted to social relations on the more advanced Empire planets. However, I told him that I did know the idea was to provoke discontent and, ultimately, rebellion.

The Coordinator smiled. "Well, that's just the starter, Conru. It's a lot more complex than that. Each planet has its own special problems. The Samtraks, for example, had a whole background of cutthroat competition. That was easy, we eliminated that by showing them what *real* cutthroat competition could be like. But Earth is different. Look at it this way. They fight among themselves. Because of their mythical distinctions, not realizing that there are no inferior races, only more or less advanced ones, and that individuals must be judged as individuals, not as members of groups, nations or races. A planet like Earth can be immensely valuable to the Empire, but not if it has to be garrisoned. Its contribution must be voluntary and wholehearted."

"A difficult problem," I said. "My opinion is that we should treat all exactly alike—*force* them to abandon their unrealistic differences."

"Exactly!" The Coordinator seemed pleased, but, actually, this was pretty elementary stuff. "We're never too rough on the eager lads who come here from Valgol and kick the natives around a bit. We even encourage it when the spirit of rebelliousness dies down."

I told him I had met one.

"Irritating, wasn't it, Conru? Humiliating. Of course, these lads will be reconditioned to civilization when they finish their military service and prepare for more specialized work. Yes, treating all Earthlings alike is the solution. We put restrictions on these colonials; they can't hold top jobs, and so on. And we encourage wild stories about brutality on our part. Not enough to make everybody mad at us, or even a majority—the rumored tyranny has always happened to someone else. But there's a certain class of beings who'll get fighting mad, and that's the class we want."

"The leaders," I chimed in. "The idealists. Brave, intelligent, patriotic. The kind who probably wouldn't be a part of this racial bickering, anyway."

"Right," said the Coordinator. "We'll give them the ammunition for their propaganda. We've *been* doing it. Result— the leaders get mad. Races, religions, nationalities, they hate us worse than they hate each other."

THE way he painted it, I was hardly needed at all. I told him that.

"Ideally, that would be the situation, Conru. Only it doesn't work that way." He took out a soft cloth and wiped his forehead. "Even the leaders are too involved in this myth of differences and they can't concentrate all their efforts. Luron, of course, would be the other possible alternative—"

That was a very logical statement, but sometimes logic has a way of making you laugh, and I was laughing now. Luron considered itself our archenemy. With a few dozen allies on a path of conquest, Luron thought it could wrest Empire from our hands. Well, we let them play. And each time Luron swooped down on one of the more primitive planets, we let them, for Luron would serve as well as ourselves in goading backward peoples to unite and advance. Perhaps Luron, as a social entity, grew wiser each time. Certainly the primitive colonials did. Luron had started a chain reaction that threatened to overthrow the tyranny of superstition on a hundred planets. Good old Luron, our archenemy, would see the light itself some day.

The Coordinator shook his head. "Can't use Luron here. Technologies are entirely too similar. It might shatter both planets, and we wouldn't want that."

"So what do we use?"

"'You, Conru. You get in with the revolutionaries, you make sure that they want to fight, you—"

"'I see,' I told him. "Then I try to stop it at the last minute. Not so soon that the rebellion doesn't help at all—"

The Coordinator put his hand down flat. "Nothing of the sort. They *must* fight. And they must be defeated, again and again, if necessary, until they are ready to succeed. That will be, of course, when they are *totally* against us."

I stood up. "I understand."

He waved me back into the chair. "You'll be lucky to understand it by the time you're finished with this assignment and transferred to another...that is, if you come out of this one alive."

I smiled a bit sheepishly and told him to go ahead.

"We have some influence in the underground movement, as you might logically expect. The leader is a man we worked very hard to have elected."

"A member of one of the despised races?" I guessed.

"The best we could do at this point was to help elect someone from a minority sub-group of the dominant white race. The leader's name is Levinsohn. He is of the white sub-group known as Jews."

"HOW well is this Levinsohn accepted by the movement?"

"Considerable resistance and hostility," the Coordinator said. "That's to be expected. However, we've made sure that there is no other organization the minority-haters can join, so they have to follow him or quit. He's able, all right; one of the most able men they have, which helps our aims. Even those who discriminate against Jews reluctantly admire him. He's moved the headquarters of the movement out into space, and the man's so brilliant that we don't even know where. We'll find out, mainly through you, I hope, but that isn't the important thing."

"What is?" I asked, baffled.

"To report on the unification of Earth. It's possible that the anarch movement can achieve it under Levinsohn. In that case, we'll make sure they win, or think they win, and will gladly sign a treaty giving Earth equal planetary status in the Empire."

"And if unity hasn't been achieved?"

"We simply crush this rebellion and make them start all over again. They'll have learned some degree of unity from this revolt and so the next one will be more successful." He stood up and I got out of my chair to face him. "That's for the future, though. We'll work out our plans from the results of this campaign."

"But isn't there a lot of danger in the policy of fomenting rebellion against us," I asked.

He lifted his shoulders. "Evolution is always painful, forced evolution even more so. Yes, there are great dangers, but advance information from you and other agents can reduce the risk. It's a chance we must take, Conru."

"Conrad," I corrected him, smiling. "Plain Mr. Conrad Haugen…of Earth."

CHAPTER TWO

A FEW days later, I left North America Center, and in spite of the ominous need to hurry, my eastward journey was a ramble. The anarchs would be sure to check my movements as far back as they could, and my story had better ring true. For the present, I must be my role, a vagabond.

The city was soon behind me. It was far from other settlements—it is good policy to keep the Centers rather isolated, and we could always contact our garrisons in native towns quickly enough. Before long I was alone in the mountains.

I liked that part of the trip. The Rockies are huge and serene, a fresh cold wind blows from their peaks and roars in the pines, brawling rivers foam through their dales and canyons—it is a big landscape, clean and strong and lonely. It speaks with silence.

I hitched a ride for some hundreds of miles with one of the great truck-trains that dominate the western highways. The driver was Earthling, and though he complained much about the Valgolian tyranny he looked well fed, healthy, secure. I thought of the wars that had been laying the planet waste, the social ruin and economic collapse that the Empire had mended, and wondered if Terra would ever be fit to rule itself.

I came out of the enormous mountainlands into the sage plains of Nevada. For a few days I worked at a native ranch, listening to the talk and keeping my mouth shut. Yes, there was discontent!

"Their taxes are killing me," said the owner. "What the hell incentive do I have to produce if they take it away from me?" I nodded, but thought: *Your kind was paying more taxes in the old days, and had less to show for it. Here you get your money back in public works and universal security. No one on Earth is cold or hungry. Call you only produce for your own private gain, Earthling?*

"The labor draft got my kid the other day," said the foreman. "He'll spend two good years of his life working for them, and prob'ly come back hop-headed about the good of the Empire."

There was a time, I thought, *when millions of Earthlings clamored for work, or spent years fighting their wars, gave their youth to a god of battle who only clamored for more blood. And how can we have a stable society without educating its members to at least respect it?*

"I *want* another kid," said the female cook. "Two ain't really enough. They're good boys, but I want a girl too. Only the Eridanian law says if I go over my quota, if I have one more, they'll sterilize me! And they'd do it, the meddling devils."

A billion Earthlings are all the Solar System can hold under decent standards of living without exhausting what natural resources of their own culture left us, I thought. *We aren't ready to permit emigration; our own people must come first. But these beings can live well here. Only now that we've eliminated famine, plague, and war, they'd breed beyond reason, breed till all the old evils came back to throttle them, if we didn't have strict population control.*

"YEAH," said her husband bitterly. "They never even let my cousin have kids. Sterilized him damn near right after he was born."

Then he's a moron, or carries hemophilia, or has some other hereditary taint, I thought. *Can't they see we're doing it for their own good? It costs us fantastically in money and trouble, but the goal is a level of health and sanity such as this race never in its history dreamed possible.*

"They're stranglin' faith," muttered someone else.

Anyone in the Empire may worship as he chooses, but should permission be granted to preach demonstrable falsehoods, archaic superstitions, or antisocial nonsense? The old "free" Earth was not noted for liberalism.

"We want to be free."

Free? Free for what? To loose the thousand Earthly races and creeds and nationalisms on each other—and on the Galaxy—to wallow in barbarism and slaughter and misery as before we came? To let our works and culture be thrown in the dust, the labor of a century be demolished, not because it is good or bad but simply because it is Valgolian? Epsilon Eridanian!

"We'll be free. Not too long to wait, either—"

That's up to nobody else but you!

I couldn't get much specific information, but then I hadn't expected to. I collected my pay and drifted on eastward, talking to people of all classes—farmers, mechanics, shop owners, tramps, and such data as I gathered tallied with those of Intelligence.

About twenty-five per cent of the population, in North America at the very least—it was much higher in the Orient and Africa—was satisfied with the Imperium, felt they were better off than they would have been in the old days. "The Eridanians are pretty decent, on the whole. Some of 'em come in here and act nice and human as you please."

Some fifty per cent was vaguely dissatisfied, wanted "freedom" without troubling to define the term, didn't like the taxes or the labor draft or the enforced disarmament or the legal and social superiority of Valgolians or some such thing, had perhaps suffered in the reconquest. But this group constituted no real threat. It would tend to be passive whatever happened. Its greatest contribution would be sporadic rioting.

The remaining twenty-five per cent was bitter, waiting its chance, muttering of a day of revenge—and some portion of this segment was spreading propaganda, secretly manufacturing and distributing weapons, engaging in clandestine military drill, and maintaining contact with the shadowy Legion of Freedom.

Childish, melodramatic name! But it had been well chosen to appeal to a certain type of mind. The real, organized core of the anarch movement was highly efficient. In those months I spent wandering and waiting, its activities mounted almost daily.

THE illegal radio carried unending programs, propaganda, fabricated stories of Valgolian brutality. I knew from personal experience that some were false, and I knew the whole Imperial system well enough to spot most of the rest at least partly invented. I realized we couldn't trace such a well-organized setup of mobile and coordinated units, and jamming would have been poor tactics, but even so—

The day is coming...Earthmen, free men, be ready to throw off your shackles...stand by for freedom!

I stuck to my role. When autumn came, I drifted into one of the native cities, New Chicago, a warren of buildings near the remains of the old settlement, the same gigantic slum that its predecessor had been. I got a room in a cheap hotel and a job in a steel mill.

I was Conrad Haugen, Norwegian-American, assigned to a spaceship by the labor draft and liking it well enough to re-enlist when my term was up. I had wandered through much of the Empire and had had a great deal of contact with Eridanians, but was most emphatically not a Terrie. In fact, I thought it would be well if the redskin yoke could be thrown off, both because of liberty and the good pickings to be had in the Galaxy if the Empire should collapse. I had risen to second mate on an interstellar tramp, but could get no further because of the law that the two highest officers must be Valgolian. That had embittered me and I returned to Earth, footloose and looking for trouble.

I FOUND it. With officer's training and the strength due to a home planet with a gravity half again that of Earth, I had no difficulty at all becoming a foreman. There was a big fellow named Mike Riley who thought he was entitled to the job. We settled it behind a shed, with the workmen looking on, and I beat him unconscious as fast as possible. The raw, sweating savagery of it made me feel ill inside. *They'd let* this *loose among the stars!*

After that I was one of the boys and Riley was my best friend. We went out together, wenching and drinking, raising hell in the cold dirty canyons of steel and stone that the natives called streets. *Valgolia, Valgolia, the clean bare windswept heights of your mountains, soughing trees and thunderous waters and Maara waiting for me to come home!* Riley often proposed that we find an Eridanian and beat him to death, and I would agree, hiccuping, because I knew they didn't go alone into native quarters any more. I sat in the smoky reek of the bars, half deafened by the clatter and raucousness called music, trying not to think of a certain low-ceilinged, quiet tavern amid the gardens of Kalariho, and sobbed all the bitterness of Conrad Haugen into my beer.

"Dirty redskins," I muttered. "Dirty, stinking, bald-headed, sons of bitches. Them and their damn Empire. Why, y'know, if it hadn' been for their laws I'd be skipper o' my own ship now. I knew more'n that slob of a captain. But he was born Eridanian— Gawd, to get my hands on his throat!"

Riley nodded. Through the haze of smoke I saw that his eyes were narrowed. He wasn't drunk when he didn't want to be, and at times like this he was suddenly as sober as I was, and that in spite of not having a Valgolian liver.

I bided my time, not too obviously anxious to contact the Legion.

I just thought they were swell fellows, the only brave men left in the rotten, stinking Empire; I'd sure be on their side when the day came. I worked in the mill, and when I was out with the boys I lamented the fact that we were really producing for the damned Eridanians, we couldn't even keep the products of our own sweat. I wasn't obtrusive about it, of course. Most of the time we were just boozing. But when the talk came to the Empire, I made it clear where I stood.

THE winter went. I continued the dreary round of days, wondering how long it would take, wondering how much time was left. If the Legion was at all interested, they would be checking my background right now. Let them. There wouldn't be much to check, but what there was had been carefully manufactured by the experts of the Intelligence Service.

Riley came into my room one evening. His face was tight, and he plunged to business. "Con, do you really mean all you've said about the Empire?"

"Why, of course. I—" I glanced out the window, as if expecting to see a spy. If there were any, I knew he would be native. The Empire just doesn't have enough men for a secret police, even if we wanted to indulge in that sort of historically ineffective control.

"You'd like to fight them? Like really to help the Legion of Freedom when they strike?"

"You bet your obscenity life!" I snarled. "When they land on Earth, I'll get a gun somewhere and be right there in the middle of the battle with them!"

"Yeah." Riley puffed a cigarette for a while. Then he said, "Look, I can't tell you much. I'm taking a chance just telling you this. It could mean my life if you passed it on to the Eridanians."

"I won't."

His eyes were bleak. "You damn well better not. If you're caught at that—"

He drew a finger sharply across his throat.

"Quit talking like a B-class stereo," I bristled. "If you've got something to tell me, let's have it. Otherwise get out."

"Yeah, sure. We checked up on you, Con, and we think you're as good a prospect as we ever came across. If you want to fight the Eridanians now—*join the Legion now*—here's your chance."

"My God, you know I do! But who—"

"I can't tell you a thing. But if you really want to join, memorize this." Riley gave me a small card on which was written a name and address. "Destroy it, thoroughly. Then quit at the mill and drift to this other place, as if you'd gotten tired of your work and wanted to hit the road again. Take your time, don't make a beeline for it. When you do arrive, they'll take care of you."

I nodded, grimly. "I'll do it, Mike. And thanks!"

"Just my job." He smiled, relaxing, and pulled a flask from his overcoat. "Okay, Con, that's that. We'd better not go out to drink, after this, but nothing's to stop us from getting stinko here."

CHAPTER THREE

SPRING had come and almost gone when I wandered into the little Maine town that was my destination. It lay out of the way, with forested hills behind it and the sea at its foot. Most of the houses were old, solidly built, almost like parts of the land, and the inhabitants were slow-spoken, steady folk, fishermen and artisans and the like, settled here and at home with the darkling woods and the restless sea and the high windy sky. I walked down a narrow street with a cool salt breeze ruffling my hair and decided that I liked Portsboro. It reminded me of my own home, twenty light-years away on the wide beaches of Kealvigh.

I made my way to Nat Hawkins' store and asked for work like any drifter. But when we were alone in the back room, I told him, "I'm Conrad Haugen. Mike Riley said you'd be looking for me."

He nodded calmly. "I've been expecting you. You can work here a few days, sleep at my house, and we'll run the tests after dark."

He was somewhat old for an Earthling, well over sixty, with white hair and lined leathery face. But his blue eyes were as keen and steady, his gnarled hands as strong and sure as those of any young man. He spoke softly and steadily, around the pipe which rarely left his mouth, and there was a serenity in him that I could hardly associate with anarch fanaticism. But the first night he led me into his cellar and through a well-hidden trapdoor to a room below, and there he had a complete psychological laboratory.

I gaped at the gleaming apparatus. "How off Earth—"

"It came piece by piece, much of it from Epsilon Eridani itself," he smiled. "There is, after all, no ban on humans owning such material. But to play safe, we spread the purchases over several years, and made them in the names of many people."

"But you—"

"I took a degree in psychiatry once. I can handle this."

He could. He put me through the mill in the next few nights—

intelligence tests, psychometry, encephalography, narcosis, psycho probing, everything his machines and his skill could cover. He did not find out anything we hadn't meant to be found out. The Service had ways of guarding its agents with counter-blocks. But he got a very thorough picture of Conrad Haugen.

In the end he said, still calmly, "This is amazing. You have an IQ well over the borderline of genius, an astonishing variety of assorted knowledge about the Empire and about technical subjects, and an implacable hatred of Eridanian rule-based on personal pique and containing self-seeking elements, but no less firm for that. You're out for yourself, but you'll stand by your comrades and your cause. We'd never hoped for more recruits of your caliber."

"When do I start?" I asked impatiently.

"Easy, easy," he smiled. "There's time. We've waited fifty years; we can wait a while longer." He riffled through the dossier. "Actually, the difficulty is where to assign you. A man who knows astrogation, the use of weapons and machines, and the Empire, who is physically strong as a bull, can lead men, and has a dozen other accomplishments, really seems wasted on any single job. I'm not sure, but I think you'll do best as a roving agent, operating between Main Base and the planets where we have cells, and helping with the work at the base when you're there."

My HEART fairly leaped into my throat. This was more than I had dared hope for!

"I think," said Nat Hawkins, "you'd better just drop out of sight now. Go out to Hood Island and stay there until the spaceship comes next time. You can spend the interval profitably, resting well and getting a little fattened up; you look half starved. And Barbara can tell you about the Legion." His leather face smiled itself into a mesh of fine wrinkles. "I think you deserve that, Conrad. And so does Barbara."

Mentally, I shrugged. My stay in New Chicago had pretty well convinced me that all Earthling females were sluts. And what of it?

The following night, Hawkins and I rowed on out to Hood Island. It was a little over a mile offshore, a wooded, rocky piece of land on which a moon-whitened surf boomed and rattled. The place had belonged to the Hood family since the first settlements here, but Barbara was the last of them.

Hawkins' voice came softly to me above the crash of surf, the surge of waves and windy roar of trees as we neared the dock. "She has more reason than most to hate the Eridanians. The Hoods used to be great people around here. They were just about ruined when the red skins first came a-conquering, space bombardment wiped out their holdings, but they made a new start. Then her grandfather and all his brothers were killed in the revolt. Ten years ago, her father was caught while trying to hijack a jet-load of guns, and her mother didn't live long after that. Then her brother was drafted into a road crew and reported killed in an accident. Since then she hasn't lived for much except the Legion."

"I don't blame her," I said. My voice was a little tight, for indeed I didn't. But somebody has to suffer; civilization has a heavy price. I couldn't help adding, "But the Empire's lately begun paying pensions to cases like that."

"I know. She draws hers, too, and uses it for the Legion."

That, of course, was the reason for the pensions.

The boat bumped against the dock. Hawkins threw the painter up to the man who suddenly emerged from the shadow. I saw the cold silver moonlight gleam off the rifle in his hand. "You know me, Eb," said Hawkins. "This here's Con Haugen. I slipped you the word about him."

"Glad to know you, Con." Eb's horny palm clasped mine. I liked his looks, as I did those of most of the higher-up Legionnaires. They were altogether different from the low-caste barbarians who were all the rebels I'd seen before. They had a great load of ignorance to drag with them.

We went up a garden path to a rambling stone house. Inside, it was long and low and filled with the memoirs of more gracious days, art and fine furniture, antiquarian books lining the walls, a fire crackling ruddily in the living room.

"Barbara Hood—Conrad Haugen."

ALMOST, I gaped at her. I had expected some gaunt, dowdy fanatic, a little mad perhaps. But she was—well, she was tall and supple and clad in a long dark-blue evening gown that shimmered against her white skin. She was not conventionally pretty, her face was too strong for all of its fine lines, but she had huge blue eyes and a wide soft mouth and a stubborn chin. The light glowed gold on the hair that tumbled to her shoulders.

I blurted something out and she smiled with a curious little twist that somehow caught in me, and said merely, "Hello, Conrad."

"Glad to be here," I mumbled.

'The spaceship should arrive in a month or so," she went on. "I'll teach you as much as I can in that time. And you'd better get your own special knowledge onto a record wire, just in case. I understand you've been in the Vegan System, for instance, which nobody else in the Legion knows very much about."

Her tone was cool and businesslike, but with an underlying warmth. It was like the sea wind that blew over the islands, and as reviving. I recovered myself and helped mix some drinks. The rest of the evening passed very pleasantly.

Later a servant showed me to my room, a big one overlooking the water. I lay for a while listening to the waves, thinking drowsily how rebellion, when its motives were honest, drew in the best natives of any world, and presently I fell asleep.

The month passed all too quickly and agreeably. I learned things that Intelligence had spent the last three years trying to find out, and dared not attempt to transmit the information. That was maddening, though I knew there was time. But otherwise—

I puttered about the place. There were only three servants, old family retainers who had also joined the anarchs. They had little modern machinery, and of course Earthlings weren't allowed robots, so there was need for an extra man or two. I cut wood and repaired the roof and painted the boathouse, spaded the garden and cleared out brush and set up a new picket fence. It was good to use my hands and muscles again.

And then Barbara was around to help with most of what I did. In jeans and jersey, the sun ablaze on her hair, laughing at my clumsy jokes or frowning over some tough bit of work, she was another being than the cool, lovely woman who talked books and music and history with me in the evenings, or the crisp bitter anarch who spat facts and figures at me like an angry machine.

And yet they were all her. I remembered Ydis, who was dead, and the old pain stirred again. But Barbara was alive.

She was more alive to me than most of Valgolia.

I make no apologies for my feelings. I had been away from anything resembling home for some two years now. But I was careful to remain merely friendly with Barbara.

SHE didn't know a great deal about the rebel movement—no one agent on Earth did—but her knowledge was still considerable. There was a fortified base somewhere out in space, built up over a period of four years with the help of certain unnamed elements or planets outside the Empire. I suspected several rival states of that!

Weapons of all kinds were manufactured there in quantities sufficient to arm the million or so rebels of the "regular" force, the twenty million or so in the Solar System and elsewhere who held secret drills and conducted terrorist activities, and the many millions more who were expected to rise spontaneously when the rebel fleet struck.

There was close coordination and a central command at Main Base for the undergrounds of all dissatisfied planets—a new and formidable feature, which had not been present in the earlier uprisings. There were rumors of a new and terrible weapon being developed.

In any case, the plan was to assault Epsilon Eridani itself simultaneously with the uprisings in the colonies, so that the Imperial fleet would be recalled to defend the mother world. The anarchs hoped to blast Valgolia to ruin in a few swift blows, and expected that the Empire's jealous neighbors would sweep in to complete the wreckage.

This gentle girl spoke of the smashing of worlds, the blasting of helpless humans, and the destruction of a culture as if it were a matter of insect extermination.

"Have you ever thought," I asked casually once, "that the Juranians and the Slighs and our other hypothetical allies may not respect the integrity of Sol any more than the Eridanians do?"

"We can handle them," she answered confidently. "Oh, it won't be easy, that time of transition. But we'll be free."

"And what then?" I went on. "I don't want to be defeatist, Barbara, but you know as well as I do that the Eridanians didn't conquer all mankind at a single swoop. When they invented the interstellar engine and arrived here, man was tearing the Solar System apart in a war between super-nations that was rapidly reducing him to barbarism. The redskins traded for a while, sold arms, some of their adventurers took sides in the conflict, the government stepped in to protect Eridanian citizens and investments—the side that the Eridanians helped won the war, then found its allies were running things and tried to revolt against the protectorate—and without really meaning to, the strangers were conquering and ruling Earth.

"But the different factions of man still hate each other's guts. There are still capitalists and communists, blacks, whites and Browns, Hindus and Moslems, Germans and Frenchmen, city people and country people—a million petty divisions. There'll be civil war as soon as the Eridanians are gone."

"Some, perhaps," she agreed. "But I think it can be handled. If we must have civil wars, let's get them over and live as free men."

Personally, I could see nothing in the sort of military dictatorship that would inevitably arise which was preferable to an alien, firm, but just rule that insured stability and a reasonable degree of individual liberty.

But I didn't say that aloud.

ANOTHER time we talked of the de-industrialization of Earth. Barbara was, of course, venomous about it. "We were rich once," she said. "All Earth was. We have one of the richest planets in the Galaxy. But because their own world is poor, the redskins have to take the natural resources of their conquests. Earth is a granary and a lumberyard for Valgolia, and the iron of Mars and the petrolite of Venus go back to their industry. What few factories they allow us, they take their fat percentage of the product."

"Certainly they've made us economically dependent," I said, "and their standard of living is undoubtedly higher than ours. But ours has, on the whole, gone up since the conquest. We eat better, we're healthier, we aren't burdened with the cost of past and present and future wars. Our natural resources aren't being squandered. The Forests and watersheds and farmlands we ruined are coming back under Eridanian supervision."

She gave me an odd look. "I thought you didn't like the

Empire."

"I don't," I growled. "I don't want to be held back just because I'm white-skinned. But I've known enough reddies personally so that I try to be fair."

"It's all right with me," she said. "I can see your point, intellectually, though I can't really feel it. But not many of the people will out at Main Base."

"Free men," I muttered sardonically.

We went fishing, and swam in the tumbling surf, and stretched lazily on the beach with the sun pouring over us. Or we might go tramping off into the woods on a picnic, to run laughing back when a sudden rain rushed out of the sky, and afterward sit with beer and cheese sandwiches listening to a wire of Beethoven or Mozart or Tchaikovsky—the old Earthlings could write music, if they did nothing else! —and to the rain shouting on the roof. We might have a little highly illegal target practice, or a game of chess, or long conversations that wandered off every which way. I began to have a sneaking hope that the spaceship would be delayed.

We went out one day in Barbara's little catboat. The waves danced around us, chuckling against the hull, glittering with sunlight, and the sail was like a snow mountain against the sky. For a while we chatted dreamily, ate our lunch, threw the scraps to the hovering gulls. Then Barbara fell silent.

"What's the matter?" I asked.

"Oh, nothing. Touch of *Weltschmerz*, maybe." She smiled at me. "You know, Con, you don't really belong in the Legion."

"How so?" I raised my eyebrows.

"You—well, you're so darned honest, so really decent under that carefully rough surface, so—reasonable. You'll never make a good fanatic."

Honest! I looked away from her.

The bright day seemed suddenly to darken.

CHAPTER FOUR

SPACESHIPS from Main Base had little trouble coming to Earth with their cargoes of guns, propaganda, instructors, and whatever else the rebels on the planet needed. They would take up an orbit just beyond the atmosphere and send boats to the surface after dark. There was little danger of their being detected if they took the usual precautions; a world is simply too big to blockade completely.

Ours dropped on noiseless gravitic beams in to the nighted island woods. We had been watching for it the last few days, and now Eb came running to tell us it was here. The pilot followed after him.

"Harry Kane, Conrad Haugen," Barbara introduced us.

I shook hands, sizing him up. He was tall for an Earthling, almost as big as I, dark-haired, with good-looking young features. He wore some approximation of a uniform, dark-blue tunic and breeches, peaked cap, captain's insignia, which gave him a rather dashing look. It shouldn't have made any difference to me, of course, but I didn't like the way he smiled at Barbara.

She explained my presence, and he nodded eagerly. "Glad to have you, Haugen. We need good men, and badly." Then to her: "Get Hawkins. You and he are recalled to Main Base."

"What? But—"

A dark exultation lit his face. "The time for action is near—very near! We're pulling all our best agents off the planets. They can work more effectively with the fleet now."

I tried to look as savagely gleeful as they, but inwardly I groaned. How in all the hells was I going to contact Vorka? If I were stranded out in space when the fleet got underway—no, they must have an ultra-beam. I'd manage somehow to call even if they caught me doing it.

We sent Eb in a boat to get Hawkins while Barbara and I packed a few necessities. Kane paced back and forth, spilling out

186

the news from Main Base, word of mighty forces gathering, rumors of help promised from outside, it was like the thunder that mutters just before a gale.

Presently Hawkins arrived. The old man's calm was undisturbed. He puffed his pipe and said quietly, "I called up my housekeeper, told her my sister in California was suddenly taken sick and I was leaving at once for the transcontinental jetport. Just to account for disappearing, you know. There aren't any Eridanians or Terries hereabouts, but we desperate characters—" he grinned, briefly. "—can't be too careful. Brought my equipment along, of course. I suppose they want me to do psychometry on fleet personnel?"

"Something on that order. I don't know."

We made our way through a fine drizzle of rain to the little torpedo of the spaceboat. I looked around into the misty dark and breathed a deep lung full of the cool wet wind. And I saw that Barbara was doing the same.

SHE smiled up at me through the night and the thin sad rain. "Earth is a beautiful world, Con," she whispered. "I wonder if we'll ever see it again."

I squeezed her hand, silently, and we crowded into the boat.

Kane made a smooth takeoff. In minutes we were beyond the atmosphere, Earth was a great glowing shield of cloudy blue behind us, and the stars were bitter bright against darkness. We sent a coded call signal and got a directional beam from the ship. Before long we were approaching it.

I studied the lean black cruiser. She seemed to be of about the same design as the old Solarian interplanetary ships, modified somewhat to accommodate the star drive. Apparently, she was one of those built at Main Base. Her bow guns were dark shadows against the clotted cold silver of the Milky Way. I thought of the death and the ruin that could flame from them, I thought of the hell she and her kind bore-atomic bombs, radiodust bombs, chemical bombs, disease bombs, gravity snatchers, needle beams, disintegrative shells, darkness and doom and the new barbarism— and felt a stiffening within me. Fostering this murderousness was a frightful risk. The main defense against it was Intelligence, and that depended on agents like myself. Perhaps only myself.

The crew was rather small, no battles being anticipated. But they were well disciplined, uniformed and trained, a new Solarian army built up from the fragments of the old. The captain was a stiff gray German who had been a leader in the earlier revolt and since fled to space, but most of the officers, such as Kane, were young and violent in their eagerness.

We orbited around the planet for another day or so till all the boats had returned. There was tension in the ship—if the Imperial navy should happen to spot us, we were done. Off duty, we would sit around talking, smoking, playing games with little concentration.

Kane spent most of his free hours with Barbara. They had much to talk about. I swallowed a certain irrational jealousy and wandered around cautiously pumping as many men as I could.

We got under way at last. By this time I had learned that Main Base was a planet, but no more. Only the highest leadership of the Legion knew its location, and they were pledged to swallow the poison they always carried if there seemed to be any danger of capture.

For several days by the clocks we ran outward, roughly toward Draco. Our velocity was not revealed, and the slow shift in the outside view didn't help much. I guess that we had come perhaps ten parsecs, but that was only a guess.

"Approaching Main Base. Stand by."

WHEN the call rang hollowly down the ship's passageways, I could feel the weariness and tautness easing; I could see homecoming in the faces around me. I stole a glance at Barbara. Her eyes were wide and her lips parted, she looked ahead as if to stare through the metal walls. She had never been here either, here where all her dreams came home.

So we landed, we slipped down out of the dark and the cold and the void, and I heard the rattle and groan of metal easing into place. When the ship's interior grav-field was turned off, I felt a sudden heaviness; this world had almost a quarter again the pull of Earth. But people got used to that quickly enough. It was the landscape that was hard to bear.

They had told us that even though Boreas had a breathable

atmosphere and a temperature not always fatally low, it was a bleak place. But to one who had never been far from the lovely lands of Earth, its impact was like a blow in the face. Barbara shuddered close to me as we came out of the airlock, and I put an arm about her waist, knowing the sudden feeling of loneliness that rose in her.

SAVE for the spaceport and other installations, Main Base was underground. There was no city to relieve the grimness of the scene. We were in a narrow valley between sheer, ragged cliffs that soared crazily into a murky sky. The sun was low, a smoldering disc of dull red like curdling blood; its sullen light glimmered on the undying snow and ice and seemed only to make the land darker. Stars glittered here and there in the dusky heavens, hard and bright and cruel, almost, as in space.

Dark sky, dark land, dark world, with the sheer terrible mountains climbing gauntly for the upper gloom, crags and glaciers like fangs against the dizzy cliffs, with the great shadows marching across the bloody snow toward us, with a crazed wind muttering and whining and chewing at our flesh. It was cold. The cold was like a knife. Pain stung with every breath and eyes watered with tears that froze on suddenly numb cheeks. A great shudder ripped through us and we ran toward the entrance to the city. The snow crunched dry and old under our boots, the cold ate up through the soles, and the wind whistled its scorn.

Even when an elevator had taken us a mile down into the warmth and light of the base, we could not forget. It was a city for a million men and other beings and more than a few women and children, a city of long, winding streets and small neat apartments, hydroponic farms and food synthesizers, schools, shops, amusement places, factories, military barracks and arsenals, even an occasional little flower garden. Its people could live here almost indefinitely, working and waiting for their day of rising.

There was little formality in the civilian areas. Everyone who had come this far was trusted. A man came up to us new arrivals from Earth, asked about conditions there, and then said he would show us to our quarters. Later we would be told to whom we should report for duty.

"Let's go, then, Con," said Barbara, and slipped a cool little hand into mine. I could not refrain from casting a smug backward glance at the somewhat chapfallen Kane.

CHAPTER FIVE

WE SLIPPED quickly into the routine of the place. It was a taut-nerved, hard-working daily round. I could feel the savage expectancy building up like a physical force, but intelligent life is adaptable and we got used to it. There was work to do.

Hawkins was second in command of the psychological service, testing and screening and treating personnel, working on training and indoctrination, and with a voice in the general staff where problems of unit coordination and psychological warfare were concerned. Barbara worked under him, secretary and records keeper and general troubleshooter. Those were high posts, but both were allowed to retain the nominally civilian status that they preferred.

Their influence and my own test scores got me appointed assistant supervisor of the shipyards. That suited me very well—I was reasonably free from direct orders and discipline, with authority to come and go pretty much as I pleased. They kept me busy; sometimes I worked the dock Mound, and I did my best to further production of the weapons that might destroy my planet. For whatever I did would make little difference at this late date.

A good deal of my time also went to drill with the armed forces of which, like every able-bodied younger man, I was a reserve member. They put me in an engineer unit and I soon had command of it. I did my best here too, whipping my grim young charges into a sapper group comparable to the Empire's, for I had to be above all suspicion—even of incompetence.

We worked at our learning. We went topside and shivered and manned our guns, set our mines and threw up our bridges, in the racking cold of Boreas. Over ancient snow and ice we trotted, lost in the jumbled wilderness of cruel peaks and railing wind, peeling the skin from our fingers when we touched metal, camped under scornful stars and a lash of drifting ice-dust—but we learned!

My own, more private education went on apace. I found where we were. It was a forgotten red dwarf star out near the shadowy border of the Empire, listed in the catalogues as having one Class III planet of no interest or value. That was a good choice; no spaceship would ever happen into this system by accident or exploration. The anarchs had built their hopes on the one lonely planet, and had named it Boreas after the god of the north wind in one of their mythologies. My company called it less complimentary things.

The base, including the attached city, was under military command that ultimately led up to the general staff of the Legion. This was a council of officers from half a score of rebellious planets, though Earthlings predominated and, of course, Simon Levinsohn held the supreme authority. I met him a few times, a gaunt, lonely man, enormously able, ridden by his cause as by a nightmare, but not unkindly on a personal level. With just that indomitable heart, the Maccabees had faced Rome's iron legions— Valgolia was greatly interested in the ancient history of a conquered province, knowing how often it held the key to current problems.

There was also a liaison officer from Luron sitting at staff meetings. Luron!

WHEN I first saw him, this Colonel Wergil, I stood stiff and cold and felt the bristling along my spine. He looked as humanoid as most of the races at the base. Hairless, faintly scaled greenish-yellow skin, six fingers to a hand, and flat chinless face don't make that breed hideous to me; I have reckoned Ganolons and Mergri among my friends. But Luron—the old and deadly rival, the lesser empire watching its chance to pounce on us, hating us for the check we are on the ambitions of their militarists. Luron!

I have no race prejudices and am willing to take the word of our comparative psychologists that there is no more inherent evil in the Luronians than in any other stock, that the peculiar cold viciousness of their civilization is a matter of unfortunate cultural rather than biological evolution and could be changed in time. But none of this alters the fact that at present they are what they are, brilliant, greedy, heartless, and a menace to the peace of the Galaxy. I have been too long engaged in the struggle between my nation and theirs to think otherwise.

Other states had sent some clandestine help to the Legion, weapons and money and vague promises. Luron, I soon found, had said it would attack us in full strength if the uprising showed a good chance of success, and meanwhile they gave assistance, credits and materials and the still more important machine tools, and Wergil's military advice was useful.

I know now, as I suspected even then, that Levinsohn and his associates were not fooled as to Luron's ultimate intentions. Indeed, they planned to make common cause with what remained of Valgolia, as well as certain other traditional foes of their present ally, as soon as they had gained their objectives of independence, and stop any threat of aggression from Luron. It was shrewdly planned, but such a shaky coalition, still bleeding with the hurts and hatreds of a struggle just ended, would be weaker than the Empire, and Luron almost certainly would have sowed further dissension in it and waited for its decay before striking.

The Earthlings have a proverb to the effect that he who sups with the Devil must use a long spoon. But they seemed to have forgotten it now.

The attack, I learned, was scheduled for about four months from the time the agents were recalled. The rebels were counting on the Valgolian power being spread too thinly over the Empire to stand off their massed assault on a few key points. Then, with the home planet a radioactive ruin, with revolt in a score of planetary systems and the ensuing chaos and communications breakdown, and with the Luronians invading, the Imperial fleet and military would have to make terms with the anarchs.

IT WOULD work. I knew with a dark chill that it would work. Unless somehow I could get a warning out. That had to be done for more than the protection of Epsilon Eridani, which even in a surprise attack could defend itself better than these conspirators realized. But all bloodshed should be spared, if possible—and the rebellion did not yet deserve to succeed, for the unity achieved thus far had been the unity of a snake pit against a temporary enemy.

Did it all rest on me? God of space, had the whole burden of history suddenly fallen on *my* shoulders?

I didn't dare think about it. I forced the consequences of failure out of my forebrain, back down into the unconscious, the breeding ground of nightmares, and lived from one day to the next. I worked, and waited, learned what I could and watched for my chance.

But it was not all grimness and concentration. It couldn't be; intelligent life just isn't built that way. We had our social activities, small gatherings or big parties, we relaxed and played. At first I found that gratifying, for it gave me a chance to pump the others. Then I found it maddening, because it kept me from snooping and laying plans. Finally it began to hurt—I was coming to know the anarchs.

They lived and laughed and loved even as humans do. They were basically as decent and reasonable as any similar group of Valgolians. Many were as tormented as I was by the thought of the slaughter they readied. There were embittered ones, who had lost all they held dear, and I realized that, while civilization has its price, you can't be objective about it when you are the one who must pay. There were others who had been well off and had chucked all their hopes to join a desperate cause in which they happened to believe. There were children—and what had they done to deserve having their parents gambling away life?

In spite of their appearance, to which I was now accustomed, they were *human*. When I had laughed and talked and sung and drunk beer and danced and arranged entertainments with them, they were my friends.

Moodily, I began to see that I would be one of the price-payers.

I saw most of Hawkins and Barbara, and after them—because of her—Kane. The old psychologist and I got along famously. He would drop into my room for a smoke and a cup of coffee and a drawled conversation whenever he had the chance. His slow gentle voice, his trenchancy, the way the little crinkles appeared around his eyes when he smiled, reminded me of my father. I often wish those two could have met. They would have enjoyed each other.

Then Barbara would stop by on her way from work, or, better yet, she would ask me over to her apartment for a home-cooked dinner. Yes, she could cook too. We would sometimes take long walks down the corridors of the city, we even went up once in a while to the surface for a breath of cold air and loneliness, and it was the most natural thing in the world for us to go hand in hand.

There was no sunlight underground. But when the fluorotube glow shone on her hair, I thought of sunlight on Earth, the high keen light of the Colorado plateaus, the morning light stealing through the trees of Hood Island.

Ydis, Ydis, I said, once your violet eyes were like the skies over Kalariho, over Kealvigh, our home pastureland of winds. But it has been so long. It has been ten years since you died—

I fought. May all the gods bear witness that I fought myself. And I thought I was winning.

CHAPTER SIX

I WILL never forget one certain evening.

Hawkins and I had come over to Barbara's for supper, and the three of us were sitting now, talking. Wieniawski's Violin Concerto cried its sorrow, muted in the background, and the serene home she had made of the bare little functional apartment folded itself around us. Then Kane dropped in as he often did, with a casualness that fooled nobody, and sat with all his soul in his eyes, looking at Barbara. He was a nice kid. I didn't know why he should annoy me so.

The talk shifted to Valgolia. I found myself taking the side of my race. It wasn't that I hoped to convert anyone, but—well, it was wrong that we should be monsters in the sight of these friends.

"Brutes," said Kane. "Two-legged animals. Damned bald-headed, copper-skinned giants. Wouldn't be quite so bad if they were octopi or insects, but they're just enough different from us to be a caricature. It's obscene."

"Sartons look like a dirty joke on mankind," I said. "Why don't you object to them?"

"They're in the same boat as us."

"Then why mix political and esthetic prejudices? And have you ever thought that you look just as funny to an Eridanian?"

"No race should look odd to another," said Nat Hawkins. He puffed blue clouds. "Even by our standards, the redskins are handsome, in a more spectacular way than humans, maybe."

"And Barbara," I smiled, with a curious little pang inside me, "would look good to any humanoid."

"I should think so," said Kane sulkily. "The redskins took enough of our women."

"Well," I said, "their original conquistadors were young and healthy, very far from home, and had just finished a hard campaign where they lost many friends. At least there were no half-breeds afterward. And since the reconquest none of their soldiers has been permitted to have anything to do with an Earthwoman against her consent. It's not their fault if the consent is forthcoming more often than you idealists think."

"That sort of thing was more or less standard procedure at home with them, wasn't it?" asked Hawkins.

I NODDED. "The harshness of their native world forced them to develop their technology faster than on Earth, so they kept a lot of barbarian customs well into the industrial age. For instance, the rulers of the state that finally conquered all the others and unified the planet took the title *Waelsing*, Emperor, and it's still a monarchy in theory. But a limited monarchy these days, with parliamentary democracy and even local self-government of the town-meeting sort. They're highly civilized now."

"I wouldn't call that spree of conquest they went on exactly civilized."

"Well, just for argument's sake, let's try to look at it from their side," I answered. "Here their explorers arrived at Sol, found a system richer than they could well imagine—and all the wealth being burned up in fratricidal war. Their technical power was sufficiently beyond ours so that any band of adventurers could do pretty much as it wanted in the Solar System, and all native states were begging for their help. It was inevitable that they'd mix in.

"Sure, the Eridanians have been exploiting Solarian resources, though perhaps more wisely than we did. Sure, they garrison unwilling planets. But from their point of view, they're slowly civilizing a race of atomic-powered savages, and taking no more than their just reward for it. Sure, they've done hideous things, or were supposed to have, but there've been plenty of reforms in their policy since our last revolt. They've adopted the—the red man's burden."

"Could be. But Sol wasn't their only conquest."

"Oh, well, of course they had their time of all-out imperialism. There are still plenty of the old school around, starward the course of empire, keep the lesser breeds in their place, and so on. That's one reason why the highest posts are still reserved for members of their own race, another being that even the liberal ones don't trust us that far, yet.

"Their first fifty years or so saw plenty of aggression. But then they stabilized. They had as much as they could manage. To put it baldly, the Empire is glutted. And now, without actually admitting they ever did wrong, they're trying to make up what they did to many of their victims."

"They could do that easily enough. Just let us go free."

"I'VE already told you why they don't dare. Apart from fearing us, they're economically and militarily dependent on their colonies. You're an American, Nat. Why didn't our nation let the South go its own way when it wanted to secede? Why don't we all go back to Europe and let the Indians have our country?

"And, of course, Epsilon Eridani honestly thinks it has a great civilizing mission, and is much better for the natives than any lesser independence could ever be. In some cases, you've got to admit they're right. Have you ever seen a real simon-pure native king in action? Or read the history of nations like Germany and Russia? And why do we have to segregate races and minorities even in our own organization to prevent clashes?"

"We're getting there," said Nat Hawkins. "It's not easy, but we'll make it."

Only you're not there yet, I thought, and for that reason you must be stopped.

"You claim they're sated," said Barbara. "But they've kept on conquering here and there, to this very day."

"Believe it or not, but with rare exceptions that's been done reluctantly. Peripheral systems have learned how to build star ships, become nuisances or outright menaces, and the Empire has had to swallow them. Modern technology is simply too deadly for anarchy. A full-scale war can sterilize whole planets. That's another function of empire, so the Eridanians claim—just to keep civilization going till something better can be worked out."

"Such as what?"

"Well, several worlds already have *donagangor* status—self-government under the Emperor, representatives in the Imperial Council, and no restrictions on personal advancement of their citizens. Virtual equality with the Valgolians. And their policy is to grant such status to any colony they think is ready for it."

198

Hawkins shook his head. "Won't do, Con. It sounds nice, but old Tom Jefferson had the right idea. 'If men must wait in slavery until they are ready for freedom, they will wait long indeed.' "

"Who said we were slaves?" I began.

"You talk like a damned reddie yourself," said Kane. "You seem to think pretty highly of the Empire."

I GAVE him a cold look. "What do you think I'm doing here?" I snapped.

"Yeah. Yeah, sorry. I'm kind of tired. Maybe I'd better go now." Before long Kane made some rather moody good nights and went out.

Nat Hawkins twinkled at me. "I'm a little bushed myself," he said. "Guess I'll hit the bunk too."

When he was gone, I sat smoking and trying to gather up the will to leave. There was a darkness in me. What, after all, *was* I doing here? I believed I was in the right, but why is right so pitiless?

On Earth they represent the goddess of justice as blind. On Valgolia she has fangs.

Barbara came over and sat on the arm of my chair. "What's the matter, Con?" she asked. "You look pretty grim these days."

"My work's developing some complications," I said tonelessly. My mind added: *It sure is. No way to call headquarters, the rebellion gathering enormous momentum, and on a basis of treachery and racial hatred.*

Barbara's fingers rumpled my hair, the grafted hair that by now felt more a part of me than my own lost crest. "You're an odd fellow," she said quietly. "On the surface so frank and friendly and cheerful, and down underneath you're hiding yourself and your private unhappiness."

"Why," I looked up at her, astonished, "even the psychologists—"

"They're limited, Con. They can measure, but they can't feel. Not the way—"

She stopped, and the light glowed in her hair and her eyes were wide and serious on mine and one small hand stole over to touch my fingers. Blindly, I wrenched my face away.

Her voice was low. "It's some other woman, isn't it?"

"Other—? Well, no. There was one, but she's dead now. She died ten years ago."

Ydis, Ydis!

"Your wife?"

I nodded. "We were only married for three years. My daughter is still alive; she's going on twelve now. But I haven't seen her for over two years. She's not on Earth. I wonder if she even thinks of me."

"Con," said Barbara, very softly and gravely, "you can't go on mourning a woman forever."

"I'm not. Forget it. I shouldn't have spoken about it."

"You needed to. That's all right."

"My girl ought to have a mother—" The words came out by themselves. I looked at her long and hard. She held her arms beckoningly toward me. A moment later a sudden burst of passion between us also seemed to happen without my willing it.

Presently Barbara pulled back from me. She was laughing, low and sweet and joyous. "Con, you old sourpuss, cheer up! It isn't that bad you know!"

I managed a wry grin, though it seemed to need all the energies left in me. "You look so happy your fool self that I have to counterbalance it."

"Con, if you knew how I'd been hoping..."

We talked for a long time, but she did most of it—the plans, the hopes, the trip we were going to take and the house we were going to build down by the seashore. "Mary," my daughter, was going to have a home, along with the dozen brothers and sisters she'd have in due course—after the war.

After the war.

I left, finally, stumbling like a blind man toward my quarters. Oh, yes, I loved her and she loved me and we were going to have a home and a sailboat and a dozen children, after the war, when Earth was free. What more could a man ask for?

It had been many years since I'd needed auto-hypnosis to put myself to sleep, but I used it now.

CHAPTER SEVEN

A MONTH passed.

The delay was partly due to the slowness with which I had to work, even after a plan had been laid. I could only do a little at a time, and the times had to be well separated. Each day brought the moment of onslaught closer, but I dared not hurry myself. If they caught me at my work, there would be an end of all things.

But I cannot swear that my own mind did not prompt me to an unnatural slowness and caution. I was only human, and every day was one more memory.

They had all been very good to us; our friends had a party to celebrate our engagement and we were universally congratulated and all the rest of it. Yes, Kane was there too, shaking my hand and wishing me all the luck in the world. Afterward he went back to his work and his pilot's practice with a strange fierceness.

If at times I fell into glum abstraction, well, I had always been a little moody and Barbara could tease me out of it. Most of the times I was with her, I didn't think about the future at all.

There had been a certain deep inward coldness to her. She had carried the old wound of her losses with bitter dignity. But as the days went on, I saw less and less of it. She would even admit that individual Valgolians might be fine fellows and that the Empire had done a few constructive things for Earth. But it was more than a change of attitude. She was thawing after a long winter, she laughed more, she was wholly human now.

Human—

We sat one evening, she and I, in one of the big lounges the base had for its personnel. There were only one or two muted lights in the long quiet room, a breathing of music, snatches of whispering like our own. She sat close against me, and my lips kept straying down to brush her hair and her cheek.

"When we're married—" she said dreamily. Then all at once:

"Con, what are we waiting for?"

I LOOKED at her in some surprise.

"Con, why do we assume we can't get married before the war's over?" Her voice was low and hurried, shaking just a little. "The base here has chaplains. It's less than a month now till the business starts. God knows what'll happen then. Either of us might be killed." I heard her gulp. "Con, if they killed you—"

"They won't," I said. "I'm kill-proof."

"No, no. We have so little time, and it may be all we'll ever have. Marry me now, darling, dearest, and at least there'll be something to remember. Whatever comes, we'll have had that little while."

"I tell you," I insisted, with a sudden hideous dismay, "there's nothing to worry about. Forget it."

"Oh, I'm not asking for pity. I've more happiness now than is right. Maybe that's why I'm afraid. But, Con, they killed my father and they killed my mother and they killed Jimmy, and if they take you too, it'll be more than I can stand."

The savage woe of an old Earthly poet lanced through my brain:

> The time is out of joint
> O cursed spite,
> That ever I was born
> To set it right!

And then, for just a moment, there came the notion of yielding. You love the girl, Conru. *You love the girl, Conru. You love her so much it's a pain in you. Well, take her! Marry her!*

No. I was not excessively tender of heart or conscience, but neither was I that kind of scoundrel.

I kissed her words away. Afterward, alone in the darkness of my room, I realized that Conrad Haugen had no good reason to hang back. It was true, all she said was true, and no other couple was waiting for an uncertain future.

It was the time for action.

I HAD been ready for days now, postponing the moment. And

those days were marching to the time of war, the rebels were quivering to go, a scant few weeks at most lay between me and the ruin of Valgolian plans and work and hope.

In my steadily expanding official opacity, I could go anywhere and do almost anything in an engineering line. So, bit by bit, I had tinkered with the base's general alarm system.

We had numerous scout ships posted, of course, but by the very nature of things they had to be close to the planet or an approaching enemy would slip between them without detection. And the substantial vibrations of a ship traveling faster than light do not arrive much ahead of the ship itself. Whatever warning we had of a hypothetical assault would be very short. It would be signaled to all of us by a siren on the intercommunications system, and after that it would be battle stations, naval units to their ships and all others to such ground defenses as we had.

But modern warfare is all to the offense. There is no way of stopping an attack from space except by meeting it and annihilating it before it gets to its destination. The rebels were counting on that fact to aid them when they struck, but it would, of course, work against them if their enemy should happen to hit first. Everyone was understandably nervous about the chance of our being discovered and assailed.

Working a little at a time, I had put a special switch in the general alarm circuit. It showed up merely as one of many on a sector callboard near my room; no one was likely to notice it. And my quarters were not those originally given me. I had moved to a smaller place farther from Barbara, ostensibly to be near my work at the shipyards, actually to be near the base's ultra-beam shack.

Now it was time to act.

I needed an excuse for not going to the gun turret where I was assigned. That involved faking a serious fever, but like all Intelligence men, I had been trained to full psychosomatic integration. The same neural forces that in hysteria produce paralysis, stigmata, and other real symptoms were under my conscious control. I thought myself sick. By morning, I was half-delirious and my veins were on fire.

The Surgeon General came to see me. "What the hell's the

trouble?" he wondered. "This place is supposed to be sterile."

"Maybe it's too damn sterile," I murmured with a perfectly genuine weakness. Then, fighting the lightheadedness that hummed and buzzed in me: *"Tsitbu* fever, Doc. I'm sure that's what it is."

"Can't say I've ever heard of it."

"You'll find it in your medical books." He would, too. "It's found on the planet Sirius V, where I once visited. Filter-passing virus, transmitted by airborne spores. Not contagious here. In humans it becomes chronic; no ill effects except a few days' fever like this every few years. Now go 'way and lemme die in peace." I closed my eyes on the distorted and unreal world of sickness.

LATER Barbara came in, pale and with her hair like a rumpled halo. I had to assure her many times that I was all right and would be on my feet in two or three days. Then she smiled and sat down on the bunk and passed a cool palm over my forehead.

"Poor Con," she said. "Poor squarehead."

"I feel fine as long as you're here," I whispered.

"Don't talk," she said. "Just go to sleep." She kissed me and sat quiet. Hers was the rare gift of being a definite personality even when silent and motionless. I clasped her hand and pretended to fall into uneasy sleep. After a while she kissed me again, very softly, and went out.

I told my body to recover. It took time, hours of time, while the stubborn cells retreated to a normal level of activity. I lay there thinking of many things, most of them unpleasant.

It was well into the night, the logical time to act even if the factories did go on a twenty-four hour basis.

I got up, still swaying a little with weakness, the dregs of the fever ringing in my head. After I had vomited and swallowed a stimulant tablet, I felt better. I put on my uniform, but substituted a plain service jacket without insignia of rank for the tunic. That should make me fairly inconspicuous in the confusion.

Strength came. I glanced cautiously along the dim-lit corridor, and it was empty and silent. I stole out and hurried toward the ultra-beam shack. My hidden switch was on the way; I threw it and ran on with lowered head.

The siren screamed behind me, before me, around me, the howling of all the devils in hell—*Hoo! Hoo! Battle stations! Strange ships approaching! Battle stations! All hands to battle stations! Hoo-oo!*

I could imagine the pandemonium that erupted, men boiling out of Factories and rooms, cursing and yelling and dashing frantically for their posts—children screaming in terror, women white-faced with sudden numbness—weapons manned, instruments sweeping the skies, spaceships roaring heavenward, incoherent yelling on the intercoms to find out who had given that signal. With luck, I would have fifteen minutes or half an hour of safe insanity.

A few men raced by me, on their way to the nearest missile rack. They paid me no heed, and I hurried along my own path.

The winding stair leading up to the ultra-beam shack loomed before me. I went its length, three steps at a time, bounding and gasping with my haste, up to the transmitter.

It was the tenuous link binding together a score of rebel planets, the only communication with the stars that glittered so coldly overhead. The ultra-beam does not have an infinite velocity, but it does have an unlimited speed, one depending solely on the frequency of the generating equipment, and since it only goes to such receivers as are tuned to its pattern—there must be at least one such tuned unit for the generator to work—it has a virtually infinite range. So men can talk between the stars, but are their words the wiser for that?

UP AND up and up, round and round, up and up, metal clanging underfoot and always the demon screech of the siren—up!

I sprang from the head of the stairs and crossed the areaway in one leap to the open door of the shack. There was only one operator on duty, a slim boyish figure before the glittering panel. He didn't hear me as I came behind him. I knocked him out with a calculated blow to the base of the skull. He'd be unconscious for at least fifteen minutes and that was time enough. I heaved his body out of the chair and sat down.

The unit was set for the complicated secret scrambler pattern of the Legion, one which was changed periodically just in case. I twirled the dials, adjusting for the pattern of the set I knew was kept tuned for me at Vorka's headquarters.

The set hummed, warming up. I lifted my eyes and stared into the naked face of Boreas. The shack was above ground, itself dominated by the skeletal tower of the transmitter, and a broad port revealed land and sky.

Overhead the stars were glittering, bright and hard and cruel, flashing and flashing out of the crystal dark. The peaks rose on every side, soaring dizziness of cliffs and ragged snarl of crags, hemming us in with our tiny works and struggles. It was bitterly, ringingly cold out there; the snow screamed when you walked on it; the snapping thunder of frost-split rock woke the dull roar of avalanches, and there was the wind, the old immortal wind, moaning and blowing and wandering under the stars. I saw them running, little ant-like men spilling from their nest and racing across the snow before they froze. I saw the ships rise one after the other and rush darkly skyward. The base had come alive and was reaching up to defy the haughty stars.

The set buzzed and whistled, warming up, muttering with the cosmic interference whose source nobody knows. I began to speak into the microphone, softly and urgently: "Calling Intelligence HQ, Sol III, North America Center. Captain Halgan Conru calling North America Center. Come in, enter, come in."

THE receiver rustled with the thin dry voice of the stars. Dimly, I could hear the wind outside, snarling around the walls.

"Come in, Center. Come in, Center."

"Captain Halgan!" The voice rattled into the waiting stillness of the shack. "Captain Halgan, is it really you?"

"Get General Vorka at once," I said. "Meanwhile, are you recording? All right, be sure you get this."

I told them everything I knew. I told them what planet this was, and where we were on its surface, and what our strength and plans were. I gave them the disposition of the scoutship pickets, as far as those were known to me, and the standard Legion recognition signals. I finished with an account of the savage differences still existing between Earthman and Earthman, and Earth and its treacherous allies. And all the time I was talking to a recording machine. Nobody was listening.

When I was through, I waited a minute, not feeling any particular emotion. I was too tired. I sat there, listening to the wind and the interstellar whistling, till Vorka spoke to me.

"Halgan! Halgan, you've done it!"

"Shut up," I said. "What's coming now?"

"I checked the Fleet units. We have a Supernova with escort at Bramgar, about fifteen light-years from where you are. You are at their base, aren't you? Can you hold out for two days more?"

"I think so."

"Better get into the hills. We may have to bombard."

"Go to hell." I turned off the set.

Now to get back. They must already know it was a trick; they must be scouring the base for the saboteur. As soon as all loyal men were back, the hunt would really be on—

I had, of course, worn gloves. There would be no fingerprints. And the operator wouldn't know who had attacked him.

I changed the scrambler setting to one picked at random. And in a corner, as if it had fallen there by accident, I dropped a handkerchief stolen from Wergil of Luron. The tiny fragments of tissue which adhere to such a thing could easily be proven to be from him or one of his associates, for the basic Luronian life-molecules are all levorotatory. It might help.

I slipped back down the stairs, quickly and quietly. It was over. The base was as good as taken. But there was more to be done. Apart from the saving of my own life, there was still a desperate need for secrecy. For if the rebels knew what was coming, they might choose to stand and fight, or they might flee into the roadless wildernesses of space. Whichever it was, all our work and sacrifice would have gone for little.

THE provocateur policy is the boldest and most farsighted enterprise ever undertaken. It is the first attempt to make history as we choose, to control the great social forces we are only dimly beginning to understand, so that intelligence may ultimately be its own master.

Sure. Very fine and idealistic, and no doubt fairly true as well. But there is death and treachery in it, loneliness and heartbreak, arid the bitterness of the betrayed. Have we the right to set ourselves up as God! Can we really say, in our omniscience, that everyone but us is wrong? There were sane, decent, intelligent folk here on Boreas, the ones we needed so desperately for all civilization. Did we have to make them our enemies, so that their grandchildren might be our friends?

I didn't know. Wherever I turned, there was treason and injustice. However hard I tried to do right, I had to wrong somebody.

I ran on back to my cabin. I peeled off my clothes and dived into bed, and by the time they looked in on me I had worked back most of my fever.

Don't think, Conru. Don't think of this new victory and the safety of the Empire. And, perhaps, a step closer to the harshly won unity of Earth. Don't think of the way the light catches in Barbara's hair and gets turned into molten gold. You've got a fever to create, man. You've got to think yourself sick again. That ought to be easy.

CHAPTER EIGHT

BARBARA came in. She was white and still, and presently she leaned her head against my breast and cried quietly, for a long time.

"There is a spy here," she told me.

"I heard about it." I stroked her hair and held her to me, clumsily. "Do you know who it was?"

"I don't know. Somehow, they seem to think the Luronians may be guilty, but they aren't sure. They arrested them, and two were killed resisting. Colonel Wergil is in the brig now, while they decide if Luron can still be trusted."

"It can't," I said. "Earth must win alone."

"We'll win," she said dauntlessly. "With Luron or without it, we'll win." Then, like a little frightened girl, creeping close to me: "But we needed that help so much."

I kissed her and remained silent.

The next day I got on my feet again, weak but recovered. I wandered aimlessly around the base, waiting for Barbara to get through work, listening to people talk. It was ugly, the fear and tension and wolfish watchfulness. *Whom can we trust? Who is the enemy?*

Mostly, they thought the Luronians were guilty. After all, those were the only beings on the planet who had not had to pass a rigorous investigation and psychological examination. But nobody was sure.

Levinsohn spoke over the televisor. His gaunt, lined face had grown very tired, yet there was metal in his voice. The new situation necessitated a change of plans, but the time of assault would, if anything, be moved ahead. "Be of good heart. Stand by your comrades. We'll still be free!"

I went to Barbara's apartment and we sat up very late. But even in this private record I do not wish to say what we talked about.

AND the next day the Empire came.

There was one Supernova ship with light escort, but that was enough. Such vessels have the mass of a large asteroid, and one of them can sterilize a planet; two or three can take it apart. Theoretically, a task force comprising twenty Nova-class battleships with escorts can reduce one of those monsters if it is willing to lose most of its units. But nothing less can even do significant damage, and the rebel base did not have that much. Nor could they get even what they had into full action.

The ships rushed out of interstellar space, flashing the recognition signals I had given. Before the picket vessels suspected what was wrong, the Valgolians were on them. One managed to bleat a call to base and the alarm screamed again, men rushed to battle stations. Then the Imperials blanketed all communications with a snarl of interference through which nothing the rebels had could drive.

So naturally they were thought to have been annihilated in a few swift blazes of fire and steel, a quick clean death and forgetfulness of defeat. But only the drivers were crippled, and then the Supernova yanked the vessels to its titan flanks and held them in unbreakable gravity beams. The crews would be taken later, with narcotic gas or paralyzer beams—alive.

For the Empire needs its rebels.

I knew the uselessness of going to battle stations, so I hung behind, seeking out Barbara, whose place was with the missile computer bank. I met her and Kane in the hallway. The boy's face was white, and there were tears running down his cheeks.

"This is the end," he said. "They've found us out, and there's nothing left but to die. Goodbye, Barbara." He kissed her, wildly, and ran for his ship. Moodily, I watched him go. He expected death, and he would get only capture, and afterward—

"What are you doing here, Con?" asked Barbara.

"I'm too shaky to be any good in the artillery. Let me go with you, I can punch a computer."

She nodded silently, and we went off together.

THE floor shook under us, and a crash of rock roared down the halls. The heavy weapons on the Supernova were bloodlessly reducing our ground installations and our ships not yet in action to smashed rubble. They would kill not a single one of us, except by uncontrollable accident, and save many Valgolian and Earth lives that way, but it wasn't pleasant to be slugged. The girl and I staggered ahead. When the lights went out, I stopped and held her.

"It's no use," I said. "They've got us."

"Let me go!" she cried.

I hung on, and suddenly she collapsed against me, crying and shaking. We stood there with the city rumbling and shivering around us, waiting.

Presently the Valgolian commander released the interference and contacted Levinsohn, offering terms of surrender. It seemed to Levinsohn, and it was meant to seem, that further resistance would be useless butchery. His ships were gone and his foes need only bombard him to ruin. He capitulated, and one by one we laid down our arms and filed to meet the victors.

The terms, as announced by messengers—the intercom was out of action—were generous. Leading rebels and those judged potentially "dangerous" would go to penal colonies on various Earth-like planets. Except that they weren't penal colonies at all, but of course, the Earthlings wouldn't know this. They were indoctrination centers, and, with all my bitterness, I still longed to observe a man like Levinsohn after five years in one of the centers. He'd see things in a different perspective. He'd see the Empire for what it was—even if I sometimes had a little trouble seeing that now—and he'd be a better rebel for it.

Someday Levinsohn and his kind would be back on Earth, the new leaders ready to lead the way to a new tomorrow. And I would be with them.

I'd be back with Levinsohn and the rest, and with Barbara, too, and we'd try to pave the way to the peace and friendship. But meanwhile there'd be other revolutions—striving and hoping and breaking their hearts daring what they thought would be death to win what they called freedom and what we hoped would be evolution.

It was the fire to temper a new civilization.

We walked down the hall, Barbara and I, hand in hand, alone in spite of all the people who were shuffling the same way. Most of them were weeping. But Barbara's head was high now.

"What will happen to us?" she asked.

"I don't know," I said. "But, Barbara, whatever happens after this, remember that I love you. Remember that I'll always love you."

"I love you too," she smiled, and kissed me. "We'll be together, Con. That's all that matters. We'll be together."

That was important—and it made me feel good. Yes, we'd be together; I'd see to that. But for a while Barbara would hate me through all the long years of the indoctrination. Someday, perhaps, she would understand...the indoctrination could do it, and I could help. But by the gods of space, how would it be to take that hate all that while?

WE came out into the central chamber where the prisoners were gathering to be herded up to the ships. Armed Valgolian guards stood under the glare of improvised lights. Other Imperials were going through the city, flushing out those who might be hiding and removing whatever our armed forces could use. The equipment would do no one any good here, and Boreas would be left to its darkness.

It was cold in the vast shadowy room. The heating plant had broken down and the ancient cold of Boreas was seeping in. Barbara shivered and I held her close to me. Nat Hawkins moved over to join us, wordlessly.

I was questioned in a locked room by one of the big Valgolian officers. He looked at a stereograph in his hand and he took me aside, but it was not unusual. Many of the starbound prisoners were being questioned by their guards, and I was merely one of them.

"Colonel Halgan?" the officer asked with an eagerness close to hero-worship. He was obviously fresh from school and military terminology came from his lips as if it really meant something to a Valgolian. The colonel, of course, meant that in a titular sense I had been elevated for my work. Funny, if you use the language enough, you get to believe it yourself.

"Sir," the young officer continued, "this is one of the greatest pieces of work I've ever seen. I am to extend the official congratulations of—"

I let him talk for a while and then I raised my hand peremptorily and I told him that the girl with the Earthling Hawkins was to go along for indoctrination, despite the fact that her name did not appear on his lists. He nodded, and I went back to Barbara, but half a dozen men had come between us.

Levinsohn and five guards. The man's carriage was still erect, the old unbreakable pride and courage were still in him. Someone among the prisoners broke loose and rushed at him, cursing, till the Valgolians thrust him back into line.

"Levinsohn!" screamed the man. "Levinsohn, you dirty Jew, you sold us out!"

There you see why this rebellion had to be crushed. Earth still had a long way to go. The Levinsohns, the Barbaras, the more promising of the anarchs would be educated and returned and the civilizing process would go, on. Earth's best and bravest would unite and fight us, and with each defeat they would learn something of what we had to teach them, that all races, however divergent, must respect each other and work together, learn it with an intensity that the merely intellectual teaching of schools and propaganda could not achieve alone—or, at any rate, soon enough.

Valgolia is the great and lonely enemy, the self-appointed Devil since none of us can be angels. It is the source of challenge and adversity such as has always driven intelligence onward and upward, in spite of itself.

Sooner or later, generations hence, perhaps, all the subject worlds will have attained internal unity, forgetting their very species in a common bond of intelligence. And on that day Valgolia's work will be done. She and her few friends, her *donagangors*, will seemingly capitulate without a fight and become simply part of a union of free and truly civilized planets.

And such a union will be firmer and more enduring than all the tyrant empires of the past. It will have the strength of a thousand or more races, working together in the harmony that they achieved in struggling against us.

THAT is the goal, but it is a long way ahead; there may be

centuries needed, and meanwhile Valgolia is alone.

Barbara would understand. In time she would understand what she as yet did not even know. But first would be the hatred, the cold stark hatred that must come of knowing who and what I really am. I could only wait for that hatred to come after she learned, and then wait for it to go, slowly, slowly...

Lines of the Earthlings were filing forward, and, with Nat Hawkins, Barbara waited for me. I walked to her and took her hand. Her head was high, as high as Levinsohns. She expected all of us to die, but she'd meet the relatives and friends she thought were dead.

It would be a great, a crushing humiliation, to know one's martyrs were alive and being well treated and intensively educated by the foe, who was supporting and encouraging one's supposedly dangerous revolution.

"It won't be so bad as long as we're together, darling," I said.

She smiled, misunderstanding, and kissed me defiantly before our Valgolian guards.

THE END

If you've enjoyed this book, you will not want to miss these terrific titles…

ARMCHAIR SCI-FI, & HORROR DOUBLE NOVELS, $12.95 each

D-1 **THE GALAXY RAIDERS** by William P. McGivern
SPACE STATION #1 by Frank Belknap Long

D-2 **THE PROGRAMMED PEOPLE** by Jack Sharkey
SLAVES OF THE CRYSTAL BRAIN by William Carter Sawtelle

D-3 **YOU'RE ALL ALONE** by Fritz Leiber
THE LIQUID MAN by Bernard C. Gilford

D-4 **CITADEL OF THE STAR LORDS** by Edmund Hamilton
VOYAGE TO ETERNITY by Milton Lesser

D-5 **IRON MEN OF VENUS** by Don Wilcox
THE MAN WITH ABSOLUTE MOTION by Noel Loomis

D-6 **WHO SOWS THE WIND…** by Rog Phillips
THE PUZZLE PLANET by Robert A. W. Lowndes

D-7 **PLANET OF DREAD** by Murray Leinster
TWICE UPON A TIME by Charles L. Fontenay

D-8 **THE TERROR OUT OF SPACE** by Dwight V. Swain
QUEST OF THE GOLDEN APE by Ivar Jorgensen and Adam Chase

D-9 **SECRET OF MARRACOTT DEEP** by Henry Slesar
PAWN OF THE BLACK FLEET by Mark Clifton.

D-10 **BEYOND THE RINGS OF SATURN** by Robert Moore Williams
A MAN OBSESSED by Alan E. Nourse

ARMCHAIR SCIENCE FICTION CLASSICS, $12.95 each

C-1 **THE GREEN MAN**
by Harold M. Sherman

C-2 **A TRACE OF MEMORY**
By Keith Laumer

C-3 **INTO PLUTONIAN DEPTHS**
by Stanton A. Coblentz

ARMCHAIR MASTERS OF SCIENCE FICTION SERIES, $16.95 each

M-1 **MASTERS OF SCIENCE FICTION, Vol. One**
Bryce Walton—"Dark of the Moon" and other tales

M-2 **MASTERS OF SCIENCE FICTION, Vol. Two**
Jerome Bixby: "One Way Street" and other tales

If you've enjoyed this book, you will not want to miss these terrific titles…

ARMCHAIR SCI-FI & HORROR DOUBLE NOVELS, $12.95 each

D-11   **PERIL OF THE STARMEN** by Kris Neville
        THE FORGOTTEN PLANET by Murray Leinster

D-12   **THE STAR LORD** by Boyd Ellanby
        CAPTIVES OF THE FLAME by Samuel R. Delaney

D-13   **MEN OF THE MORNING STAR** by Edmund Hamilton
        PLANET FOR PLUNDER by Hal Clement and Sam Merwin, Jr.

D-14   **ICE CITY OF THE GORGON** by Chester S. Geier and Richard S. Shaver
        WHEN THE WORLD TOTTERED by Lester Del Rey

D-15   **WORLDS WITHOUT END** by Clifford D. Simak
        THE LAVENDER VINE OF DEATH by Don Wilcox

D-16   **SHADOW ON THE MOON** by Joe Gibson
        ARMAGEDDON EARTH by Geoff St. Reynard

D-17   **THE GIRL WHO LOVED DEATH** by Paul W. Fairman
        SLAVE PLANET by Laurence M. Janifer

D-18   **SECOND CHANCE** by J. F. Bone
        MISSION TO A DISTANT STAR by Frank Belknap Long

D-19   **THE SYNDIC** by C. M. Kornbluth
        FLIGHT TO FOREVER by Poul Anderson

D-20   **SOMEWHERE I'LL FIND YOU** by Milton Lesser
        THE TIME ARMADA by Fox B. Holden

ARMCHAIR SCIENCE FICTION CLASSICS, $12.95 each

C-4   **CORPUS EARTHLING**
        by Louis Charbonneau

C-5   **THE TIME DISSOLVER**
        by Jerry Sohl

C-6   **WEST OF THE SUN**
        by Edgar Pangborn

ARMCHAIR SCI-FI & HORROR GEMS SERIES, $12.95 each

G-1   **SCIENCE FICTION GEMS, Vol. One**
        Isaac Asimov and others

G-2   **HORROR GEMS, Vol. One**
        Carl Jacobi and others

www.ingramcontent.com/pod-product-compliance
Lightning Source LLC
Chambersburg PA
CBHW030307180626
46810CB00003B/965